KT-503-657

HAWKHURST

2 0 FEB 2018

1 4 OCT 2014
2 6 JAN 2015

1 8 JUN 2019
- 5 AUG 2023

1 0 MAR 2015
2 1 APR 2015

- 1 SEP 2015

2 7 NOV 2015

Please return on or before the latest date above.
You can renew online at *www.kent.gov.uk/libs*
or by telephone 08458 247 200

CUSTOMER SERVICE EXCELLENCE

Libraries & Archives

Kent
County
Council

00884\DTP\RN\07.07   LIB 7

C161008091

Rakes Who Make Husbands Jealous

Only London's best lovers need apply!

The League of Discreet Gentlemen has only one priority—providing the women of London with unimaginable pleasure. The secrecy demanded is expensive, but satisfaction is definitely guaranteed!

The League pride themselves on knowing *everything* about desire. But they're about to discover that whilst seduction is easy falling in love can be very hard indeed…!

Don't miss this incredible new quartet by dazzling
Mills & Boon® Historical Romance author

Bronwyn Scott!

SECRETS OF A GENTLEMAN ESCORT
(Mills & Boon Historical Romance)

AN OFFICER BUT NO GENTLEMAN
(Mills & Boon Historical *Undone!*)

A MOST INDECENT GENTLEMAN
(Mills & Boon Historical *Undone!*)

LONDON'S MOST WANTED RAKE
(Mills & Boon Historical Romance)

AUTHOR NOTE

Here it is—the finale to my *Rakes Who Make Husbands Jealous* mini-series! I hope you've enjoyed it. I know I have. The series explores the different aspects of this premise: sex is easy, love is hard. In Nick's story—SECRETS OF A GENTLEMAN ESCORT—we met (or, if you're just joining us, you will meet) a man who defines himself by his bedroom abilities. It's quite transformational for him to move beyond that definition of himself with his heroine, Annorah.

Even if we're not professional escorts, how many of us end up defining ourselves by our jobs or titles? Or define our success in material gains and accomplishments?

In Jocelyn and Grahame's *Undone!* short stories we met two men who are all about the thrill of the game—until they discover love offers something better: the thrill of for ever. Don't miss their exciting tales.

That leaves Channing Deveril, the mastermind behind the agency. The series wouldn't be complete without the leader of the League of Discreet Gentlemen meeting his match in Alina Marliss, the Comtesse de Charentes. She too is a 'gamesman' when it comes to bedroom politics—the perfect opponent for Channing. The game is good fun until they realise being opponents isn't enough—but perhaps their game has gone too far for it to be any different. Love will require exposing their secrets, revealing their pasts, and trusting each other with the hard truths behind their game.

Does Alina's name sound familiar? If so, you probably remember seeing it in the Christmas anthology, A SPRINKLING OF CHRISTMAS MAGIC. She's the guest Channing brought to the holiday house party. Now you know what happens after the party!

Enjoy the last of these gentleman escorts!

Check out my blog for updates and giveaways at www.bronwynswriting.blogspot.com

LONDON'S MOST WANTED RAKE

Bronwyn Scott

All rights reserved including the right of reproduction in whole
or in part in any form. This edition is published by arrangement with
Harlequin Books S.A.

This is a work of fiction. Names, characters, places, locations and
incidents are purely fictional and bear no relationship to any real
life individuals, living or dead, or to any actual places, business
establishments, locations, events or incidents. Any resemblance is
entirely coincidental.

This book is sold subject to the condition that it shall not, by way of
trade or otherwise, be lent, resold, hired out or otherwise circulated
without the prior consent of the publisher in any form of binding or
cover other than that in which it is published and without a similar
condition including this condition being imposed on the subsequent
purchaser.

® and TM are trademarks owned and used by the trademark owner
and/or its licensee. Trademarks marked with ® are registered with the
United Kingdom Patent Office and/or the Office for Harmonisation in
the Internal Market and in other countries.

First published in Great Britain 2014
by Mills & Boon, an imprint of Harlequin (UK) Limited,
Large Print edition 2014
Harlequin (UK) Limited, Eton House, 18-24 Paradise Road,
Richmond, Surrey TW9 1SR

© 2014 Nikki Poppen

ISBN: 978-0-263-23981-2

Harlequin (UK) Limited's policy is to use papers that are natural,
renewable and recyclable products and made from wood grown in
sustainable forests. The logging and manufacturing processes conform
to the legal environmental regulations of the country of origin.

Printed and bound in Great Britain
by CPI Antony Rowe, Chippenham, Wiltshire

KEN
ARTS & LIBRARIES

Bronwyn Scott is a communications instructor at Pierce College in the United States, and is the proud mother of three wonderful children (one boy and two girls). When she's not teaching or writing she enjoys playing the piano, travelling—especially to Florence, Italy—and studying history and foreign languages.

Readers can stay in touch on Bronwyn's website, www.bronwynnscott.com, or at her blog, www.bronwynswriting.blogspot.com—she loves to hear from readers.

Previous novels from Bronwyn Scott:

PICKPOCKET COUNTESS
NOTORIOUS RAKE, INNOCENT LADY
THE VISCOUNT CLAIMS HIS BRIDE
THE EARL'S FORBIDDEN WARD
UNTAMED ROGUE, SCANDALOUS MISTRESS
A THOROUGHLY COMPROMISED LADY
SECRET LIFE OF A SCANDALOUS DEBUTANTE
UNBEFITTING A LADY†
HOW TO DISGRACE A LADY*
HOW TO RUIN A REPUTATION*
HOW TO SIN SUCCESSFULLY*
A LADY RISKS ALL**
A LADY DARES**
SECRETS OF A GENTLEMAN ESCORT††

And in Mills & Boon® Historical *Undone!* eBooks:

LIBERTINE LORD, PICKPOCKET MISS
PLEASURED BY THE ENGLISH SPY
WICKED EARL, WANTON WIDOW
ARABIAN NIGHTS WITH A RAKE
AN ILLICIT INDISCRETION
HOW TO LIVE INDECENTLY*
A LADY SEDUCES**
AN OFFICER BUT NO GENTLEMAN††
A MOST INDECENT GENTLEMAN††

†*Castonbury Park* Regency mini-series
**Rakes Beyond Redemption*
***Ladies of Impropriety*
††*Rakes Who Make Husbands Jealous*

and as a Mills & Boon® special release:
PRINCE CHARMING IN DISGUISE
(part of *Royal Weddings Through the Ages*)

Did you know that some of these novels are also available as eBooks? Visit www.millsandboon.co.uk

DEDICATION

For my Brony, who firmly believes in
the lesson of 'The Quackling'
(a French nursery tale):
you can never have too many friends.

Chapter One

The sex was killing him! Channing Deveril shifted carefully, so as not to wake the brunette asleep against his shoulder, and sighed. There, that was better. He hadn't slept in his own bed for the last seven nights and he was sorely missing the luxury of a big bed all to himself where his long limbs could spread out at will.

It was a sentiment that would surprise a certain population in London who believed Channing Deveril was the luckiest man alive. While they strutted and postured their way through boring musicales and tedious outings to the park, and dedicated their nights to dancing at Almack's without the benefit of strong drink, all in the effort of competing for the few true prizes on the marriage mart, Channing had women competing for *him*. Not just any women, but the best sort of women, the sort one could bed and not have to marry—the rich ones looking for exciting bed sport. And if rumour was to be believed, they even paid him for his presence in their beds. It was something else that a certain population's pride would never admit to, but who couldn't do with a little extra blunt and who wouldn't mind earning it that way? In their opinion, Channing Deveril was living the dream; all the sex and money he could manage.

Right now he wasn't managing the dream very well. That certain population would also be surprised to note that his first thought upon waking, other than the sex was wearing him out, was a calculation of the odds: what were his chances of getting out of Lady Bixley's lavender-scented sheets *and* to the door before she woke up? Marianne Bixley had been a tigress. Nothing had slowed her down—not the ropes, not the blindfold, not even the extra shot of brandy.

This was closely followed by the third thought: he just wanted to go home. The 'luckiest man in London' was tired, his mouth tasted like stale liquor and he wanted a few hours' sleep in his own bed before it began all over again. Channing blew out a breath and tried an experimental move. Marianne Bixley murmured, but didn't move. His arm was free. Now all he had to do was wait a few moments and roll.

How was he going to last the Season if he was this tired already? The Season hadn't even started. These last two weeks had merely been the preamble. The Easter break was coming and then the Season would begin in earnest. Already, the agency, his very popular League of Discreet Gentlemen, was struggling to keep up with demand.

The League of Discreet Gentlemen had become such a success he was having difficulty scheduling his men to fill the requested appointments while still keeping the League discreet, as its name suggested. The latter had been a problem ever since the previous year when Nicholas D'Arcy, one of his top men, had almost been caught tupping a lord's wife *in* the lord's town house, an episode that had done much for the League's popular notoriety and little for preserving the secrecy Channing preferred.

Providing a woman's pleasure was not a topic for public purvey in his opinion and he rather liked the idea that most of London's *ton* hadn't originally been sure if the existence of the League was fact or fiction. These days, it was becoming harder to preserve the mystique of the unknown. Everything was becoming harder.

But that wasn't why he'd stepped in to take on a few additional assignments. Usually, most of his days were spent administering the programme and that was work enough. He could rationalise the decision to step back into the role of full-time escort as the business's booming need, but he knew his motives were more selfish than that. Lady Marianne Bixley was supposed to be the cure for what ailed him. So far, he didn't think it was working.

Beside him, Lady Marianne gave a soft moan. It was working for her, however. He'd done his job well last night. He'd be doing it again, too, if he didn't extricate himself from her sheets quickly. Just the thought that he *wanted* to get out of a beautiful woman's warm bed was testament to the cure's failure. Not even the persuasion of a morning erection and the warm comfort of Lady Bixley's lush curves could compel him to stay.

Channing lifted the sheets and rolled out of

bed. He held his breath as Lady Marianne stirred briefly, then settled. He began to dress, quickly, quietly. Since when had sex not cured everything for him? From boredom to loneliness to physical satisfaction, sex had been his go-to antidote since he'd turned sixteen, his constant companion. Now, it was letting him down most thoroughly. The past year and a half had been peppered with disappointment in that regard.

Channing reached for his boots. He was almost free! He would put them on in the hall to avoid making additional noise. It wasn't that he couldn't perform. Lady Marianne was proof enough that he could please even the most demanding of sensual appetites. He gathered up the remaining package of French letters on the nightstand and stuffed them into his coat pocket. Leaving them behind might give her the idea he was hoping for a repeat engagement. He made for the door with stealthy footsteps.

He was almost out when her voice, sultry with sleep, caught him, his hand on the knob. 'Leaving so soon? Come back to bed.'

Channing turned, pasting a regretful smile on his face. 'I wish I could. Unfortunately, I have an appointment I need to prepare for.' It was true. Amery DeHart, one of his up-and-coming new escorts, had requested a meeting, but that wasn't until later this morning. He could see from the pouting frown on Lady Marianne's lips she thought it was another woman.

'I'm sure I'm more exciting,' she purred, letting the sheet drop a bit to reveal the swell of full breasts. Her eyes lowered to his trousers where his morning glory still flowered heavily against the fabric. 'Your cock certainly thinks so.'

'I'm sure you are, but business is business.' Channing made her a small bow and took the chance to exit while she unravelled his comment. She was a smart woman, she would understand the reference and, when she did, she would be none too pleased to be categorised as an appointment. Appointments with the likes of Amery DeHart were business, but appointments with the likes of Lady Marianne were business, too, even if they were conducted at night. The sun had come up and it was time to move on with his day.

Channing was finding it hard to move on three hours later even after a bath and a change of clothes. He'd had to forgo the nap and it had left him struggling to focus. Channing pushed a hand through his hair, trying hard to concentrate on whatever it was Amery DeHart was saying. His thoughts kept returning to the question that had taunted him this morning: when had sex failed to meet his needs? Maybe his dissatisfaction with the act was a sign he should retire, close up shop altogether or hand the business over to someone else who had an appetite for it the way he had when he'd started the whole affair. Either way, perhaps it was time for him to get out.

'I think it's time for me to get out.'

Channing didn't hear the rest. Amery's words roughly jerked Channing's attention front and centre. For a moment he worried he'd spoken his own thoughts out loud. 'I beg your pardon?'

Amery gave him a disapproving stare that suggested he knew Channing hadn't been listening. 'I said I think it's time for me to get out to the country and see the family,' he repeated patiently.

'You're not thinking of quitting, are you?' The last time Channing had sent an escort to the country, it had been Nick D'Arcy and the dratted man had got himself married. Channing wasn't sure what he'd do without Amery. He'd come to rely on the younger man quite regularly in the past year with the departure of his three veteran rakes. Amery had been good with training the new gentlemen Channing had hired as replacements and the ladies liked him.

'Not permanently,' Amery clarified. 'I've had a letter from home. I'll be gone three weeks to a month. My sister is getting married and there's some other family business to see to.' Channing knew Amery liked his job, but he loved his family. If Amery was going home for a wedding, he'd be bringing his sister the finest wedding dress to be had in London. Channing handled all the finances and was aware just how much money Amery sent home to his mother.

Amery sighed apologetically and there was no doubting the sentiment was genuine. 'I don't like the idea of handing off an assignment halfway through, but my client and I were slated to attend a house party out of town for the Easter break.'

Channing flicked his gaze to the calendar on his desk. The Easter break, the last dash to the country before the Season began in earnest, was just three days away.

'There's no way I can make it,' Amery was saying. 'It would hardly be fair to desert her halfway through.' Amery winked. 'In all honesty, I think she'd do better with you anyway. She's rather mature.'

'I'm only thirty, Amery, hardly in my dotage.' Channing tried not to feel offended by the comment. Just because he was contemplating retirement and had spent the morning fleeing a lusty woman's bed did *not* mean he was old, only that he might be in the market for a new adventure.

'It's not age, it's the maturity of her thinking, her mannerisms. It's hard to explain.' Amery groped for words. Interesting. Amery was never at a loss for what to say. Then he came out with it. 'Oh, hell, Channing, she's beyond me,' Amery admitted baldly. 'She's too sophisticated. She's got the Continent written all over her.'

'Who were you assigned?' Channing did a mental sort through the recent placements, but came up blank. Amery was slated to take the Misses Bakers to the opera on Wednesday since their brother couldn't come up to town just now; he was escorting a diplomat's wife to a fête at the Belgian embassy on Thursday. Multiple assignments at once were one way of keeping everyone guessing about the fact or fiction of the League, but none of the women on Amery's roster fit his description.

'You wouldn't know her. She's one of the clients I took on while you were gone for your nephew's birth. Her name is Elizabeth Morgan.'

Ah, that explained it. He'd left Amery in charge while he'd gone home for a few weeks in February to see the new family addition.

'I don't think any of the new fellows will do,' Amery went on, making his case. 'Perhaps Nick or Jocelyn could have done it if they were around, but...' Amery gave a shrug as his words dropped off to imply the impossibility. Nick and Jocelyn were happily married.

'Amery, do you ever feel as if you're the only bachelor left in London?' Channing gave a chuckle, but it wasn't funny, not really. Dear lord, weddings were thick on the ground these past twelve months. Nick and Jocelyn had married, as had Grahame, all three of them his veteran escorts. Both of his sisters had married last August in a double ceremony at his family's estate.

And, of course, his older brother, Finn, had

married their childhood friend, Catherine Emerson, even before that and had wasted no time in begetting an heir, a squalling, red little thing with a shock of black hair who had melted his rather cynical heart on sight and had done much in resolving some of the lingering tension between he and Finn after his last visit home.

Amery merely smiled. 'I'm a bachelor and proud of it. Marriage is fine for some, but men like you and I need the spice, the thrill of a single life.'

Channing knew the thrill Amery spoke of: the thrill of sex as a tool for pleasure or power. The games one could play were limitless. He'd learned years ago those games served him far better than anything more emotional, more meaningful. Sex in that particular arena left one too vulnerable. Although that specific game had been heady, he'd not cared for the aftermath of that experience or the woman who had served it to him. Since then, he'd limited himself to the business of pleasure and women like Marianne Bixley.

Amery leaned forward. 'Will you do it, Channing? I would be for ever grateful.'

There was nothing for it. There was no one

else to send and he did owe Amery for filling in for him in February. It was only fair. Channing nodded. 'I'll do it. Now, go on and pack.'

Channing leaned back in his chair, pushing his hand through his hair again, this time in restlessness. He hadn't intended to be out of town. He'd hoped to use the Easter lull as a chance to catch up on paperwork, go over the League's accounts and maybe work with some of the new escorts before the Season. But perhaps a house party was what he needed to shake himself out of these megrims. He did admit, even in his current state of exhaustion, a twinge of curiosity over meeting a woman who'd managed to rout Amery DeHart.

He hoped the party had a decent hostess. He should have asked Amery where it was being held. The right activities were the key to any house party's success. If not, given his current state of mind, this was going to be the house party from hell, no matter how 'Continental' Elizabeth Morgan was.

Chapter Two

This was going to be the house party from hell. Lady Lionel's Easter getaway was not where the sophisticated and worldly Comtesse de Charentes would have chosen to be of her own accord. The venue promised to be bland and boring, the mediocre tone of the guests currently assembled already attesting to her hypothesis. But the *comtesse* had a mission and it had to be accomplished here. She was looking for men, two men to be precise.

The *comtesse* surveyed Lady Lionel's drawing room with a cool sweep of her eyes, her aloof exterior giving away none of the hot temper that simmered beneath the surface.

Her eyes landed briefly on her quarry: Roland Seymour. Her pulse quickened, her temper rising at the sight of him. The bastard stood twenty feet away and she could do nothing, *yet*. But when the time came, she was going to rip his balls off. Seymour had stolen money most insidiously from her family and then attempted to compromise her sister into marriage in order for the family to make their money back. But Seymour had made a tactical mistake there. No one touched her sister. One bad marriage in the family was enough. That was where ball-ripping came in. For that, she needed the second man, who was most notable by his absence.

Another sweep of the room confirmed Amery DeHart wasn't there. She certainly hoped he'd arrive soon. At the least he'd liven things up, at the best she could start to put her plan into motion. Without him, she could not effect the introduction to Seymour she needed.

Aside from what was going to be a tardy arrival, she liked the young escort with his manners and wit. Her plans for his balls were somewhat gentler than what she'd planned for Seymour, although she couldn't imagine actually bedding DeHart with any large degree of interest. In her experience, young men in bed usually lacked a certain finesse. She appreciated something a bit more refined when it came to the art of *amour*. Not that she was in the market for an *affaire*. There was no time for such a dalliance. She was, however, in the market for revenge and that made DeHart's easy-going mannerisms useful.

She was counting on him to befriend Seymour and then introduce her. His introduction would make it easier for her to insinuate herself into Seymour's circles without raising suspicions. Once in, she would take things from there.

A stir at the doorway drew the *comtesse*'s eye. A surge of energy flowed from the hall. Amery must be here at last. It was the kind of excitement his presence could generate. She smiled, relieved. She hated to be kept waiting, it made her anxious. But her smile froze when a different man stepped through the doorway: Channing Deveril. The most arrogant Englishman to walk the earth. Out of all the house parties in England, he'd chosen this one. Well, that made three sets of balls she'd have to deal with.

She wanted to be wrong, but even at a distance there was no mistaking those blond good looks, the tall, slender grace of his movements, the impeccable fashion with which he wore his clothes. Today it was a coat of blue superfine, the buff trousers tightly fitted to show the perfection of his physique and perfectly polished high boots. There was a sensuality to everything he did. Even the simple gesture of greeting their hostess took on an intimate cast as she watched him bow over Lady Lionel's hand. She had not seen him in over a year, not since they'd parted badly at a Christmas house party she'd hired him to escort her to, and it was like seeing him all over again for the first time, so striking was his appearance. A woman could look at him all day and never tire of the view. But it would not be in her best interest.

The *comtesse* knew how dangerous all that handsome sensuality was. Beneath the good looks and laughing blue eyes lay a master of bedroom politics. She'd experienced a tangle in those sheets on two occasions. The first time had been in Paris, a brief but explosive affair during her marriage that had not been carnally consummated, but had not been less explosive for the lack of it. It had ended poorly and that had admittedly been her fault for even starting it. She'd been young, desperate, vulnerable. But the second time—oh, the second time she held him fully accountable.

It had been here in England a few years later. She had hired him as an escort who could help her reintegrate into decent society after so many years abroad. It was to have been business only between two mature adults who knew the rules. She had not understood how deeply he held Paris against her, or how compelling he could be, how he could make her believe it wasn't only business for him. He'd made her believe what he felt for her wasn't only a job, but genuine emotion, and then he'd dropped the pretence most cruelly. In doing so, he'd had his revenge. She had yet to forgive him. No one made a fool out of the Comtesse de Charentes. Roland Seymour was about to become one example of that and Channing Deveril could be the second if he chose to engage.

She could make it easy on them both and await Amery in the gardens just outside. But the thought occurred too late. Before she could quietly slip outside, Channing spied her and she was caught in the web of his blue gaze.

He inclined his head in her direction in sardonic acknowledgement and query, his eyes registering quickly veiled surprise over her presence. What was *she* doing here? She returned his nod with the cool, regal smile she'd cultivated for the men of Paris, the smile that invited men to look, but reminded them they touched at their own peril.

Well, at least she could take consolation in the fact that Channing's presence meant Amery was close behind. It stood to reason that, as friends, Amery and Channing would have shared a coach and come together. It was not beyond the scope of possibility that Channing had been hired by another lady at the party. But a glance beyond Channing into the hall revealed nothing. Perhaps Amery was still out at the coach, making arrangements for his trunks.

A few minutes more passed and Amery had still not appeared, although Channing continued to linger by the door, talking with the hostess. Something was wrong. Lady Lionel's fair brows had knitted together in consternation, just before Channing took his leave and began to cross the room towards her.

Within moments he stood before her, bowing over her hand much as he'd bowed over Lady

Lionel's. 'The Comtesse de Charentes, *enchanté,* although I suppose I shouldn't be surprised.' The blue eyes holding hers were full of mischief, secretly laughing. Channing was always laughing with his eyes, with his mouth. It had, unfortunately, been a rather endearing quality in the past.

'I have a bit of a dilemma and I thought perhaps you could help? I am looking for a guest, only Lady Lionel is not familiar with her, which I find extremely odd. After all, it's her party and her guest list.'

'And you thought you'd ask me,' she finished with cold politeness.

'Well, yes, since you seem to know these sorts of things.'

She understood the mischief in his eyes now. It was true. She did know everyone. She'd made it a point to know as many people as possible since her return from the Continent over a year ago. She'd been gone too long and acquaintances had lapsed. She'd done her best to restore those lines of friendship, although not everyone had welcomed her overtures. But it was more than that. 'These sorts of things' implied Channing had his suspicions about the identity of Elizabeth Morgan. His mind was fast like that.

'I will be glad to assist if I can.' Alina smiled politely, but inwardly her concern was growing. Where was Amery? Her gambit was off to a shaky start. 'I do need to let you know, however, that I am waiting for someone. He should arrive momentarily.' It was a weak ploy at best. If Channing had come with Amery, he'd already know that.

Wherever Amery was, Alina wished he'd hurry up. Even so, it was too late to avoid explanations. She'd given Amery a false name when she'd applied for the League's assistance this second time, wanting to avoid Channing. 'Who are you looking for?' she asked Channing. The faster she could help him, the sooner he'd leave her alone.

'I'm looking for a Mrs Elizabeth Morgan. Perhaps you know her? Amery DeHart was to meet her.'

She'd been right to worry, not that she'd let Channing see it. Her stomach churned as she realised the implications of Channing's presence. If Channing was looking for Elizabeth Morgan, it meant Amery wasn't coming. She had two choices: either brazen it out and confess or deny knowledge of the name and send Channing home, which would leave her on her own with Seymour, unless the perverse man decided to stay and make the house party miserable for her anyway, something he just might do given their track record.

She opted for the former, her chin going up a notch in defiance. 'Amery DeHart was supposed to be meeting me. I am Elizabeth Morgan.'

Channing's face hardened. She could see that he'd already grasped the basic tenets of the situation. The quick acuity of his mind made him a dangerous opponent, a reminder that everything she'd counted on would have to be rethought. Amery would have done her bidding with no questions asked. But Channing would ask. He'd want to know why she was using one man to meet another. He would demand explication and perhaps much else—after all, he was a man of extraordinary passions. *You are not in the market for the 'much else,'* she told herself sternly. Things had a habit of going badly when she and Channing were together.

His mouth formed one word. 'Liar.'

She took the verbal blow with aplomb. 'Fabulous. I see you've come to ruin another house party.

Ah, so she hadn't forgiven him for the débâcle at Christmas—not last Christmas, but the Christmas before that. 'Angry and beautiful, just as I remember you,' Channing said calmly, knowing it irritated her to no end that he wouldn't rise to the bait of her temper.

Her pale blue eyes flashed with an icy fire. Beautiful was something of understatement when it came to describing Alina Marliss, Comtesse de Charentes, an Englishwoman turned French countess, and now a returned Englishwoman. She was like a living diamond with her platinum hair and flawless skin. She sparkled from every facet. Not all of those facets were physical. Her personality sparkled as well. She could be positively charming when she chose. She was not choosing to be so now when she was on the defensive. Channing decided to push his offence.

'You lied. You gave Amery a false name. Why don't we stroll in the garden and you can tell me all about it? I find it quite interesting you needed to give an alias when you already have so many other names to choose from. Now we can apparently add Elizabeth Morgan along with Miss Alina Marliss and the Comtesse de Charentes.'

'Don't call me that,' she hissed, falling in step beside him, but she did not, he noted, take his arm. The minx was determined to declare her independence at every turn.

'I thought a widow got to keep the title as a matter of honour. Was I misinformed?' Channing answered in low tones. He'd known beforehand how much she despised the title. She'd tried to shun it, but society had forced her to keep it at every turn.

'You were not misinformed. However, if it were up to me, I would prefer not to wear his brand.' Her tone left no doubt about the unpleasant depths of that marriage. Of course she would detest it, would see it as a man's attempt to label her from beyond the grave. Alina Marliss belonged to no one. It was what made her such an intriguing and delicious challenge. But despite her efforts to simply be Lady Marliss, society would not let her forget she'd once had access to a higher title, even if it was French.

Out of doors, the gardens were full of sunshine

and the quiet conversations of others who strolled there. Channing guided them to a less-populated walkway and changed his tack. 'Perhaps you could enlighten me about your arrangement with Mr DeHart?' Part of him hoped that arrangement might be more superficial. He didn't want to know if Amery was sleeping with her. It shouldn't matter. This was just a job and objectivity was as important in this line of work as discretion.

'Why isn't he coming?' she answered with a question of her own.

'He has a family wedding to attend. His sister is getting married. Now, about that arrangement?' Whatever her answer, they were both adults. They could muddle through a week together at a house party. They'd be surrounded by others. There would hardly be any time at all to be alone. Not all escort jobs included sleeping with the client. Amery certainly wasn't sleeping with the Misses Bakers when he took them to the opera.

She gave him a coy smile as if she'd read his mind. 'Do I detect a hint of jealousy beneath your attempt at bland enquiry?'

'You detect a hint of self-protection,' Channing

replied. 'I want to know what I'm up against. When we were last together, I ended up with a vase thrown at my head.'

She snorted at this and dismissed it with a wave of her hand. 'You deserved it. You made me look like a fool.'

'I'm sorry about Christmas. I can only apologise so much,' Channing said stiffly. She was not without grounds to complain. The unfortunate incident had happened eighteen months ago. It was to have been her first foray into decent English society and she'd hired him at considerable expense to ease her return into that society, which he had. From an objective standpoint, he'd discharged his duty admirably. However, there had been what one might call 'interpersonal complications'. But how had this turned into an interrogation of him when he'd meant it to be an interrogation of her? 'I'm here now and I would like to fulfil whatever contractual obligations you had with DeHart.'

'Really?' She drew out the word into a provocative drawl as she gave the idea consideration, tapping one long, perfectly manicured finger against her chin. Channing felt another primal stab of possessiveness as the thought recurred. Was she sleeping with Amery? How did he feel about taking Amery's place in her bed or, for that matter, how did he feel about Amery having taken *his* place? The League never shared clients in that regard.

She gave a throaty laugh. 'DeHart and I have a purely social arrangement. He introduces me to people I want to meet and I've discovered that regularly having the same gentleman by my side has defused the amount of unwanted attention someone in my situation might attract.'

By 'situation' she meant widowed and wealthy and that made her available to all manner of advances. It did not help that her husband had been a French count and everyone knew life on the Continent was far looser, morally, than it was in England. There were even some who felt a good English lady was better off coming home than remaining among such a debauched set. That was a story Channing had spun.

Channing had spent a good deal of his time that Christmas setting the script into play for her and in the intervening months the story had hatched into plausibility, even if their relationship had hatched into disaster.

'What is it that you need from me? An introduction or a shield?' Thanks to his efforts, Miss Alina Marliss had been accepted back into society. But they both knew that acceptance was tentative. One false move on her part and society would not hesitate to expel her.

'Both.' Alina flicked open the fan she carried about her wrist, a pretty white-lace affair with painted pink flowers, the kind of accessory a decent Englishwoman would carry and a testament to how carefully she crafted this facet of her persona. 'I need to meet Mr Roland Seymour.'

'I'm afraid I don't know him.' He didn't sound like someone Amery would know either. Mere misters were not their speciality.

'But you *will* know him. That's the point of house parties, isn't it? To mingle and hopefully expand one's social network in useful ways?' Alina waved the fan back and forth in a slow languid gesture. The action called subtle attention to the expanse of bosom on display in a deceptively demure afternoon dress of soft pink muslin.

Channing gave a wry grin and tried to keep his eyes above her neck, but it was deuce difficult and *he* knew *she* knew it. 'You want me to befriend him and then insinuate you into his crowd,' Channing divined.

'Essentially. Play a little billiards.' She smiled at him over the top of her fan. 'Shoot a few things, preferably not each other, whatever it is gentlemen do.' She was trying awfully hard to distract him; smiles, fans and bosoms. It made him suspicious, especially coming from a woman who'd been icily distant a few minutes ago.

'Why?' Even knowing she was playing with him, he couldn't help but flirt back. Channing leaned closer, breathing in the light rose fragrance of her soap. She'd even gone so far as to smell like an Englishwoman.

'I wish to pursue some business with Mr Seymour.'

Channing raised an eyebrow at this. 'Are you going to tell me what sort of business?'

'No.' She laughed and took a step backwards. 'Now, you have work to do and I have ladies to ingratiate myself with. If you'll excuse me?'

It was a clear dismissal and he let her go. Amery

had not been wrong when he said the Continent was stamped all over her. She'd cut her teeth in the salons of Paris where Channing had first met her, the extraordinary Comtesse de Charentes. She'd been a married woman then, but that had not stopped the thrill of flirting with her. That same thrill had been present today even among all of his misgivings. She could get to him in ways the Marianne Bixleys of the world couldn't. He wished all the lush perfection of her didn't affect him so thoroughly, but it did and that didn't begin to address the layer of intellect and wit.

She was every man's fantasy. Perhaps that was her greatest trick. She could make herself all things to all men. He had yet to meet a man who had not fallen under her spell. It made Channing angry and intrigued all at once. Angry because he prided himself on being less susceptible than other men when it came to sexual politics, but in her case he seemed to be no different than the rest; intrigued because he did wonder who she was when no one was looking.

Was there anyone to whom she showed her true self? Once upon a time, he'd spent too many hours contemplating who that true self might be and how he might convince her to show that self to him. It was one of the innumerable fantasies he had about her.

He wasn't alone. Channing watched the eyes of the other men in the garden track her progress to the French doors leading inside. Their thoughts were fairly transparent. Lord Barrett, married with three children, was thinking how he could arrange an affair back in London. Lord Durham was thinking of how he could get into her room at the house party, tonight even. Lord Parkhurst's son, blond and indolent, was calculating whether or not his allowance could afford her if he set her up as his mistress, as if Alina would allow such a thing. Channing hoped he wasn't as obvious as the rest of them. No wonder she felt she needed Amery's presence as protection.

He eyed his own target across the garden, deep in discussion with Elliott Mansfield, whom he did know. He and Elliott were both members at White's. It was time to presume upon that acquaintance. Channing couldn't help but wonder: if he was there to protect Alina from unwanted advances, who was going to protect Roland Seymour from her? Business with Alina Marliss was guaranteed to be dangerous. He was living proof of it. The beginning of all his own woes could be traced back to her. Channing was starting to think it was the *comtesse* who had ruined him for other women.

Chapter Three

There was no competing with the Comtesse de Charentes when the company gathered in the drawing room for dinner that night. Alina made a grand entrance, alone, at five minutes after seven, exuding confident sensuality in a watered sage-green satin that commanded the attention of every male in the room and the jealousy of every female.

The choice was carefully calculated on her part. There was no doubt in Channing's mind she'd done it on purpose. It was a bold strategy, one that said she was ashamed of nothing. She would meet head on the stories that had already started circulating in fits and starts after tea. They were the same stories that always accompanied her: her husband had died suddenly without reason. It made her both a tragic figure and a suspicious one. He'd heard the tale and had immediately gone to work steering it in a useful manner. He'd done so, he clarified for himself, not out of any lingering empathy for the *comtesse,* but because Amery would have done so if he'd been here. It was his job.

The rise of the old story was not unexpected. This was a crowd to whom the *comtesse* was only partially known. Some of the more high-brow guests like Durham and Barrett had encountered her in London, but the others present did not run in such high circles or stayed closer to home at their country estates. They were entirely reliant on gossip in forming their first impressions of this relative newcomer. Still, she had come to this house party where she knew what she'd be up against when surely there were easier invitations to accept, making this a most interesting and almost illogical choice. Now she stood among a room of strangers, garnering all their attention, both good and bad.

That, he could understand. Channing saw her stratagem at once. She had cast her net wide to catch all the fish in the hopes of catching the attention of the one that mattered most. In this instance, that fish was Roland Seymour. The gambit had worked, Channing noted. Seymour's eyes followed her about the room just as every other man's had.

For his part, Channing wasn't much taken with Seymour and he was hard pressed to imagine what Alina saw in him. For that matter, he didn't know what Alina saw in this house party. Lady Lionel's circle wasn't exactly the *haute* elevations Alina had so painstakingly cultivated.

The supper bell rang and Channing silently commended Alina's choice of timing. Like all else about her, it was immaculate. She'd come down in enough time to command attention, but close enough to the bell so that she wouldn't have to make small talk, or worse, risk a cold shoulder from jealous matrons.

Lady Lionel was fussing over getting everyone paired for the dinner parade, another sign that this was not the high set he or Alina were used to frequenting. In his circles, people knew their place in line implicitly and needn't be herded. Channing rather resented the parade that separated natural couples and pitted social ranks against one another. When he was growing up, his mother had assured him it was to facilitate the meeting of new people. But Channing felt the only thing it facilitated was the prevention of people associating with others of an inappropriate station.

However, he did fight back a twitch of a smile as he watched Lady Lionel struggle with where to place Alina. As a countess, she was the highest-ranking woman in the room next to Lady Lionel, but she was a French countess who teetered on scandal, which was quite different than being an English countess of good standing. Lady Lionel erred on the side of caution and partnered Alina with her husband. Alina tossed Channing a smug victory glance over her shoulder.

He'd take that as a gauntlet being thrown down. So they were to play, were they? He wondered if she'd meant to play with Amery or if this was a signal that they were to resume their usual warfare. There was power in sex and they both knew it well. It didn't matter that he was paired with a baronet's daughter or that he was sitting a little further down on the opposite side of the table. He was adept at flirting at a distance. He smiled politely at something the baronet's daughter said and offered her his arm. Supper was about to get interesting.

* * *

The meal turned into a covertly wicked affair. He cupped the bowl of his wine glass; she stroked the stem of hers, idly, of course, and without even looking at whom the message was intended. That was the trick of the game, not to get caught. He bit into the duck as if it were the most tender of flesh. She bit into a berry and used a quick flick of her tongue to wipe a droplet of juice from her lips.

That had been risky, almost too overt. The other trick of the game was to keep the gesture questionably vague so that anyone who happened to pick up on it could only wonder if the gesture was actually meant for them. Roland Seymour had caught the lick and from the sly smile on his face was even now contemplating whether that lick was meant for him.

By the time the cherry ices arrived, Channing was contemplating other things beyond spoon sucking that could be done with the refreshing after-dinner treat. He wondered if Seymour was as well. He rather regretted the ladies' departure for the drawing room. Buttonholing the port around the table wouldn't be nearly as much fun. But it would be a chance to further Alina's agenda, whatever it was, with Roland Seymour. Channing settled into making himself agreeable. He knew two or three of the men present and Sir Lionel made it easy.

'So, Seymour, Durham here tells me you're an investor.' Lionel filled his glass and slid the decanter to the right. 'What do you invest in?'

Seymour gave an unnatural smile, one that Channing thought the man must practise in front of the mirror to achieve the proper amount of wryness. If so, he could use more practice. It didn't quite ring true. 'In land, it's the one thing that will outlast us all. I believe it's the only true investment out there. It won't short-change you and it will always hold its value.'

A few of the older gentlemen at the table exchanged uncomfortable looks. They were weighing the acceptability of such a profession or even if it was a profession at all. That was the sticking point. A profession wasn't acceptable at all. A real gentleman didn't work. Did investing qualify as work? A few of the younger men present seemed intrigued, however.

'Do you develop the land? What do you do after

you invest in it?' Parkhurst's son asked. Channing's gaze drifted back to Seymour. It was a trick question. Was Seymour well-bred enough to know it? Land development would definitely classify as work, whereas simple land ownership and real estate could be excused. Channing himself held several deeds for properties all over London. Buying was all right. It was a show of wealth.

Seymour took a swallow of his drink. 'I hold on to it until it's time to let it go,' he replied vaguely. Channing was starting to dislike Seymour more and more. The conversation shifted to other things and Channing used the opportunity to take Seymour's measure.

Dark-haired and of medium height, Channing supposed women would not find him unattractive. He'd probably appear more attractive one on one with no other males around for comparison. But there was an insincere quality to him that gave him the perception of being oily, a certain slickness that branded him as bourgeois. He wasn't Alina's type at all for business or for pleasure. She'd been adamant it was business in this case, but Channing had to wonder—why Seymour? If she wanted to dabble in real estate, he could recommend a better quality agent with more suitable credentials.

Not that it's your business who she does business with, Channing cautioned himself. He had to remember she'd hired Amery, not him. He was not here as her friend—those days were long past. He'd offered her friendship, more than friendship once, and she'd shunned it. He was here only as a substitute and as the result of co-incidence. He would do himself a favour by re-maining detached. It was his job to act as a shield against unwanted advances if they arose and to help smooth any slanderous gossip. It was *not* his job to tell her how to do business or with whom. Still, he could make a polite suggestion before things went any further and leave it at that.

A well-placed hint here and there would re-direct Alina's 'business' as soon as the gentle-men rejoined the ladies for tea in the drawing room, but a quick scan of the drawing room in-dicated Alina was not present. Had something happened in the interval? With a reputation as precarious as hers, that was always a hovering possibility. Asking Lady Lionel was out of the question. It was too obvious and it made Alina a point of interest on his behalf, something he'd rather avoid. A flash of white in the darkness beyond the French doors caught his eye and Channing made his way discreetly towards it. She'd gone out. That decided it. He could do with a bit of fresh air himself.

He'd found her. Alina straightened at the railing, keeping her back towards the door, refusing to acknowledge him by turning around. 'I knew you'd come.' He'd had a few hours to contemplate the situation. Now the questions would start. Perhaps she could stall them with a polite freeze.

'It's uncanny how you do that. I tried to be extraordinarily quiet this time.' Channing refused to be put off by her cold shoulder. He was all friendly affability as he moved to stand by her at the balustrade. Not that she believed the act for a moment. 'What gave me away this time? Don't tell me it was my cologne, it's hardly heavy enough to be noticed.'

'It was the warmer air and the slight change in light patterns when the door opened,' Alina confessed in aloof tones, making clear that he was not welcome, that she'd come out here to be alone, not to invite private conversation. 'How did *you* know *I* was out here?' For two people who did not do well together, they had a knack for always knowing when the other was near.

Channing tapped his head with a finger and grinned. 'Your hair. All that platinum is like a star in a night sky. Still, you'd make an admirable spy. Have you thought of offering your services to the Home Office?' he joked.

'I'll pretend that's a compliment, not a criticism.' She was having none of it. A careless woman was too easily sucked into his easy flattery and then it was too late. Alina forced him straight to the chase. 'What did you really come out here for?'

'Fresh air and answers.' Channing's voice was sharp and quiet in the darkness as he, too, discarded any veneer of civility. The people they'd once been had been forged into new people who were harder, stronger, people who were built to last.

Of course he'd want answers. He'd had a few hours to contemplate the situation. Now the questions would start as he tried to fill in the pieces.

'I met Seymour,' Channing began. 'He doesn't seem like your sort. Perhaps you might tell me what you need an introduction for.'

She was not going to make it easy on him. 'I'm the one paying your fee.' Let him be reminded that for all his tricks and flattery, she was the one in charge here. She'd hired him, not the other way around.

'I can terminate the contract at any point if I am not comfortable with the terms,' Channing reminded her. 'Perhaps you mean to lead me into nefarious crimes as an unwitting assistant.

'Scandal? You? Hah!' Alina snorted in a most unladylike fashion. What he posited was ridiculous, all things considered. 'It won't work, you know, you standing there posturing like a virgin with a reputation to protect. You're Channing Deveril, the "luckiest" man in London; a new woman, a new bed, every night. You're worried about scandals? You *are* a scandal.'

'I will not blindly get you an introduction and find myself embroiled in scandal,' Channing repeated calmly.

She met him with silence. This would be a perfect opportunity for him to go back inside and in his manly pride feel he'd emerged from the encounter triumphant. But the dratted man didn't take the chance.

'If you won't tell me about Seymour, why don't you tell me about dinner?' Channing said rather drily. 'I should point out to you that Seymour noticed our little table game. From his response, it wasn't clear he understood the game wasn't for his benefit. Or was it? You clearly have his attention. Why do you need me to approach him?'

Channing was a dog with a bone. This question wasn't really about dinner. It was still about Seymour, just from a different angle. She gave a throaty laugh. 'You should know, a lady never promotes herself to a gentleman on her own behalf. It would be too pushy by far.'

'Yes, well, that being said, I must inform you that a lady also doesn't stroke the stem of her wine glass as if it were a man's phallus.'

Her voice lit with dark humour. 'Why, Channing Deveril, what a naughty mind you have! And to think you got all of that out of the way I held my wine glass. Along those lines, one might think you were cupping the underside of a woman's breast the way you held yours.'

'Maybe I was.' Something hot and dangerous sparked between them. At some point in their exchange they'd turned towards one another, neither of them looking out over the expanse of garden any longer. The space between them was negligible. If she drew a deep enough breath, her breasts would brush the front of his dinner jacket. This was where she had to be careful. The line was so very close, so very easy to cross. If she crossed it, she'd have to be cautious—what was work, what was pleasure?

For him it was always work. She would do best to remember it because she'd forgotten once to her detriment. This hot détente could not last. She glanced over his shoulder into the drawing room. 'Shall we go in?'

Channing turned his head to catch the scene through the doors. 'Ah, is it bedtime already?'

'What a rather clumsy segue for you. Usually you are more...' She waved a hand to indicate she was looking for a word.

'Suave? Debonair?' Channing supplied.

'Subtle.' She raised her brows, sensing her chance to even the playing field. He'd come out here looking to clarify their situation. She'd give him some clarity, then. 'Since we're *not* being subtle at the moment, let me remind you, I'm paying you for protection. I'm not paying you for sex.' She gave him a knowing look and ran her gaze down the length of him in provocative suggestion. 'I've had that from you before for free.'

'I would remind you, nothing is free, *comtesse. Bonne nuit.*' Channing bowed smartly over her hand and was gone.

Chapter Four

Had she done it on purpose; turned the conversation from business to an exchange of wits that fell somewhere into a grey area between flirtation and warning? Channing wondered as he undressed for bed. Such techniques might have distracted other men, but she'd have to try harder than that to distract him.

He knew better than anyone that she saw everything as a strategic seduction. Conversations, people, all were delicious games to be played and won. Such knowledge kept his own guard up. Only a foolish man would assume the *comtesse* needed anyone. He was far from a fool these days. He wasn't the soft-hearted young man she'd encountered in Paris. She'd have to do a far sight better than flutter a fan and stroke a wine goblet if she meant to distract him.

Channing stretched out on the bed, revelling in the novelty of being alone. Maybe it was worth coming to the house party simply to have his own bed. Well, almost worth it. Alina made things tricky. He had a careful line to walk with her. Yes, he was here to honour Amery's contract and that technically put her in charge. But, no, he would not blindly do her bidding if he questioned the legitimacy of her motives and he was questioning them.

On the most obvious front, something wasn't right. This house party didn't fit her profile, the one she'd worked so hard to cultivate since returning from France. Seymour didn't fit her circles either. After listening to him talk over port, Channing didn't care for the oily bastard one bit. Whatever business Alina had with him, it was no good. Both those items added up to trouble.

Alina had to be cautious here. Her image among society was not pristine. There were still those in London who took the conditions of her husband's death and the accusations that followed quite seriously. She might have gained some respectability in certain circles, but one false step on her part and that thin cloak of respectability would be stripped away. If that happened, there would be no second chances, no benefit of the doubt extended to her another time. It made Channing wonder what she wanted from Seymour to justify such a risk.

Wondering was bad, Channing scolded himself. It led to curiosity and curiosity led to evil things when it came to the *comtesse*. He'd learned in Paris during their brief affair that she knew how to use a man and how willing a man could become to being used. He would not let curiosity make him that vulnerable to her again. He told himself, he was only wondering about her circumstances now out of a sense of self-protection. He hoped that was the truth. It was no wonder Amery had felt out of his depth. This was an assignment that pitted one master against another. She might be good at these games, but he was good, too. Damn good.

She'd been very good the prior night. Alina stretched in the morning sun as it fell across the wide expanse of her bed. She was still revelling in her little victory of last evening. Her strategy had worked divinely. A flirtation at dinner and then later on the veranda had neatly deflected Channing away from further enquiries about her business with Seymour.

It had been work of a sort, but that didn't mean it hadn't been energising. Flirting with Channing was *invigorating,* perhaps because it was dangerous. He would not hesitate to strike back, perhaps because it was a challenge. Channing embodied a healthy amount of resistance to her charms and that was novel in itself. He wasn't overcome with her looks or her wit. Not like Parkhurst's scion who was so obviously infatuated he might as well just offer her *carte blanche* on the back of a calling card and let her run roughshod over him. She was not interested.

Alina rolled over and yanked on the bell pull next to her bed. There would be more of the same kind of work to do today. Yesterday had just been the beginning. An easily obtained gentleman held no appeal for her. Perhaps that was why Channing's parting comment, *Nothing is for free,* still lingered in her thoughts. She wasn't even sure what he'd meant by that, but it had been enough to keep her thinking about it, keep her thoughts going back to a certain moment, to a time she wanted to remember as much as she wanted to forget it. Still, she could make use of it.

The comment was the perfect launching point for the next level of her distraction game. She wanted Channing to be so busy sparring with her, pursuing her, he'd not be watching her transactions with Seymour. At least that was what she told herself. Her choice of gambit had nothing to do with a pair of disarmingly blue eyes and a ready smile set amid the perfect planes of elongated squared cheekbones and a length of straight aristocratic breeding.

Her maid, Celeste, was prompt, bearing with her a tray of morning chocolate. Celeste had been with her since her disastrous marriage to the French *comte* and was arguably the best thing she'd taken away from her time abroad. *'Bonjour, madame,'* she sang out, always cheery, as she set the tray on a table by the window and turned to the wardrobe. 'There's a ride planned for this morning, *madame*. There's to be two groups, one for casual riders and one for the more advanced group.'

'I'll need the blue habit with the jaunty little hat. We'll put my hair up in that twist you do so well, Celeste.' Alina got out of bed and went to sit beside the tray, her thoughts already starting to work: what to wear, what to say, where to ride, how to subtly create the right impression to draw Seymour in.

Celeste tossed a knowing smile over her shoulder. '*Oui,* the young blond lord will like that. He likes to look at your neck.'

Alina sipped her chocolate. 'It's not for him. It's for Seymour.'

Celeste made a pouting moue as she laid out the riding habit. 'I like the young lord better.'

'This is business, Celeste.' Alina said sternly. She'd decided last night after the veranda she could no longer wait for Channing to procure an introduction to Seymour. It wasn't that she doubted Channing's ability to get the introduction. He would get it and he'd have it by the end of the day. But he would make her pay for it with questions and enquiries. He'd want to know what she intended to do with the introduction and she had no intention of telling him. If he knew, he'd want to get involved. 'Which group is Seymour riding with?'

'The advanced group, *madame*. Mr Deveril is riding with them as well.'

'Send word I'll want a suitable horse for that group, too,' Alina instructed, finishing the last of the chocolate. She would have liked to have lingered in the sunny bower of the window, but there was work to be done and elegance like hers didn't come easy. Alina crossed the room to the dressing table where her pots and brushes were laid out. 'Time to work your magic, Celeste.'

Then she would work hers. At least on the ride she'd have both men where she could see them. One could play with a man like Channing, flirt a little, but one couldn't trust them—couldn't trust them to leave well enough alone, couldn't trust them not to get under one's skin without even trying. And because of those reasons, she couldn't wait for him to get the introduction. She had to do this her way and she had to do it fast before Channing could step in. She'd already paid twice in the past for his involvement in her life, once physically and once emotionally. The first time she'd been naïve. She could forgive herself for that. The second time, she'd simply been a fool who had trusted the wrong man. Well, no more.

The Comtesse de Charentes had emerged from the fires of her marriage, wiser to the ways of men.

The drive in front of the house was full of milling people and horses by the time she arrived downstairs. A honey-bay mare was waiting for her, prancing eagerly. Alina eyed the prancing horse warily. She was a competent horsewoman, but she'd rather have ridden with the casual group, more time for talk and conversation. This feisty girl was going to demand her attention, starting with getting on. Alina looked around for a mounting block.

'Need a leg up?' Channing materialised at her side. He stroked the mare's shoulder, looking golden and handsome in the morning sun. There was nothing for it. The mounting blocks were all busy. But she would have refused if she could. He had a way of touching a woman that made her feel special even when she knew better, even when the task was as mundane as mounting a horse. Perhaps she imagined his hand lingered at her leg a moment longer than necessary as he checked the girth.

'Are you riding with this group?' A line creased his brow between his eyes.

'Yes,' she answered smartly, gathering the reins. 'You're not worried, are you?' She didn't want him concerned. It made him warm, likeable.

'Are you sure you can handle the mare? She's a fine horse, well trained but spirited, too,' Channing quizzed.

Alina gave him a confident smile. 'I can handle her. I've ridden bigger horses than this one.' The gelding she had had in France had been nearly seventeen hands.

He gave her a naughty look. 'Size isn't everything.'

She laughed and moved her horse forward. A line was beginning to form. She wanted to get closer to Seymour at the front. 'You'd better mount up if you mean to come.'

'Oh, the things I could do with that statement.' Channing gave a loud laugh and drew several eyes their direction.

'Hush, will you?' Alina scolded.

He smiled and stepped back, relenting. 'I'll be along shortly. I need to find a servant to take care of something before I can ride out.

* * *

She couldn't keep up. After the first two miles, it was apparent the mare was willing. It was her own skill that would not allow her to take certain risks. She could ride the flat ground well enough, giving the horse its head over the wide meadows, but she didn't dare take the jumps over hedges and logs at full speed. She took them at a slower, cautious rate. That put her at a disadvantage and whatever ground she'd made up on the flat was soon lost, putting her at the back of the ride while Seymour continued to ride in the front.

Alina reined the mare to a trot, giving the horse a chance to breathe and herself a chance to think. She would never catch Seymour at this rate. She needed a short cut, a detour that would take her around the designated course and bring her up with the leaders. She caught sight of a path cutting through the woods to the side of the course. Ah, some luck at last. Alina veered to the path and into the woods.

This was better. There were no logs or hedges to jump, only the occasional tree root to navigate and her horse was sure footed enough. She'd make up time fast enough now. But that was before the screech of a hawk split the quiet of the woods and her mare took off as if it were a clarion call to arms.

She had no time to react. It was a testament to her competence that Alina stayed on as long as she did. A forest at full tilt was no easy trail. There were dangers aplenty in low-hanging branches and jutting roots. One stumble on the horse's part would be all it would take to dislodge a rider.

Alina gave up any attempt at steering. The horse had a mind of its own and Alina sensed the mare was running not so much out of the crazed urgings of a spook as it was because it wanted to and nothing, certainly not she, was going to stop it. Her only option was to stay on and ride the mare out. That worked fairly well until they came to a tree lying across the path.

With no idea of what might lie on the other side, Alina pulled at the reins in a final attempt to stop the racing mare. It was the wrong choice. It slowed the horse, but not enough to turn away from the jump, only enough to take it with a little less momentum than she needed. The mare cleared the log, but the landing was shaky. The mare stumbled in the soft mud, depositing Alina in the shallows of a forest stream on the other side. It was a most ignoble finish to a gallant ride.

The mare recovered her feet and trotted to a stop on the other side, whinnying happily as if this were the greatest of larks. Alina smacked the water with an angry fist and shouted, 'Don't you dare laugh at me, you silly horse!'

It felt good to vent some of her frustration, but there was still plenty of it left. She'd never get to Seymour first at this rate. Her habit was soaked. 'You've ruined everything, you know,' she scolded the horse. 'I'll never get to the picnic now. I'll have to go back to the house and change. You have no idea what you've done. Channing will get to Seymour first and then he'll have all these questions.' She hit the water again for emphasis.

'Hey, don't hurt the water!' a cheery male voice called out and Alina froze. Within a moment, Channing appeared around the edge of the log, leading his horse by the reins. It occurred to her briefly to get up out of the stream. But why? Her humiliation was already complete. Of all the people who could have found her in this situation, it had to be Channing Deveril. Getting up now wasn't going to change that or dry her clothes any faster. She might as well wallow in it.

'Are you hurt?' he asked, tethering the two horses together on a low bush.

'Just my pride.' She struggled to stand. Her skirts were heavy and she was embarrassed to find she couldn't quite manage it.

'Wait, let me help you or you'll fall again.' Channing extended a hand, his boots sinking into the muddy bank.

She took his hand and resisted the temptation to pull him in with her, but he'd already sacrificed his boots to the cause and she opted not to be petty. 'How did you know I was out here?'

'I was behind you, quite a way, but I saw you veer off into the forest. I wanted to make sure you were all right.' He leaned against a tree trunk while she sat on a stump, wringing out her skirt. Channing shrugged out of his coat and offered it to her.

She didn't want to take it, but it felt good after the cold water of the stream. The day itself was warm and she'd dry soon enough, but for now the warmth of his coat was irresistible. The coat smelled of him, all spice and vanilla. It was like being wrapped in his arms, a most dangerous place to be. She knew from experience it was a place full of a false sense of security. He was a seductive man, but he wasn't for her, *couldn't* be for her. Sons of earls didn't marry women widowed under a cloud of suspicion. Besides, she didn't want another marriage anyway. One disaster was enough. Although with Channing, it would be a disaster of a different sort.

'What were you thinking, to strike off on an unknown trail with a horse you'd never ridden before?' Channing stroked the long nose of her horse. His tone was less cheerful.

'This is not my fault.' Alina answered with a certain amount of terseness. 'It's *her* fault.' She nodded towards the mare who was perfectly docile under Channing's attentions. 'We were doing fine until she heard a hawk and took off.' She dropped the folds of her skirt. She'd got out as much excess water as possible, but the wringing had left the skirt wrinkled and she could do nothing about the mud stains.

'I'll have to go back to the house,' she said, disappointed.

Channing shrugged. 'Maybe. We might have an alternative to that. First, tell me why you came this way? You haven't answered my question yet. Does it have to do with Seymour?'

From anyone else, it would have been a shot in the dark. From Channing, it wasn't a lucky guess. 'You always could read minds,' Alina admitted ruefully. 'I wanted to put myself in his sphere of influence.' She could confess that much at least. It was no more than what he would have heard her shouting to the horse about as he came upon them.

Channing pushed off from the tree and came to stand in front of her. 'Tut-tut, that's almost a lie. As in I almost believe you, but not quite. Why would you do that when there's no need? Your little flirtation at the table last night securely put you in his sphere of influence. Seymour noticed you. I told you that much on the veranda. Second, I am going to befriend him at the picnic, at your request, I might add. By nightfall you would have had your introduction just as you planned. Thus, there's no need to further your efforts.'

At this declaration, Channing began to pace in front of her, giving her a fine view of long legs and tight buttocks encased in riding breeches, her absolute favourite piece of male attire. She was regretting not pulling him into the stream after all. The breeches would be spectacular wet. Other things would be spectacular, too.

'What?' Channing stopped his dissection of her motives, which were all too on the mark for her taste. She hated how he could see right through her. It was time to change that, time for him to be the one off balance for a change.

She closed the small distance between them and twined her arms about his neck, her voice low and sultry. 'I was just thinking it's been a while since I've seen you naked.'

'It has been.' Channing's teeth nipped at the column of her neck. A tremor ran through her at the delicious contact. Her mouth claimed his in a long kiss full of tongues and tastes.

She pressed her hips lightly against his. 'You're wrong, you know, size does matter.' He murmured something hot and husky against her neck and she reached for him through his breeches, intending to cup his length. But he stepped back.

'I'm not that easy, *comtesse*. I'm sorry if you felt I was.'

'What I felt wasn't "easy,"' Alina shot back, letting anger disguise her disappointment. The little interlude had been nice until he'd gone and ruined it along with her plans for distraction.

'Perhaps I should clarify. When I said easy, I meant easily distracted.' Channing returned to his tree and folded his arms, an amused smile playing across those kissable lips.

'Can't a girl just give a man satisfaction in the forest?' Alina retorted. She would have been more coy about it if she thought it would have worked.

Channing laughed. 'You never change. Do you really think I don't know what you're doing?'

'I don't know. Why don't you explain what it is you think I'm doing and I'll tell you if that's right?'

'I'll do better than that. I'll cut straight to the chase.' He fixed her with an intense blue stare that would have singed lesser mortals. But Alina knew how to stand her ground against anyone, even handsome Englishmen who thought they had her best interests at heart.

'Others would conclude your haste in rushing to Seymour's attention is that you doubt my ability to get you the introduction. But that's not it. It's just the opposite. You know I'll get that introduction and you've decided you don't want me to. I wonder why? Am I close?'

'Amery has more tact than you.' Alina snorted. She pulled off his coat and handed it to him

'Amery isn't here. Perhaps that's for the best. He doesn't know you the way I do.' He reached out and took his coat, but instead of taking it, he used it to tug her to him. His hands rested at her waist. When he spoke again the edge was gone from his voice. 'Since I've known you, you've never let anyone help you. You rush your fences and not always for the best. There's a difference between taking decisive action and being impulsive. You're rushing your fences now with Seymour. I think you're missing the potential consequences. It will not look good if you are too forward with him. You know what people will say.'

He meant the gossips—anyone looking for her to behave inappropriately would say she was throwing herself at Seymour. She knew Channing was right. She'd thought the same thing herself. It was why she'd decided to bring Amery to the house party. But the risk of Channing becoming too involved had outweighed her need for caution.

Alina shook her head. This was how he'd got to her the last time, pretending all this concern. 'Don't do this, Channing. One minute you're castigating me for a little flirtation, the next you're my sincere adviser. I have hired you to be neither.' She tried to step away, but he held her fast. 'The truth is, I'd rather not have you involved in this business I have with Seymour. You and I aren't good together.'

'Except in bed,' came Channing's answer, 'and Lady Medford's gardens, the Duke of Grafton's library, that little closet in Lady Stanhope's town house—do you remember the one, it was at the end of the hall on the second floor?'

'Except in bed,' she echoed, refusing to be goaded. He was simply mirroring her technique from last night of mixing business with reminders of pleasure, reminders of a time when she'd thought he was more than a hired escort. She held his hot eyes, letting his gaze burn her. What was in the past needed to stay there except for the lessons it had taught her.

'I'm afraid, in this case, it won't be enough.' She had to be firm here or she'd regret it. She could not afford to let those lines blur again. 'Now, if you'll excuse me, I need to go back and change out of these clothes.'

'No, you don't.' A smile played across Channing's mouth. 'I had a spare outfit sent ahead to the picnic.'

'When did you do that?' The gesture touched her unexpectedly, but she couldn't think of when he'd have had time to do it. He'd been in the drive with everyone else long before she'd arrived.

'Do you remember that I had something to do before I could leave this morning?' Channing was grinning now as he boosted her into the saddle. He swung into his own and winked. 'I suspected you might be over-horsed.'

'I was *not* over-horsed,' Alina protested. But yes, she recalled he'd mentioned something about an errand. She remembered it just as clearly as she remembered that closet at Lady Stanhope's.

Chapter Five

Channing was as good as his word. By the time Alina sat down at the tables for cards after dinner, all was in order. Channing had arranged to partner her while they played against Roland Seymour and a Mrs White from Richmond. It was the most subtle of organisations from which natural conversation and association could grow. She couldn't have asked for a better opening. Seymour would have no reason to be suspicious of her motives.

But that didn't make sitting down next to such a man any easier. It galled her that she had to sit there, concentrating on cards, laughing and pretending to have a good time, while all she wanted to do was strangle him, or call him out and expose him to the present company for the fraud he was. Strangling was unfortunately against the law. She wasn't sure about ball-ripping though, there might be some potential there. Either way, torture would have to wait. She didn't have the proof she needed, not yet. But she would soon. The house party was just the beginning of what she intended for Mr Roland Seymour, deceiver of widows and unsuspecting families. Under the table, Channing's foot kicked her leg. 'It's your play, *comtesse.*'

'Thank you, my mind must have wandered.' She gave Seymour an apologetic half-smile and fingered the pearls at her neck while she studied the current trick in play. 'Perhaps you could remind me what was led?'

'Your partner has led the ten of hearts, Mrs White has followed with the jack,' Seymour supplied helpfully with a touch of the patronising in his tone.

Alina kept her tongue in check. There were things she'd like to say to that tone, but demure was the watchword for tonight. If last night had been more dramatic, tonight was about showing a slightly softer side to the *comtesse*. Seymour might be more open to the tragic, exposed French *comtesse.* Goodness knew he had a penchant for helpless women.

Channing kicked her again under the table. This time it had nothing to do with wool-gathering. He knew she was out of hearts and wanted her to trump the trick so she could lead back with a spade that played to his voided suit. Alina would have sluffed a club just to be irritating if she thought he wouldn't risk another kick. Her shin was likely to be black and blue tomorrow if he kept it up and she was already sore from her fall in the stream. But Channing was competitive and she was, too. If she had to choose between giving in to Channing or losing to Seymour, she'd choose the former. Alina tossed down the trump.

'That gives us the second game,' Channing declared an hour later, setting down the pencil beside the score pad. They'd won the first game, too, although it had been close. Mrs White and Seymour had played well, or perhaps, Alina thought, she and Channing had played well enough to give the illusion of closeness. Around them, other games were breaking up and people were beginning to mill about the room, waiting for the evening tea cart.

Alina rose and smoothed the aquamarine folds of her skirts. 'I thought I might take a stroll before tea. I've wanted a moment to admire the painting on the far wall.' She gave Seymour a hopeful glance and played with her pearls, drawing the eye to her discreetly displayed expanse of bosom.

'Might I accompany you?' Seymour predictably offered.

'I would like nothing better.' Alina smiled coyly through her lie. There were a million things she'd like better, starting with seeing him deported for his crimes, both those he'd committed and the ones he'd meant to commit. How many young women had there been before he'd tried to marry her sister?

'Are you enjoying the house party, *comtesse?*' Seymour began with the usual small talk as they strolled the perimeter of the room. Others had followed suit, perhaps exploring potential new relationships formed at the picnic that afternoon.

'Yes, very much. It's a blessing to be away from town for a while.' Alina sighed. 'There's so much business to take care of and I often fear I haven't the head for it. What do I know of rents and crops? I know fashion and parties.' She forced herself to brighten. 'But those are my troubles, not yours. I should not burden you with them. It's just that I didn't think being alone would be so difficult.' She let her words drop off, infused with a reflective tone while she waited to see if he would bite.

'My dear *comtesse,* I know we are but new acquaintances. Still, I would offer my services. I cannot bear to see a lady in distress. I have some knowledge of land matters. If I could help, I would be glad to do so.'

Alina smiled softly as if she couldn't believe her good luck. 'I would be grateful. Your offer is most generous.'

The tea cart arrived shortly after that and Alina made sure to mingle carefully, not spending any more time in Seymour's company although he was certainly willing to continue their association. It would be best to leave him wanting more. There was no need to appear too clingy, too desperate. Even snakes like Seymour appreciated a small show of strength. It served to make the appeal for assistance all the more sincere—here was a woman who didn't ask for help often, but she'd asked him. He would be feeling quite assured. She was careful also to avoid Channing. No good would come of being too closely associated with him. It would make Seymour wonder why she'd simply not asked Channing for help, why seek out a stranger when Mr Deveril was prepared to dance attendance on her?

Channing was among the first wave of guests to head upstairs. She waited and exited with the last so that Seymour could clearly see she was unattached. Not that such visual evidence meant anything at house parties when one dissected the logic of it. Everyone knew there would be several furtive journeys in the dark to various bedrooms not one's own before the sun rose.

Alina opened the door to her bedchamber and stifled a scream. She would not give Channing the satisfaction of knowing he'd startled her. The arrogant man hadn't even bothered to be furtive. He'd come up and directly helped himself to her bed. There he lay, hands behind his head, legs crossed at the ankles and looking entirely too comfortable. She boiled to take him down a notch. 'I think the rule is that you're supposed to wait until the house settles for the night.'

Alina set down the lamp on the dressing table and crossed her arms. For all her bravado, she was startled to see him. After his lecture at the stream about the need to protect her reputation, this seemed to do the opposite. 'Did anyone see you come in?' She had just put the next step of her plan in motion and it depended on convincing Seymour she was alone.

'Of course not,' Channing scoffed at her worries, arrogant in his own way.

'What are you doing here? I'm sure there's nothing that can't keep until morning.' Alina unfastened her pearls. 'Unless it is an apology for kicking me all night.'

Channing snorted. 'I kicked you twice and you deserved it. You were flirting with Seymour. Which raised a burning question in my mind. I don't think I could sleep without an answer.'

'If I tell you, will you go away?'

Channing shrugged. 'Maybe. This bed is pretty comfortable, though.' He paused and fixed her with his gaze, the humour fading. 'Why is it you insist on seeking out men you don't like?'

There was a great riposte in that, but this was not the time for teasing. 'What makes you so certain I don't like Seymour?' Alina slowly pulled the pins from her hair, gathering her thoughts. It was easier to think when she was doing something. There was less time for her brain to be distracted by the sight of Channing lying on her bed.

'You wanted to eat him alive at cards tonight, not exactly an attitude that matched the soft colours, and innocent pearls.' Ah, Channing had noticed. He was far too perceptive. 'Whatever "business" you have with Seymour, I'm starting to think it's not friendly.' And now he was meddling, too, just as she'd feared.

She shook down her hair, letting it fall over her shoulders. Channing shifted on the bed. He was in a poor position to hide any effects of her *toilette*. Well, good, let him be the uncomfortable one for a change. 'Are you going to come over and help me with my gown?' She made a show of reaching for the impossible back fastenings.

Channing rose from the bed and came to her, standing close enough to smell, close enough to kiss. She thought she had him, aroused and distracted. Even in dark evening clothes, the former was evident. But apparently she hadn't succeeded with the latter because his answer surprised her. 'No. I am not going to help with that gown. We both know what will happen if I do. It won't stop there.' His words were a whisper between them, part anger, part a seduction of his own. 'I don't want you like this, Alina. I'm not a game. I will not be used.'

Alina would not retreat. Her arms went about his neck, her lips kissed his throat. 'I thought you said those two weeks in France were the best of your life,' she whispered.

'They were, which is why I refuse to tarnish them with something like this,' Channing growled, setting her away from him. 'Not all men are like your husband, Alina. Not everyone can be manipulated with sexual favours, nor does everyone expect to be.'

She froze at the words, all thoughts of distraction fleeing in the wake of her anger. 'Are you calling me a whore? Considering your line of expertise, that would be quite like calling the kettle black.'

'Am I mistaken? I thought it was you who was so fond of saying there wasn't much difference between prostitution and marriage because we all did it for money in the end.'

'You would know. You've done it more times for money than the rest of us.' They were hurtful words. She knew what the League of Discreet Gentlemen meant to him. She knew it was about more than the money and the sex. But she hurled the words anyway because he'd hurt her and she was angry. She made a sharp gesture towards the door. 'Get out!' She was shaking with rage. 'Don't even think you can lecture me on the way I managed my marriage. You don't know what that man was like. You don't know what I had to do to win my freedom.' She'd told no one about the degradations that had gone on behind closed doors. Not even Channing with his keen intuitions could guess at half of it.

'A thousand pardons, *comtesse*.' Channing gave her a frigid stare and exited the room.

Well, at least he'd dropped the matter with Seymour. But it was small consolation. This had not been how she'd wanted to do it. Still, she'd known from the start how things could explode with Channing. They'd been too intimate, too close, once upon a time. They knew each other far too well for objective games of manipulation to work without consequence. They knew just how to prod the sleeping lions each carried within them as this last demonstration had proved.

Alina rang for Celeste, disappointment blooming where anger had resided. Channing had been a source of strength for her once. Those two weeks had given her power, had taught her that she was strong, that she had value, the taint of a bad marriage could not diminish.

She was facing another important trial right now in exposing Seymour. Channing's strength would be welcomed. But she couldn't risk it. She didn't want him involved. He had the League to protect. If her plans went sour, there'd be a scandal and she couldn't promise he wouldn't be exposed along with it. She'd never contemplated involving Amery when she'd hired him. She had no intentions of involving Channing now no matter how much he pushed, which was why she'd be sleeping alone tonight.

He'd be sleeping alone tonight because he hadn't pushed, not in the right direction at least. Channing yanked off his cravat with an angry pull. He couldn't remember the last time he'd been thrown out of a woman's bedroom. He had only himself to blame. He'd done it all wrong, broken every basic rule of relationship management. He'd called her attempt at seduction a manipulative ploy and by extension he'd implied rather blatantly she was prostituting herself in order to distract him from the true issue.

It had been a low blow no matter what. A gentleman never called a lady a whore. It was an especially low blow because he knew what her experiences would cause her to make of the situation. He'd accused her of being no better than the *comte,* a man whom she had thoroughly despised.

Channing undressed himself without assistance. He was in too poor of a mood to inflict himself on the unsuspecting valet. He should apologise. Once he did that, he could seduce her, which is what he should have done in the first place. Everyone knew you caught more flies with sugar than vinegar and he'd been nothing but vinegar. He'd rebuffed her efforts in the forest and he'd picked a fight with her tonight. Neither of those were classic recommendations for winning a woman's favour or her trust. He needed both if he was going to uncover her business with Seymour and, if need be, protect her from her own impetuosity. She was paying the agency for protection and he was damn well sure she was going to get it even if it was protection from herself.

Why do you even care? his mind challenged. *She's been nothing but trouble to you since the day you met her and likewise she thinks the same of you. Yet you can't seem to stay away from her.* But Channing knew why. She was beautiful and strong and yet more vulnerable than she understood. There was a *joie de vivre* in her laugh, a magic in her wide smile, an exhilaration in the lightest of her touches. He'd never met a woman like her who could captivate a room so effortlessly by simply walking into it, who could captivate *him*, a man who had known so many women in his time and who could have any woman.

And yet you remember everything about her. You remember the first time she looked at you from across a Parisian salon, how she smells, how she freezes a man with a glance and how she stokes him with one as well. Channing blew out the lamp and climbed into bed, knowing full well the night was a lost cause. He was going to dream of Paris until the sun came up.

The *comtesse* might be genuine. Roland Seymour yawned sleepily from his discreet post in the hall. Perhaps she was truly alone. There'd been no questionable entrances or exits from her room since he'd taken up his position shortly after one in the morning. To have come sooner would have aroused suspicion. The house had not yet settled. He didn't think he'd missed anything though; the *comtesse*'s maid had only left a few minutes ago, suggesting to him that there was no man inside her room. He'd give it another hour and then take himself to bed. No one would be showing up at three only to have to be out by five before the house servants started their rounds.

He intended to enjoy his brief association with the *comtesse*. She was everything a Continental woman should be, elegant and refined, sensual and passionate. He'd seen the tenacity with which she'd played a simple card game, perhaps an indicator of what awaited a man who garnered her favours. And yet, she was a woman and that meant she had limitations, limitations which she had freely admitted to him during their stroll. The business of running estates weighed on her. He fully expected she'd come forward with a more specific request for help tomorrow. Hopefully, she was in her room right now contemplating the wisdom of taking his offer. If not, he'd gently push that direction. He was fully confident he would know her situation by tea time.

Of course, he knew a little of her situation even now. She was a widow of two years according to the rumours circulating the house party. But rumour also suggested the marriage had been bad and the husband's death somewhat suspect. What could one expect when one married a Frenchman? Still, there were those at the house party who were less generous in their thoughts: Why marry a Frenchman in the first place?

He'd listened to the gossip because it proved that she was alone. Even at the party there were no staunch allies for her, no one she could turn to with real problems. He would make himself that man. If he could bed her all the better. Women gave up all kinds of secrets in bed.

Chapter Six

Channing was right. He was going to dream about her all night. But he was wrong if he thought it was a waste of an evening. His dreams took him back to the first time he had ever seen her, a time of perfection, a time when he was young and still full of his father's ideals of love and women.

He'd been to Parisian salons before but this one was different. There was an energy that emanated from the room. It didn't come from the excellent décor, although the large drawing room was well appointed in blues and creams. It didn't come from the exquisite collection of art hung on the walls representing significant schools of painting, although the collection certainly spoke well of the patron who had acquired it. Nor was it the comfort with which the room was designed. There were plenty of chairs grouped together for easy, intimate conversations, and more seating around the centre point of the room where the main event of the salon, a reading from a playwright's latest work, he'd forgotten whose, would take place later.

Then he saw it, or rather her, the source of the energy, sitting slightly to the right of the room's centre and surrounded by guests. She laughed and fluttered a fan at something a guest had said. In doing so, she turned his direction and he was stunned. She had white-gold hair, a platinum really, such a unique and unmistakable colour. That would have been enough to make her remarkable, but there was more: the sharp blue of her eyes, the pertness of her nose, the curve of her cheek and, perhaps most of all, the wide generous mouth invitingly painted in the palest of pinks to match the gown she wore, a frothy chiffon confection that contrived to be sophisticated, avoiding the immaturity that often accompanied such frills. She wore pearls at her neck to complete the picture of freshness and innocence.

'It is the coup de foudre *for you.' His friend,*

Henri, who had brought him, nudged him as the woman made a gesture with her fan to approach. 'I will introduce you, but you have to remember to speak,' he joked. 'Many men are tongue tied in the presence of la comtesse.*'*

Up close, he could see that she was young, perhaps not older than his own age of three and twenty, and when she spoke he could hear the accent beneath the words. She was not French, but English, even though her French was flaw-less. When she smiled at them, declaring she was glad Henri could come and doubly glad he had brought a friend, someone new to enliven their little circle, Channing was struck again by the quality of her freshness, the vibrancy in every expression. He was struck, too, by the realisa-tion that she was married to Monsieur le comte *and he knew something akin to devastation. She belonged to another. She could never be his. It was a ridiculous sentiment upon a first meeting.*

Then she singled him out and all else ceased to matter. 'Has Henri shown you the garden? No? Ah, Henri, it is remiss of you when you know the gardens are the best feature of the house.' She tapped Henri on the arm with her fan. 'Come,

Mr Deveril, I will give you a tour. We have a little time before the reading begins.'

He supposed the gardens were lovely. He supposed he made the right obligatory comments about plants and the pond. He just wanted to stare at her, just wanted to listen to her. She could talk about anything and he'd listen. 'The garden seems almost English,' he offered as her tour wound down. He didn't want to go in, he wanted to stay out here with her.

She smiled softly, her eyes meeting his fleetingly and then flying away. 'I hope so. I wanted to create a little piece of England for myself so I'd have some place to remind me of home.'

'Do you miss England?' It had not occurred to him that the comtesse *was not happy here in Paris.*

'I don't know that I miss England, but I do miss my home and my family. My sister and I were close, she is dear to me. Still, this is a good marriage for a girl like me. I could not have expected to do better and Monsieur le comte *lets me do as I please most days.'*

Channing shook his head 'A girl like you? What is that?'

'*My family is gentry. We are neither low born nor high. We're not part of the peerage and we're not wealthy enough to attract their attentions. In England, I could not have hoped for a great match. But here in France, the system of nobility is different. I could expect a great deal here. My parents want me to be financially secure and not need to worry for anything. They are older, you see, and there is my younger sister to consider.*'

Channing did not like the way she said it, as if she were trying to justify the choice to herself.

'*It appears they have succeeded.*' *Channing smiled.* '*Have you been married long?*'

'*Nearly a year.*'

He'd missed her by a year. It was illogical to think of it in those terms but the thought came anyway. '*Is the marriage all you hoped it would be?*' *Channing asked quietly. It was an intensely personal question to ask on short acquaintance.*

The blue of her eyes met his. She smiled but there was sombreness in her gaze. '*Monsieur le comte is away much. I do not see him often, but I am well provided for.*' *She looked past his shoulder.* '*Our guest is ready to begin his reading. I need to go and play hostess.*' *She gave him an apologetic smile for her upcoming absence as if she sensed he would not stay long now that he was deprived of her presence. 'Do you read much, Mr Deveril?'*

'On occasion,' Channing answered vaguely. He wasn't a reader, it was not something that came easily to him. But he'd become one if it mattered to her.

'Then perhaps you'd like to come tomorrow? We are discussing one of Voltaire's letters, purely an academic exercise and a chance to debate. But the group will be smaller, just a few of my intimates, and afterwards we'll walk in the garden.'

'I would be delighted.'

The part of him that knew he was dreaming wanted to pull her into his arms, anything to keep her from going back inside. But that part of him knew, too, that such a move would end the dream, it always did because nothing of that nature had happened in the real memory, not then anyway. So, he let her go....

Channing awoke with a start, his brain still foggy with sleep and wanting. Even seeing her in dreams took his breath away. He'd peppered

Henri with questions about her all the way back to their lodgings that evening. Henri answered each of them with a laugh. What kind of flowers did she like? What was her favourite colour? But always Henri's answers became vague when he asked about her marriage and the *comte*. Something was not right there. His sleep-fogged brain didn't want to contemplate those reasons at the moment, it wanted only to drag him back into pleasanter thoughts and pleasanter times and he let it take him back to his days in Paris....

The comte *seemed to matter very little, though, in the weeks that followed. The man was merely a technical spectre that lay on the periphery of his growing relationship with* la comtesse. *In the month Channing was in Paris, the* comte *did not make a single appearance and it was easy to forget he even existed. It was easy to forget a lot of things existed, so entranced was he with* la comtesse. *And it seemed she was entranced with him.*

She invited him everywhere and he delighted in showering her with little gifts; beautifully wrapped bon bons, a rare copy of Voltaire's English letters. All appropriate of course, nothing that would cause the errant husband any anger. His father had raised him well. He knew the rules. But Channing had anger aplenty as his time in Paris drew to a close. His business for his father was concluded and he had no excuse to stay longer. How dare le comte *neglect his wife!*

'If you were mine,' he'd told her on their last afternoon as they strolled the Luxembourg Gardens, 'I would not leave your side for a minute. I think it's a shame your husband is so perennially absent.' By English standards it was a shocking thing to say. The French were much more given to such exaggeration as a form of flattery and flirtation. He was not her only admirer.

The comtesse *had turned to him and put a firm hand on his sleeve, her blue eyes intense. 'You must not think such things. It can change nothing,' she scolded, seeming far older than her years in that moment. 'Besides, I prefer it this way.'*

She preferred the comte's *absence. The realisation hit him hard. His intuition had not been wrong. All was not right inside the* comte's *marriage. That was when he began to suspect, too, that she had not experienced the joys of the mar-*

riage bed and it fuelled his anger in a different direction. Neglect, it seemed, had many different forms.

In the next moment, her scold was gone. 'In August, I will go to Monsieur le comte's home in Fontainebleau. It is beautiful in the summer. Perhaps you will come and spend some time? I am inviting several of my friends down or I shall be too lonely. Besides, what is the good of having a lovely country home and no one to share it with?' She gave a little smile that suggested he was forgiven for his earlier transgression. This second chance served as a warning, too. He was not to make such enquiries again or there would be no more forthcoming visits to Fontainebleau or anywhere. He would be shut off from her.

Channing raised her hand to his lips and kissed it. 'I would be honoured to come.' He'd have to lie about it, though, to his family. They would have too many questions about his newfound infatuation with France.

He did go to Fontainebleau that August, the best two weeks of his life. It was every bit as beautiful and as torturous as he'd expected, to be near her and know that near was all he could have. They spent their days walking the gardens, going into the village, picnicking in the meadows. He savoured every glance, every laugh, every light touch even though they were surrounded by others of her select coterie, men and women alike.

'When shall I see you again?' he'd asked as the visit came to a close. Monsieur le comte *had written, requesting her presence in Paris at the end of August, something neither of them cared to speculate on.*

'Perhaps it is best you do not come again,' she said softly. 'It is hard on both of us, I think.' It was as close to a declaration of affection as she'd ever got and he treasured it, each word a precious pearl.

In itself, the request was not odd. Everyone was returning to town, the summer was over, but as the days wound down, he knew she carried unease about the reunion. The comte *himself had spent the summer months in a villa on the northern Italian lakes with friends she did not care for. 'I will go to Paris with you,' Channing had offered impulsively, his head immediately filled with ideas of challenging* le comte *to a duel, or spiriting her away to some far part of the world where no one would ever find them. Honour had kept him from her in the most carnal of senses, but he was regretting such ethics now. Perhaps shared passion would have bound her to him.*

'No!' Her answer was vehement and swift, her eyes flashing. 'You must never do that.'

He'd not been ready to give her up. When they said goodbye the next morning, Channing had a wild plan, as young naïve men often do when faced with the full throes of first love. The simplicity of it even now embarrassed him in the dark of his room. 'Come away with me. We will go where we cannot be found. The British Empire is big and America even larger if it comes to that. I will wait in Paris for three days.' He'd pushed a folded slip of paper in to her hand with an address on it. 'Come to me and we will leave straight away.'

'He will not let me go.' But something akin to hope had flared in the depths of her eyes even as she offered the protest. There was a fierce set to her jaw as she debated the option he put before her. He'd not known then exactly what he'd offered her relief from, only that he could

*not live without her. It was a selfish young man's
invitation.*

*He'd gripped her hands with all of his pas-
sion. 'I don't care. You will be the wife of my
heart with or without the sanction of law. We can
go where no one will know, no one will mind.'
He'd heard of soldiers who kept wives in India
and wives in England. Surely such a deception
wasn't that hard to pull off with the wide ocean
between them. His family loved him, they would
recover from the blow and in time they'd come
to love her as he did.*

*He'd kissed her then, long and hard. What it
lacked in finesse, it made up in ardour. They'd
been hot for each other in that last embrace, his
hands everywhere, her cries in his mouth as he
devoured her, joy surging through him that she
would be his one day very soon.*

He awoke, aching and hard beneath the sheets,
his body drenched with sweat. The dream had
been intense as were his waking emotions as they
tangled with the fingers of sleep. Drowsy anger
rose still after all these years, righteous anger on
behalf of the young man he'd been and the be-

trayal that young man had suffered—a betrayal of his heart, of his ideals. It had changed everything for him. He had waited, not three days, but five. She had not come and the dreams that claimed him now were not as rose-tinged as the ones that had come earlier.

It was Henri who had borne him the news of her betrayal. The comte *and she were as reunited lovers, Henri told him. Henri had been to their home for a supper and he'd walked with them in their garden holding hands as they strolled with their friends. The* comte *had showered her with new gowns and a king's ransom in jewels, among them a diamond collar worth a small estate in itself.*

Jealousy stabbed him hard as he imagined her in those gardens walking with another, even if that other was her rightful husband. Those were their gardens, his and hers, where they'd first strolled, where they'd walked so many times after her salons. Never mind that they walked there with others, always surrounded by others. That was a fact a lovesick swain conveniently forgets. His mind, too, made arguments for him. She doesn't love him. She loves you, it was you she gave her sum-mer to. Ah, yes, the cynic in him began to rise. You and the myriad other guests who flitted in and out of the house in Fontainebleau.

The man in the dream had seen then in hind-sight how he hadn't truly had the full sum of her attentions. He was one of many. She'd made him feel special, that was all.

It would have been best if he'd accepted defeat quietly, graciously and gone home to England at that point. But his blood ran hot where the com-tesse *was concerned and Henri's report wasn't enough to dissuade him. Foolish boy that he was, he'd forced Henri to tell him where she might ap-pear in public since it was clear she wasn't going to invite him to her home. Henri had reluctantly told him she and the* comte *would be at the Lux-embourg Gardens on Sunday for a picnic with friends. He'd gone and watched her from the periphery of their group, although it took all his will-power not to approach her directly.*

She'd been stunning that day. She'd worn pink, a deep, bright, true pink that brought out her hair and complexion brilliantly. Around her neck, she wore an expensive diamond collar that dripped with wealth just as Henri had reported. Never could he afford such jewels, Channing had thought. He was comfortably provided for as a second son, but he hadn't the comte's *wealth. Her circumstances would be somewhat reduced if she'd come with him.*

He'd waited and watched for an opening, on the hope that she'd leave the comte's *side and he'd have a chance to speak with her. He had no luck. She'd spent the day beside her husband, a tall, dark-haired man with olive skin who looked like the Italians he'd summered with. He was well dressed, too, and full of manners. He smiled at his wife, fingered the diamonds at her throat and laughed at whatever she said.*

She'd answered such attentions with attentions of her own. She had eyes for no one but the comte, *except the one brief moment when she had spied him on the edge of the company, hanging back by the hedges. Her eyes had gone cold and she'd looked right through him as if he were nobody, as if they had not clung together so fiercely in those last moments at Fontainebleau, as if she had not considered throwing all this away for him just a few days ago. She'd made it clear in a single, heart-piercing gaze she would not contemplate such an action now. She had made her choice: silks and jewels and the sporadic affections of an oft-absent husband over the passions of a second son. The woman whom he'd believed was different from others was no different at all. The dream was over.*

Channing stretched on his bed and rolled over, looking for a cool space in which to reclaim some comfort. The sun was coming up and he realised too late he'd not shut the curtains. It hardly mattered, he wouldn't sleep again, his thoughts were churning. He remembered what had happened next. He'd gone home, his heart broken, his ideals shattered, his lesson learned: pleasure and passion were right and good as long as one did not engage in them to an emotional extent. He'd merely been a tool she'd used to assuage a need her marriage had not met. He'd rather other young men not learn such a lesson in such a brutal way and he'd set out to do something about it.

He'd formed the League of Discreet Gentlemen, a service that would save men and women alike from heartache while providing them with the pleasure they sought. He'd formed an agency, a league of gentlemen dedicated to a woman's pleasure. There should be no more empty lives, no woman abandoned in her marriage, but, more importantly, no young men ruthlessly used and discarded when there were escorts who could be paid for the experience without jeopardising hearts and emotions.

The organisation had flourished, but not once had he told anyone the inspiration behind it, not even his best friend, Jocelyn Eisley, who had helped him. What was the point? He was never going to see her again, never going to go to France again. But fate had a way of intervening and, as it turned out, he hadn't had to go to France to encounter her again after all. She'd come to him, ironically because of the League, the very agency he'd formed to save others from *femme fatales* like her.

He remembered her vividly, sitting in his office at Argosy House explaining her case. She had wanted to re-integrate into English society. She was widowed and wanted to be home. She'd hoped to use the Little Season and the holidays that followed as a first opportunity to show herself. She'd been a veritable ice princess with her white-gold hair and travelling gown in a deep blue; her new signature colour, no more pinks. There was an edge about her that leant her a sensual, sophisticated edge that appealed to him greatly. They were new people, different from whom they'd been in Paris. They were people who could take pleasure at will.

It had not taken long for them to fall into bed, into whatever room was convenient. The winter holidays had been heated and the new man he'd become, the man who sought pleasure with detachment, had finally bedded the woman of his rather naïve dreams.

Channing rubbed his eyes against the sun streaming through his window. His head hurt and his cock throbbed for an impossible woman, one that had spurned him. Yet his body still wanted her and he had to go downstairs, eat breakfast and pretend it didn't. Or maybe not. A thought came to mind as his head cleared. Perhaps the best way to get her secrets out of her would be to seduce them, not an entirely unpleasant prospect. He could bed her as long as he didn't mistake it for something else. For that, he'd need a plan.

Chapter Seven

He was going to have to apologise, too. Principle and practicality demanded it. On principle, he'd not behaved the way a gentleman of the League should have, no matter who the client was. On the level of practicality, alienating Alina didn't help him determine her business with Seymour. He ought to be seducing her trust, not turning it away like he had last night.

Channing knew how he wanted to do it. There was to be an egg hunt in celebration of the Easter holiday after breakfast that morning. Already, Lady Lionel was starting to circulate through the places where people lingered over morning coffee and tea with an urn full of names. Everyone was to draw for a partner. He would make sure he drew Alina's name. If he was going to be successful with her, this would be a case of keeping one's friends close and one's enemies closer. Alina was somewhere in between.

Channing put on his best smile and approached Lady Lionel with a light touch on her arm. He kept his voice low and private. 'Might I have a quiet word with you?' He drew her into the hall away from the other guests. She would not appreciate every male guest engineering their partners for the egg hunt. 'I have a favour to ask. I would like to partner the Comtesse de Charentes, if I may? I am sure you could arrange it,' he said, implying that she was a hostess of great skill.

She blushed under the flattery. 'I don't know, it's not how the game is supposed to work.'

Channing nodded. 'I understand, and while I would love to partner any of the ladies, a circumstance has arisen where I need to make amends with the *comtesse*.' Lady Lionel looked interested now. She could smell a bit of gossip in the wind, a fair trade for his request. Channing pushed on. 'I fear I may have offended her last evening after cards and I do not want her to feel uncomfortable for the rest of the house party.' That was all true and a safe admission that would not show Alina in a poor light. As a member of the League, he was sworn to discretion even if Alina was not.

She smiled. 'I think we could make an exception in this case.' She moved over to the console set against the wall and dumped slips of paper out with names carefully printed on them. Channing helped her sort through them, looking for Alina's. 'I don't know the *comtesse* well,' Lady Lionel began. 'How is she enjoying her return to England?'

The lady was fishing for more gossip and trying to determine just how well *he* knew the *comtesse*. Channing was too savvy of a player to fall for such a basic ploy for information. 'I assume she is doing well—she is here, after all.' Lady Lionel would hear the compliment in that. 'Ah, I've found her name.' Channing held up the slip of paper. 'A thousand thanks, Lady Lionel.' Now all he had to do was wait for Alina to come down.

She came down at the stroke of eleven and not a moment sooner. He'd not expected her to. Alina wasn't a breakfast eater, nor was she an early riser. She would have chocolate and toast in her room and take her time with her *toilette* before showing her face to the world. It was always worth the wait. Today was no exception. She descended the stairs in a sea-foam walking ensemble with dyed-to-match kid boots that peeped from beneath her skirt. She carried a straw leghorn in her hand for protection against the sun, but for now her platinum hair was on display, carefully put up in what looked to be a casual up do, but what probably took Celeste the better part of the morning to fix. It was the kind of arrangement men's fingers itched to take down.

Lady Lionel was already calling for gentlemen to find their partners. Channing moved through the crowd of milling guests to her side before she could make her way towards Roland Seymour. Along with apologising, he was determined to figure out exactly what sort of business she hoped to conduct with him before it went any further.

'*Comtesse,* I believe we are partnered for the event.' He swept her a gallant bow and she shot him a thunderous look.

'You arranged it, I am sure,' she replied frostily.

Channing gave her a boyish smile. 'Of course I did. You're the best partner here and I want to win. The prize is jewellery of some worth. Other than that detail, Lady Lionel is being secretive about it.' He dropped his eyes to her neck, to the spot where her delicate collar bones almost met. If they were alone he would have touched her there, but it was far too intimate a move to make in a crowd.

Her eyes met his, two hard, glittering blue gems. But they did not glitter from a sense of mischief. 'Do you think jewellery is apology enough? That you can just throw me a pretty trinket and all will be forgotten? That's a pretty big assumption, especially since we haven't won yet.' Was she thinking of other times she'd traded jewels for apologies?

'No, I mean to apologise so all will be forgiven.' In the background, he could hear Lady Lionel going over the rules of the egg hunt. He drew Alina to the side, away from the crowd. 'I am sorry for last night. It was poorly done of me.'

She arched a pale brow. 'Is that all? You aren't going to follow it up with all the reasons why you behaved poorly? No justification of your actions?'

She was trying to bait him. Channing folded

his arms and smiled, refusing to bite. 'You're such a jade.' He knew the kind of apology she was talking about, the kind that came with a 'but' statement and it would have been simple enough for him to have added: *I am sorry I behaved poorly, but your lack of forthcoming information prompted me to such bad behaviour.*

'That's how men apologise, isn't it?' she answered tartly.

'Not all men, not me,' he answered her challenge evenly, but his body was starting to become aroused by those flashing eyes and that sharp tongue of hers, which he could definitely put to better use than trading barbs in Lady Lionel's hall. 'There's no need to play the jade with me, Alina. You know me.'

'Yes, I do and that's all the more reason to be suspicious of your apology.' She tapped a long, well-manicured finger with its perfectly filed and rounded nail against her chin. 'It does make me wonder—what is it that you want, Channing, that you would be willing to apologise for it?' They were playing a different sort of game now, a seductive teasing one where they were competing for the upper hand.

Channing leaned an arm against the wall over her head, bringing his body close to her, his mouth at her ear, and took an outrageous chance. 'You. I want you, right now up against this wall.' He did. More than he wanted to know about Seymour, more than any other consideration, he wanted her viscerally, physically. The remnants of last night's dreams were riding him hard. 'I want to drag my hands through all that platinum perfection until the pins fall out. I want to feel your legs about my waist, gripping me, squeezing me as I plunge into you.' He kissed the spot beneath her ear. 'I want to feel you come apart with me inside.'

He was being arrogant, but she needed to know he was no plaything and that she was not in charge, not completely.

Her eyes darkened, her pupils widened. The pulse at the base of her throat did a rapid beat. She was not immune to this game. 'Do you think you're the only man in this room who wants that?'

'I think I'm the only man in the room who can have that.' Channing took a soft bite at her ear lobe.

She gave a throaty laugh that sounded more of

midnight than midday and Channing wished they were anywhere else but a back corner of Lady Lionel's hall. Alina ran a finger down his chest. 'I see you are still London's most-wanted rake, women falling at your feet everywhere you turn. You can't help yourself, you never could.'

'Do I detect a moment of sentimentality?'

'You detect the game about to start.' Alina side-stepped away from his arm just in time as the crowd started to move towards the doors in an excited wave of motion, but not so excited that someone wouldn't have noticed them standing inappropriately close together.

'Which game would that be?' Channing couldn't resist as they joined the throng.

She tossed him a hard stare, but she wasn't angry. Far from it. The next question was what could he do about it and where? The egg hunt would certainly lend itself to answering the 'where'. Whether Lady Lionel intended that to be the case or not, there were definitely possibilities, there always were when couples were paired up outdoors and given permission to wander off, especially if one was a rake and knew where to go. Strawberry picking was another good activity for mischief, too, come to think of it. But that would have to wait for another time.

Channing scanned the wide lawn. 'Everyone else is heading west towards the bridle trails. Let's head east towards the lake.'

They discreetly separated from the crowd and went towards the lake, a move that paid off in competitive terms. Lady Lionel's staff had hidden more than three hundred decorative eggs on the grounds and Channing and Alina encountered three of them in various places on their way to the water.

'Aren't they adorable!' Alina held one egg-shaped casket up to the sun, letting the glass and paste decorations catch the light. 'There's a clasp, too.' In her excitement she looked for a moment like the girl he'd first met in Paris. 'Do you think it's the one with the prize?'

Channing laughed. 'I hate to ruin your fun, but all the eggs have clasps. You'll have to open it and see.'

She gave a wide smile. 'It doesn't ruin my fun to know there are prizes in *all* the eggs.' She flicked the clasp open and gave cry of delight. 'Bon bons. Two of them. Good, I'm hungry.'

'Hey, one of those is mine. It's not my fault you didn't eat breakfast,' Channing protested with good humour.

She shut the egg and her eyes danced as she studied him. 'Very well, you can have one, but first you'll have to catch me.' And she was off, skirts in one hand, egg in the other, her laughter floating back to him on the breeze. It was like being in Fontainebleau again before everything was ruined.

He was happy to give chase and she led him a merry one into the woods on the edge of the lake, around tree stumps, over logs and back out again until he had her breathless and cornered in the summerhouse—or was it she who had him cornered and breathless? He suspected the latter. 'You planned this,' he accused with a laugh, bending over, hands on knees, to catch his breath. 'You knew exactly where you were going.'

Her hand was at her waist as she tried to steady her breathing. 'I knew where I was going, I just didn't know if I'd get there. I thought you had me at the tree stump.' She set down their little basket of eggs on the table, her eyes still twinkling with amusement. 'In fact, I don't think you've technically caught me yet. We're just standing here. That doesn't qualify as a catch.'

Channing grinned wolfishly. This would be short work. The table was between them and an old cushioned sofa behind Alina.

There were two choices. They could dance around the work table for ever or he could go over it.

Alina started to dart a bit to the left, clearly opting for the former, but Channing vaulted the table and seized her about the waist. The momentum of his surge easily carried them to the sofa and he pinned her with his body, both of them laughing hard.

After a moment he rose up on his elbows and peered down at her. 'There, that should qualify as a catch.' God, she was beautiful looking up at him with those blue eyes and her hair falling about her shoulders. Celeste would be so disappointed, or maybe not. Perhaps the art of those coils was that they were meant to come down.

'Now, about those bon bons.' She started to shift out from under him, but he wasn't ready to let her go, not with those hips wriggling against his. 'Not so fast, my wicked tease,' he scolded. 'I will claim a victor's prize first.'

'I thought the bon bons were the prize.' She moved beneath him again, but he could tell it was purposely done. The little minx knew precisely what she was doing.

'Perhaps I have something sweeter in mind.' Channing whispered, pressing his lips to the column of her throat. He moved the trail of kisses up to claim her mouth, then the delicate line of her jaw, the tiny lobe of her ear.

'Channing—' she breathed beneath him '—don't start something you can't finish.' There was hope there and a warning, too, a warning for them both.

'Shh. No talking.' Channing returned to her mouth and covered it with his own.

No talking. It was an easy enough of a command to comply with. As if she could talk *or* think when being kissed by a master! *The* master. Channing wasn't the first man she'd bedded, but he was the only man she'd found pleasure with. Part of her had started this game today to see if that pleasure still existed, could still be called up between them. She wished it could be different, she wished she didn't want him so much. Beyond the pleasure, he was bad for her, so very bad because nothing could come of it as he'd proven so astutely a year and a half ago. But it was hard to remember that when he pressed his body to hers, when his mouth claimed hers, when his every touch ignited a fire in her blood, his every word a provocative promise.

She arched against him, her arms twining about his neck. It had been so long and she had asked for this, made the opening overtures for this with her invitation to chase. He was going to hold her to that. Well, that was fine. She made a hasty negotiation with herself. She could have the pleasure as long as that was all. No more fanciful notions of what lay beyond the pleasure, no more reading into it.

His hand moved to her skirts. Yes, she wanted them up, wanted her legs free to bend around him, to invite him in. Her body was hungry for this even as her mind tried to encourage her to take its advice. The warning she'd uttered was as much for him as for herself. But it was no use. Her hands worked the fastenings of his trousers, eager to push them over slim hips, eager to free the hot length of him.

Her hand closed over him, urging him into position. Channing gave a hoarse laugh. 'My dear, have patience, I know where it goes.'

'Then show me.' Her own voice was as throaty as his with need and excitement over what would follow. It would be rough and fast; circumstance and need dictated the necessity of such a coupling. One did not risk a languorous coupling in an unprotected summerhouse where anyone could walk in on them, especially when the grounds were teeming with guests. Still, there would be pleasure at the end of it.

Channing came into her swift and sure with a commanding thrust that obliterated further thought. There was only feeling now and the sensations evoked by the advance and retreat of their rhythm. Her hips arched, her body bucked. A moan came from her lips. It was too much, too much; she could not endure it, could not tolerate it without shattering. Channing gave a final thrust, his own body tight with the tension of need; she felt the coil of him spring apart just as she broke.

'I always feel like Humpty Dumpty afterwards,' Alina murmured what seemed quite a while later. It took ages to get her feet under her. Channing could reduce her to a boneless heap, a boneless bon bon-eating heap at the moment. Her head was in his lap and he was popping chocolates into her mouth. There'd been more in the other two eggs and she was making quite the meal of them.

'That means we did it right.' Channing might have managed to sit up afterwards, but he was lethargic, too. It was a consolation of sorts to know she wasn't the only one so thoroughly affected. He fed her another chocolate.

'All I want to do is take a nap,' she said around the bon bon.

'Hmm. Me, too.' Channing smoothed her hair back from her forehead, a reminder that they were going to have to try to fix it before they returned to the party.

'Do you think anyone found the diamond necklace yet?' She'd forgotten about it.

'No.' Channing drew a lazy line between the valley of her breasts. She wished she was naked.

'There's to be a horn blown once the ground prize is found.'

'Oh. This hunt might go on all day,' she suggested with a hint of naughtiness.

'I think that was Lady Lionel's intention.' He paused. 'But I wouldn't risk it if I were you. Someone's bound to come in this direction before much longer.'

She laughed. 'How did you know that's what I was thinking.'

Channing grinned. 'I almost always know what you're thinking.'

'Almost. That's the key.' With a quick turn of her head to where his trousers still lay open, she took him in her mouth, her tongue flicking over the head of him. 'There, you didn't know I was going to do *that*.'

Channing laughed. 'No, I didn't, but now that you have, you'd better not have started something you won't finish.'

'Don't worry, I can finish.'

Chapter Eight

They were at it again. Roland Seymour leaned against a tree trunk at the edge of the woods giving on to the lake and spat into the ground. He'd avoided taking a partner in the Easter egg hunt for the purpose of following the lovely Comtesse de Charentes. He needed to determine how much of her façade from last night was fact or fiction before he took things with her any further. In spite of his offer to the contrary, he had no intentions of 'helping' someone who couldn't help him. By that he meant he wasn't going to set himself up to be ambushed by someone who expected foul play. The more helpless she was, the better.

Was she playing the helpless maid in the summerhouse right now? Was Deveril on top of her, pumping into her hard and fast while she cried out? Or was she riding him, her hair unbound, her hands on her tits as she slid on his cock? Seymour shifted his weight to accommodate his growing arousal.

The muffled sounds coming from the summerhouse had done as much to fire his imagination as had the *comtesse* herself. She could arouse a man simply by walking beside him, by her elegant hands toying with the jewellery at her neck. She knew enough tricks to keep a man hard all night without even touching him.

Seymour reached deep into his trouser pocket to discreetly handle himself—the visions of the *comtesse* naked were too much to withstand. Ah, that was better. He was going to need to keep moving along. After an hour of waiting, he wasn't sure he had the answers he wanted. But he had some he didn't and they were followed by more questions.

For starters, she was attached more intimately to Mr Deveril than she'd let on if the activity in the summerhouse was any proof. But did that mean anything? Last night, he'd sensed a lack of logic in her choice to confide in him if she had another man in the picture. It was the 'if' that mattered. Still, perhaps Mr Deveril was just a sensual diversion to pass the party with, hardly an outlandish diversion for a worldly woman like her. Being with Deveril didn't necessitate spilling her private business to him. That's where the 'if' came in.

If the attachment went beyond the house party, however, Deveril might become an awkward accessory. Fortunately, he knew how to eliminate those types of obstacles. Everyone had secrets they wanted to protect. The more status a man had, the more important it was he preserved it. An earl's son would be more than eager to keep certain aspects of his life concealed: illegitimate children, debts. Seymour was sure Deveril was no different. Whatever the secret was, he would find it and Deveril would suddenly find the *comtesse* less attractive.

Seymour threw a rock idly in the lake and slunk back into the woods. He wouldn't learn anything he didn't already know by staying.

'We can't stay here all day.' But Channing's words held little conviction. He stretched his arms above his head in an attempt to rouse himself, but with little success. He'd rather stay at the summerhouse and see what other surprises Alina had in store for him. She'd completely outdone herself with her head in his lap.

Alina sat up, her hair spilling down her back in disarray. All the pins had come out by now and she looked like a fairy-tale enchantress; a sensual, otherworldly creature. 'That prize is still out there,' she suggested, a soft fire lighting her eyes. 'I bet we could still find it. I was thinking, if I was Lady Lionel and I wanted my hunt to last all afternoon, I'd hide the necklace at the furthest point.'

'And delay the finding of it with minor distractions like eggs with bon bons in them strewn between the guests and the prize's location,' Channing finished with a laugh. Although he was sure Lady Lionel hadn't expected the bon bons to provide quite the diversion they'd taken in the summerhouse.

'It's obvious where it is,' Alina continued. 'There's a folly on the eastern edge of the estate. Lady Lionel mentioned it in passing the other day.' She stood and began arranging her clothing. He rose, too, albeit reluctantly, and went through the process of tucking in shirttails and fixing up his trousers, but his heart wasn't in it. Sex with Alina was always all-encompassing; it left him incapable of thinking of anything else. Part of him wished it wasn't. It would be easier if she was like his other women, people he could walk away from when the contract was done and feel no need for further attachment. But with Alina, it was far more complicated. It didn't help knowing she was the one woman he should walk away from.

He could only imagine what his family would say, what Society would say if he married a French countess, widowed under peculiar circumstances. Well, married was certainly putting the cart before the horse. Channing wasn't sure where that thought had come from. If Alina was complicated, marriage to anyone was even more complicated for him. Marriage would necessitate a final decision about the agency, about the life he'd led for the last seven years. It was quite a lot to turn his back on. There were people counting on him. What would become of them if the agency were to close? No, marriage was a most precipitous thought, indeed, on all accounts. Better to focus on the present.

'Let me do that.' Alina disengaged his hands from his cravat, scolding gently, 'You're going to ruin it.' She had it tied within moments. Her hands were at his shoulders, smoothing his coat.

'You'd make a fine valet,' Channing murmured, breathing in the light floral scent of her.

She slid her arms about his neck and he pulled her close. Maybe leaving the summerhouse wasn't a foregone conclusion, after all. But her next words disabused him of the notion. 'Channing,' she whispered, pressing a kiss to his neck, 'find me that prize. I want to wear it when we make love tonight.'

That wouldn't be a problem if his cock was a compass. It was steering true north right now. 'What else will you be wearing?'

'Nothing, Channing, nothing at all.' She nipped at his neck and stepped away, holding out her hand, a sensual smile on her lips. 'How about it, Mr Deveril? Shall we find Lady Lionel's secret jewels?'

Outside the sun was bright overhead, the day fair, perfect for a hike. 'Which direction is the folly?' Channing asked, scanning the horizon. They were still alone, none of their fellow egg hunters had ventured this way yet.

'Through the woods.' Alina pointed to the little cluster of trees.

He let her take him by the hand and lead them forward but at the edge of the woods, he caught sight of something disturbing: the deep imprints of a man's boots in the mud. There was no smaller, potentially female counterpart with them, nullifying the idea that a pair of partygoers had fleetingly passed that way. Channing said nothing to Alina, who was too intent on pulling him forward to notice. Someone had been there. From the depth of the impressions, that someone had stood there for a while. Channing shot a look over his shoulder to the summerhouse. From here, a person would have a good view of the place and what might be going on in it without the occupants being aware of anyone's presence. The realisation swept through him, leaving a cold, clammy feeling behind. Lucifer's balls, they'd been watched!

Not that he cared. He wasn't bothered by the concept of being seen naked, or even by the idea someone had seen him in the act. He was, however, bothered by what someone with nefarious purposes would do with the information. Then again, he was London's most-wanted rake, such a juicy titbit would only serve to enhance his reputation.

He had little to fear. That wasn't true of Alina. Taking a lover in the bright light of midday, out in the open where apparently anyone could see, would be damaging to her. The careful reputation she'd pieced together for herself would be shattered by such a revelation, proving to everyone she was no better than she ought to be, a woman corrupted by the loose ways of the Continent.

The old desire to protect Alina rose as sure as it had risen that day so long ago when he'd offered to wait for her in Paris. It wasn't supposed to. He was supposed to be beyond such chivalrous susceptibilities. This time he knew her full measure. She hadn't accepted his offer back then and he feared she wouldn't accept it now if the need arose. She was too independent, too stubborn. They might have had incredible sex in the summerhouse, but that didn't mean she wasn't hiding something from him. There was definitely something she wasn't telling him.

They came out of the forest where the path converged with others coming from different directions on the property and Channing could see others had the same thoughts as Alina. They were no longer alone—a handful of couples waved to them, holding up baskets full of eggs. Another worry came to him. Would the three eggs they'd found look suspiciously few? Behind the lead couples, larger groups were converging on the path to the folly. Alina tugged at his hand with urgency. 'Come on, or we'll be too late.'

They beat the other couples to the folly only by a few minutes, the others having stopped to search the area at the base of the hill in the hopes of finding more eggs. Apparently, there was also to be a prize for the team with the most eggs. 'That's what we get for not listening to the rules.' Alina gave him a saucy smile as they crested the hill.

Their first few guesses as to where the last egg was hidden turned up false, but they did gather a couple more bon bon–filled eggs. Their basket looked more respectable. By then, the other couples had joined them. That was when Channing saw it—an egg tucked up in the crumbling battlements of the folly. He took Alina's hand and whispered, 'Up there, on the left. We must be stealthy or we'll give away its position.' And other couples were closer if they noticed. Alina's face glowed with anticipation. It was Alina who went up into the battlements while he ran diversionary tactics down below, frantically searching under rocks and in nooks as others crowded the hillside.

'I've got it!' came Alina's cry at last. Channing looked up and smiled. Alina stood at the top of the battlement, the necklace dripping from her hand in a glittering cascade, looking like a regal medieval queen in her triumph. Night, Channing thought, couldn't fall fast enough. Diamonds were about to become his best friend.

'Diamonds become you, *comtesse.*' The words startled Alina into alertness. She gathered her thoughts and remembered to smile. She'd worn the necklace to dinner as an honour to her hostess and to commend the success of the ingenious egg hunt. She'd not seen a way out of it without being rude, but diamonds were not her friend. She'd wished with all her heart the prize had been anything but a diamond necklace, the one piece of jewellery she'd come to despise above all else, the one thing she intensely associated with the humiliations of her marriage: the diamond collar she'd worn the day Channing had come to the park, the same collar she'd worn at the *comte*'s command whenever he wished her to remember her place, at his feet like a dog.

She put a hand to the jewellery where it lay against her neck. 'Thank you, Mr Seymour. Did you enjoy the egg hunt?' Alina enquired out of politeness. She had no doubt the event would be the talk of London when everyone returned to the city in a couple days. Lady Lionel had certainly succeeded there.

She'd been wool-gathering. Shame on her, when she should have been working. The evening had slipped by; dinner had given way to a pleasant evening of music and cards. Here it was, nearly time for the tea cart and she hadn't made her next move with Seymour. Time was running out. There was only the ball tomorrow and the party would be over.

She caught sight of Channing starting to cross the room and quickly slipped a hand through Seymour's arm. If she meant to take the next step with Seymour, she needed to have him to herself. Channing would only serve to scare Seymour off. She guided Seymour towards the doors leading outside.

'I did. I made several interesting discoveries.'

Too bad he hadn't choked on his bon bons, Alina thought. But then she wouldn't have the pleasure of catching him out and seeing him ruined. She gave a pout, letting her expression cloud. 'I had such a good time today, so you can imagine how disappointed I was to return and find a letter waiting from my solicitor.' She looked up at him from underneath her lashes, suddenly reticent. 'Did you mean it last night about wanting to help me? I wouldn't want to burden you.' She hesitated ever so slightly.

'My dear *comtesse,* it would be no burden at all,' he replied silkily. Good lord, the man could barely keep the avarice out of his eyes. He was disgusting.

'I have a property that is failing. It's a good property,' she added hastily, 'but it needs improvements in order to turn a profit and improvements are beyond my current budget.' She fingered the necklace and gave a rueful smile. 'Perhaps not now, though. I suppose I could sell my necklace. I was going to ask if you might be able to help me arrange for a loan, but now I think I might ask if you could pawn my necklace for me?' She conjured a watery gaze. 'These kinds of arrangements are unknown to me. I fear I would be taken advantage of if I attempted them on my own.'

'I hate to see a lady sell her jewels for something as mundane as farming implements and tenant roofs.' Seymour cocked his head as if an idea had just surfaced. 'I don't think such a prize should be sold. It will be a wonderful memento of this day.'

'But I have no choice,' Alina gently reminded him.

'I could loan you the money,' Seymour suggested.

She let herself brighten at the prospect. 'You could? You would do that for me? It would be perfect. It would be private? No one needs to know?'

'No one needs to know,' he echoed, covering her hand where it lay on his sleeve. She fought the urge to withdraw it. 'I am the soul of discretion, *comtesse*.'

She sighed. 'But there is a problem. I haven't any collateral. I have no way of securing the loan and I don't want to take advantage of you.'

He smiled again. 'Never mind about that, here's how we'll do it.' He explained the process and she managed to nod in key places. 'Do you understand, *comtesse?* It's all very simple really. We'll have your property turning a profit in no time.'

'Yes, I understand perfectly.' She understood all too well. There was no problem in what he suggested, only in what he did when the property was under his purvey. 'Thank you, Mr Seymour, you've made this much easier than it could have been otherwise.' It was all true, only not in the way he thought she meant it. His greed had made him a pigeon ripe for the plucking. Channing was on the move again and, this time, she let him find her. It was the ideal manoeuvre for disengaging herself from Seymour without giving the appearance of leaving him abruptly on her own accord. She'd let Channing take care of that.

'There you are, *comtesse*.' Channing did not disappoint. 'Lady Lionel sent me to find you. She wanted you to have the first piece of cake as the victor of our egg hunt.' It was perfectly timed, the tea cart just rolling in.

'If you'll excuse me, Mr Seymour?' Alina gave him a smile and moved to Channing's arm.

'Of course, my dear. We'll speak again in the morning.' He gave her a bow and she could already feel Channing's muscles tighten beneath her hand.

'What does Seymour wish to speak about in the morning?' He fairly bristled as they walked.

'Business.' She cast him a sly glance and touched the necklace in subtle reminder. 'Don't be jealous, what I have planned for us is all pleasure.'

Channing gave an imperceptible arch of his eyebrow. 'Makes me want to skip the tea cart altogether,' he murmured huskily.

'I'd advise eating.' She gave a throaty laugh. 'You'll need your strength.'

'Minx. You really are irresistible.'

You are, too. The afternoon had been a delightful foray into pleasure and play. It had proven that the pleasure still existed between them. That was half the problem. The other half was that she didn't even want to try to resist on afternoons like today when she'd been swept away in the fun of being with him. Giving herself over to that kind of abandon hadn't worked out for her in the past. *This time,* she reminded herself, it would be different. She was smarter, wiser and she knew what she was after: just the pleasure, nothing else. *This time* she wouldn't forget: out of bed, Channing Deveril had limitations.

Chapter Nine

Those limitations didn't apply inside the bedroom, however. Nor did they apply for the duration of the house party, Alina decided as she readied herself for Channing's visit. She had her mental ground rules firmly in place. There was no reason why she should not carry on a wicked flirtation with Channing that served both her purposes of distraction and pleasure. Surely, after all she'd endured, she deserved a little pleasure as reward. There was no harm in it as long as she kept perspective.

She would have to be subtle, starting with tonight. Channing had seen right through her other attempt from the start and he had no tolerance for being someone's plaything, especially not hers. What he perceived as her betrayal all those years ago would not allow for it. Alina paused in front of the mirror over her vanity and studied the reflection. She'd chosen a white-silk dressing gown that belted at the waist and flowed over her curves. She wore nothing underneath. Her hair was up, loosely held in place with a clip. It would come down easily and quickly. For now, she liked the image it created, as if she was fresh come from her bath. But her neck was bare. She'd decided long ago she would not wear the diamonds for Channing or any man. The necklace was prettily laid out on her vanity, catching the candlelight, but it would not grace her neck.

The woman in the mirror had long known the power of sex to bend men to her will. Without it, she would not have survived the cruelties of her marriage to the *comte*. Slowly, she unbelted the robe and drew the robe apart, revealing her nakedness to the mirror. She cupped her left breast and lifted it, exposing the underside. The faint remnants of his mark were still there, hidden from view, especially in the dark. But she knew and he'd known it was there.

Alina drew her fingers gently over the tiny impressions of the scar. It had faded over time, but it would always be there. It was the night he'd gone too far. He had not liked the way she'd looked at a gentleman, an English visitor, over dinner. Frankly, he'd not liked Englishmen since he'd discovered Channing's infatuation with her. Alina squeezed her eyes shut, pushing back those memories. She'd been too young, too naïve to do anything then but bear it. She'd done nothing to inspire this new Englishman, but the *comte,* in his paranoia, believed otherwise.

He'd called her to him in his chamber that evening and she'd known it would go badly, that she'd be blamed for some imagined slight, even though it was by his own orders that she graced his table and consorted with his guests. He'd been in a rage and he'd been planning. She saw too late that his signet ring had already been heating in the fire. She'd tried to run, tried to fight him. She'd not yet learned that such attempts excited him to frenzy. He'd ripped the fabric of her gown from her and pinned her to the wall with his weight while he'd pressed the scorching ring into her soft flesh, all the while she screamed, knowing no one would answer her cries.

Alina drew the folds of her robe together and rebelted it. She'd changed that night. She'd gone from being a meek wife whose strategy for survival had been invisibility and quiet acceptance of her fate to a woman empowered by her assets. Maybe she didn't have the brute strength to counter him physically or to stop him, but she had the power to deny him the satisfaction of watching her break. Harnessing that power had required her to be bold, to go against the teachings of childhood when it came to a woman's duty and obedience. She'd had to acquire skills no decent Englishwoman learned in the schoolroom, but she'd done it. Sex became a game, a source of power and control, and she'd survived.

It was not until she'd met Channing again in England upon her return, that she'd learned there could be pleasure. Even that lesson had been hard learned. He'd shown her how to soar like Icarus to the sun, then he'd let her crash. But tonight, she would have both the power and the pleasure.

Alina gave her appearance a final glance. Satisfied, she checked the supplies in the drawer beside the bed. The *capotes anglaise* were prepared, one of them already out of its package so there would not be much interruption when the time came. She moved to the table and chairs set before the fire. Little vials of oil stood discreetly ready on the table top along with the more obvious bucket of champagne. She picked up one of the oils and removed the stopper, letting the scent of sandalwood fill the room. But that was not the one she was going to use on him. She had a nice vanilla-scented oil for *that*. All was in place.

A thrill ran through her at the prospect of what lay ahead. Games and pasts aside, this was going to be a delightful seduction. The interlude at the summerhouse ensured it. It had served as an ice-breaker of sorts. The fast, heated, playful love making had paved the way for something more sophisticated and lingering, something that could take all night if they wanted. They would not repeat the mistakes of the previous night with a quarrel and insinuations from pasts neither of them fully understood. Better to live in the present.

There was a quiet scratch on the door and her pulse raced for a moment with anticipation of what was to come. Sex with Channing Deveril was one of the highlights of her life as long as it was just sex, as long as she remembered the rules of the game and what she wanted at the end of it.

Channing slipped inside and shut the door softly behind him. He was dressed in a robe, too, and his feet were bare. 'I hope no one saw you.' Alina let her gaze sweep his form. He was obviously naked beneath the robe. More than a hint of bare chest was visible between the lapels of the robe and his legs were uncovered. No one catching him in the hall would believe he was on his way to the library to pick out some night reading.

'I didn't want to waste time.' Channing smiled, his hand going to the belt at his waist. It gave with a yank, the robe falling open to confirm his nakedness. In the next moment it was off, a dark pool at his feet. From there, her eyes went up past trim calves and muscled thighs, to the golden nest between his legs where his maleness rested. Only it was not at home just now, but rising strong and firm in anticipation of the evening. Beyond that, lean hips gave way to the expanse of his chest and the muscled smoothness of his arms and shoulders.

Some men disappointed once the clothes came off, but not Channing. He was muscular, not in the way of a strong, stocky farmer who worked the land, but in the way of a gentleman who knew how to take care of himself and who had deliberately done so with hours on horseback and time spent in the male preserves of Jackson's or Manton's when in London. 'I had forgotten how magnificent you are without clothes,' she whispered, letting her eyes unabashedly drift back to the core of him. Of course, she remembered his body abstractly, the idea of him and how he felt. But this was so much better, so much more concrete.

'Then I am pleased to remind you.' He let her look, in no hurry to rush to the next stage of the night.

She liked his boldness. He was not ashamed of his nudity or his blatant love of the sexual. The body was meant to be explored, each new body a chance for new discovery. She matched it with a boldness of her own. Alina undid the sash of her robe, her eyes moving to his face, holding his gaze. She wanted to watch him watch her when she did this.

Alina shrugged the dressing robe from her shoulders, letting it slide from her body without touching it. It was an erotic little trick that implied a certain metamorphosis, an emergence from a cocoon, ready to take flight as a sensual butterfly.

She pulled the clip from her hair and shook it down. It, too, was a beautifully calculated move to draw the eye from her face down the length of body as the viewer watched her hair fall past shoulders and over breasts. The gown at her feet, a glimmer of white in a dark room, ensured the viewer continued to look down to long slim legs and the carefully groomed silver pelt between them.

Channing's breath caught. 'I don't think Aphrodite could be any lovelier.' She knew exactly what Channing liked and it pleased her to please him. That perhaps was the difference between Channing and her other lovers.

There'd been no time in the summerhouse to appreciate the other's body, only time to appreciate what their bodies could do to one another, *for* one another. She gestured to the chair and small table by the fire. 'Will you come and sit? I have champagne chilling. Moët's Imperiale Rose— your favourite, I believe.' Her favourite as well. She never travelled without it, which was why she'd just happened to have two bottles with her. She'd certainly not expected Lady Lionel to have any in her cellar. She'd had it chilling since the return from the egg hunt.

She opened the bottle herself, her back to the firelight, knowing full well the sensual nature of what she presented—a naked woman, pulling the cork from a champagne bottle. The effect was immediate. Channing's blue eyes darkened to deep sapphire. She poured him a glass and then one for her. 'To a long and satisfying night,' she toasted.

The coldness of the champagne sliding down one's throat was a titillating contrast to the heat of the fire. 'Is there anything more decadent than this?' Channing said with a happy sigh. 'Drinking champagne naked.'

'I can think of a few things,' she offered coyly, her eyes dropping briefly to his phallus.

'Are you going to sit?' Channing nodded to the empty chair.

Alina set aside her champagne and reached for the vial of vanilla oil. 'No, I'm going to kneel.' She gave him a wicked smile and took up her position between his legs. She poured oil into the cup of her hand, holding Channing's gaze, and blew on it. No one in their right mind would actually believe *she* was in the submissive role here. Of course, men weren't usually in their right minds, which accounted for the belief that this sort of pleasuring by mouth was a subservient act. Alina had no such illusions. She had all the power. Channing's broken exhalation of 'Have mercy, Alina, I'm only a mere mortal', was proof enough of that.

'Pleasure, then mercy,' she murmured. She massaged his inner thighs first, relaxing the muscles as she worked in the oil, enjoying the reminder of his excellent physique. A man who took care of himself was a confident man, capable of taking care of others, a man who believed in his own prowess, his own value. There was a certain aphrodisiacal quality to that knowledge. Her thumbs made a habit of occasionally brushing the edges of his sac as she massaged. Channing moaned in appreciation and she moved her massage on to more intimate parts. She gently drew her fingernail across his balls and felt them tighten.

'Vixen!'

She looked up and placed a kiss on his phallus. 'You're magnificent, Channing.' Then it was time to take him in hand. She loved stroking him, truth be told, loved the feel of the hot length of him, the radiant power of him contained in this living centre, loved knowing she could call it to life with a look, a touch, a press of her lips against its tender head. She stroked him until he begged, 'Your mouth, Alina, *please.*' He'd slid down in the chair and his hands had dug into the wood of the arm rests.

She was happy to comply. She tongued his tip and then his length, tasting the salt of him mingled with the vanilla , a sweet-sour combination as heady as the man himself. It was nearly as arousing to her as the act was to him. She could feel her core weep as she took him, her body knowing her own turn at such pleasure wasn't far away.

'Alina!' His body tensed and the hoarse cry was all the warning she had. She slipped her mouth from him and took him in her hand, holding him, catching him, as his body climaxed. She was prepared for that, too. Soft hand towels were waiting beneath the table, out of sight until needed. She cleaned him, delighting in the intimacy of such an act, and delighting, too, in the nature of a man who was bold enough, comfortable enough with himself, to allow such a thing. A French lover would certainly not have minded, but the English were not at ease with any ounce of evidence of the sexual act, another reminder of how much she'd changed in her years away.

She felt Channing's hand cover hers as she finished her ministrations. His voice was full of husky promise. 'Come to bed, let me return the favour.'

Channing led her to the bed, their hands entwined, a most intimate walk knowing the outcome that waited for her. But Channing was in no rush to claim that outcome. Ah, he knew how to prolong the delicious anticipation. He kept them upright, taking her mouth in a long kiss that licked and sucked and promised a dilettante's pleasure. 'Good things come to those who wait,' Channing murmured, his lips moving over hers.

'But he who hesitates is lost,' she whispered, giving his lower lip a little bite.

He didn't make her wait much longer. He swept her up in his arms and deposited her on the bed. It was not the playful, rambunctious dumping that had accompanied his tackle in the summerhouse today. It was the laying down of a treasured lover, a prince preparing to claim his princess. 'There, now I can look at you properly.' Channing lay down beside her, his golden head propped in his hand, his blue eyes intense with desire.

His hand was splayed in the valley between her breasts before he moved to cup each one, his thumb flicking across each nipple in turn until she arched against him, a mewl of delight on her lips. Even the lightest of his touches was exquisite, every touch building anticipation and want for the more intimate touches that would come. Then his hand was there at last, on her silvery mons, his fingers gently parting her folds, searching for her feminine pearl. He found it with unerring accuracy.

'You're beautiful by candlelight.' Channing's voice was rough.

'Don't take me all the way, Channing. I want it to come with you inside me,' she breathed the command.

'Come both times. Why do you have to choose?' Channing kissed her mouth then, his tongue making a fair reproduction of the strokes of his finger over her tight bud until she thought she'd scream from the dual sensations. And he was right. Why choose when she didn't have to? Channing brought her to the brink and toppled her over it in a wave of pleasure that shattered on a far shore. But he wasn't done yet. He took what he needed from the little drawer beside the bed and he moved between the cradle of her legs. He began the ultimate act, the one they'd been building towards all night. Her fears that their extensive foreplay would deplete their resources were for naught. Her body stirred to life, her legs wrapping around his hips, urging him to take her, the rhythm claiming them both.

She met his thrusts, arching into him, their cries mingling until they were both lost in the other. She was aware in an abstract sense of consciousness that his hair had fallen over his face, that his head was buried at her shoulder. She was aware, too, that she was no longer in charge, that Channing had taken over the interaction entirely and was directing it, driving them with each thrust to an explosive conclusion. She was consumed entirely with the act as he pumped furiously into her one last time.

He held her to him, letting the power of the climax consume them both. He was her anchor in these precious moments where her mind was blank, empty of everything but the enormity of what they had wrought between them. Surely this was the eighth wonder of the world? She did not want to let go. She was content to stay wrapped in his arms, his phallus still inside her as it recovered, their breathing beginning to slow, his heart beating against hers, skin to skin in an ever-steadying rhythm. Then came the moment he withdrew from her and rolled to his side. She felt strangely bereft except for the connection of his gaze, binding them, connected as if this was more than sex, as if it mattered. No wonder he was London's finest.

'Do you look at all the women you bed like this?' Alina asked drowsily. She felt him tense momentarily and winced. In her current state, she had not thought that last question out.

But Channing played along as if nothing were amiss. He drew a circle around the aureole of her breast and smiled. 'And how is that exactly?' It was a heart-stoppingly sincere smile that would have melted her had she not already been a pile of useless, disconnected bones.

'As if I am your rapture,' Alina ventured.

Channing gave a laugh. 'Oh, that way. Then the answer is no. Only you. I look at only you that way.'

'I suppose you say that to all the girls,' she flirted a little.

'No, not all of them.' He favoured the side of her neck with a kiss. 'Just the ones who serve me champagne naked.'

He was teasing her now and she was more awake, her senses recovered. She propped herself up on an arm and reached for him. 'You're a wicked tease, Channing Deveril, and for that you should be punished.' He was stirring against her hand already.

'What do you suggest?'

'I suggest this.' She kissed him hard on the mouth and rolled on top of him. 'I get to ride you in revenge.' She put her hands behind her head so that her breasts were in full relief and rose up over him, coming down to take him inside, feeling him harden within her as she slid down his length.

'Ah, this is why they say revenge is sweet.' Channing grinned.

Chapter Ten

Channing's internal clock, the one every gentleman of a certain repute carried within him to urge him out of bed before the house roused, nudged him awake around five in the morning. But that healthy dose of self-preservation, the one that had rolled him out of Marianne Bixley's lavender-scented bed and encouraged him to leave immediately failed him. The sight of Alina asleep beside him, her hair spread on the pillow like a pale fan, created a powerful argument to stay. Her maid, Celeste, wouldn't mind if she came in and found her mistress abed with him. It wouldn't be the first time.

Channing stifled a groan. This was where it got complicated, the game within the game—was it real or did it just *seem* real? Last night, she'd seduced him like the best of Venetian courtesans, everything carefully, artfully choreographed for maximum effect and yet executed so effortlessly that it appeared natural and one soon forgot that perhaps it wasn't.

It was the 'perhaps' that bothered him the most. Like himself, she was a sensual, sexual creature at heart. In the bedroom arts, she matched him pleasure for pleasure, fantasy for fantasy. But how much of it meant something? Any of it? None of it? Was she playing with him the way he'd played with so many women who'd come to the League over the years, looking for something temporarily satisfying in their mundane lives?

Why did he do this to himself? His logical mind knew these answers and it was laughing at his less-logical self that insisted on taking these questions out yet again and exploring them. First, he knew empirically she had the capacity to play with him. She'd shunned him brutally in Paris after he'd offered her the world, traded his offering for satins and jewels. Second, she'd been attempting to distract him since he arrived. She'd made it clear she didn't want him probing into her business too closely. Last night might have been fun, but the more fool he was if he didn't acknowledge it was also just another level of distraction. He wasn't the only one playing a game within a game here.

But he was also a fool if he didn't acknowledge how it had made him feel. Being with Alina could not be compared to any of his other assignments. Those were mere exercises in the physical. This was something *more.* Which was likely why he kept revisiting the same old question: did this mean anything? Could he let it mean anything? Even though he knew the risks and had done all he could to protect himself from hurt.

He knew his rules: seduce the information and nothing else. She could not be trusted with anything else. She'd broken his young man's heart once upon a time. He should know better. Yet he couldn't say he was making much headway there. He was no closer to knowing what she wanted with Seymour than before the summerhouse. He gave a little laugh. He hadn't meant to do it out loud. If at first you don't succeed, try, try again. Well, that was certainly an adage he wouldn't mind employing with Alina.

'You're thinking too much,' Alina murmured

beside him, snuggling into the notch of his shoulder.

'I was thinking about you.'

'That gives us something in common. I was thinking about *you*.' Her hand disappeared beneath the sheets. A moment later he felt it close around his cock, warm and sure.

'What about your maid?' Channing asked, but it was pro forma. At the moment, he could not care less if the whole house party walked in on them.

'Don't worry—' Alina smiled '—she likes you.'

'And you?' Channing was fishing in deep waters now, but he'd been lucky so far. 'Do you like me?'

Alina leaned over and kissed him on the mouth, her thumb running over the head of his penis in a delicious caress. 'What do you think?'

It was not an answer, but he was too smart to press his advantage. He'd let her be in charge for the moment. He'd have his chance later. He had a little game of seductive Q and A in mind that would help further his cause. The competitive part of him felt as if he was running in second place. She had what she wanted—he'd got the introduction for her—*and* she had the pleasure of his company in bed to boot. What did he have? Certainly nothing he'd thought to use the latter to acquire. Was she using him again? Was he letting her?

He gave a gasp as her thumb hit a sensitive spot. He didn't mind right now, but he was going to. He'd promised himself he wouldn't let her use him again

The lack of an explicit response from her had nagged at him the rest of the day. It had nagged him throughout the picnic to yet another nearby set of Roman ruins and it was nagging him still by the time he returned to his room to dress for dinner and the ball that was to follow. The house party would end the day after next, giving the guests time to recoup after the late evening of dancing tonight.

Technically, his obligation to Alina ended then, too. Amery's contract would be fulfilled. He should feel relief, but he didn't. After having reconnected with her, he felt nothing but loose ends at the prospect of leaving her. In part, those loose ends were the situation with Seymour. But also, the loose ends stemmed from things done but never spoken of in their past. Did they dare address Paris? Did they dare address the Christmas party? They would quarrel certainly, which was no doubt why they'd not brought either episode up. And what would it solve?

Channing dismissed his valet and headed downstairs, tucking a sapphire stick pin in the snowy folds of his cravat as he went. Still, he could tie up some of those loose ends tonight in regards to Seymour.

By his estimate, he was a little early. Alina would not be down yet. She would make her entrance as always right before the dinner bell. But when he entered the drawing room, he found he was absolutely mistaken.

Alina was present early and she was already engaged in conversation with none other than Roland Seymour. A spear of intense dislike stabbed through him. He was seldom a jealous man. Women came and went through his life and he spared them little covetous thought once their time together had passed. It was the nature of his business. But this—watching Alina focus all the attention of her blue eyes on the undeserv-

ing Seymour, knowing she stood close enough
that Seymour could smell the delicate floral scent
of her, that he could even drop his eyes a shade
lower and glimpse a peek at her exquisite cleavage—this was torture.

Seymour leaned close. Alina laughed up at him
and Channing knew raw envy. It was primal and
poorly done for a man of his sophistication and
experience. She couldn't possibly be interested
in the likes of Seymour, not when she had had
him in her bed. He'd given her pleasure last night,
she'd gifted him with pleasure as well. One didn't
go to such lengths for a man who meant nothing:
the Moët, the intimate caress of mouth and hands
on him by the fire. It would be a long time before the memory of her naked body silhouetted
by the flame, the Moët in her hand as she poured
for him, would fade to respectable proportions.
A man could die happy after a night like that.

And yet she had come down early and sought
out the questionable Roland Seymour, who, even
at this late date in the house party, remained on
the fringes, having failed to penetrate the inner
circle of the more elite guests like Durham and
Barrett. Even the host spared only the required

amount of time politeness demanded with Seymour. So what did Alina mean by it?

It seemed he was asking that question about a lot of things she did, yet clearly Seymour meant something to her. She needed him for something, something important enough to drag her to this house party, which, aside from its inspired egg hunt, was not so special in its location or guest list. The Comtesse de Charentes surely had better choices for how she spent the short break before the Season began and for how she dared to risk her reputation.

'You're staring.' Elliott Priest came up beside him, a friend from the London clubs who'd been invited, too. 'I can't say I've ever seen you stare before. But then, there aren't many women like her. I can't blame you. I'd stare, too.' He was silent for a moment. 'I wonder what she sees in him?'

Channing gave a short laugh. 'I was wondering the same thing myself.' Elliott provided an excellent diversion. It would serve him far better to pass the time before dinner chatting with Elliott than it would to be caught staring at Alina. So for the sake of appearances he applied himself to

Elliott's conversation, letting his gaze drift only occasionally to the corner of the room Alina occupied with Seymour.

He was watching her. Alina could feel the intensity of his gaze even at a distance, as brief as it was. Thank goodness Channing had stopped staring outright. It had been difficult to pretend she wasn't aware, difficult to give Seymour all of her simpering attentions. Play the game, she'd admonished herself. But it was hard to keep all the games straight. Only the first one was going well. She had Seymour right where she wanted him. She had Channing right where she wanted him, too—in her bed, but that game was becoming murky, probably because it had ceased to be one. She knew better. The last thing she needed was Channing around to poke his nose into her business with Seymour. It was bad enough he was staring daggers across the room at her and he didn't even know exactly what she was up to. He would certainly not like it any better when he heard the particulars. 'Do you think Mr Deveril will be a problem?' Seymour's comment forced her to focus.

'I shouldn't think so. He's not a man of business, after all,' Alina said dismissively, implying that Channing's pursuits were more leisurely in nature.

Seymour cocked a knowing eyebrow in her direction. 'I don't doubt that at all—one hears things, you know.'

Alina fought the urge to bristle. It was one thing to be dismissive; it was another to be derisive. A man like Roland Seymour had no right to sit in judgement on the son of a peer. But she hated herself for the quick defence. This was the problem with Channing, he was so likeable even when she knew better. It was his *job* to be likeable. He'd made likeability into an art form and into a fortune as the head of the League of Discreet Gentlemen, something most of London had yet to empirically verify.

She put a hand on Seymour's sleeve. 'Thank you for signing the contracts before dinner. I will be able to enjoy my evening now, knowing that everything is in your capable hands.'

The dinner bell rang and the gentleman she was supposed to walk in with came to claim her. Alina felt a sense of relief. In England, a decent woman didn't leave one man to seek the company of another, but she hated being trapped with Seymour now that her business was conducted. There was nothing more to do on that end but wait and watch. He would reveal himself soon enough and she would be there to ensure he never took advantage of another woman again.

Dinner was festive. Everyone was in high spirits from the picnic and the anticipation of the dancing to come. She made conversation with the married gentleman on her left and the single gentleman on her right, miles down the table from Channing, which suited her purposes at the moment. She wanted to avoid his questions about Seymour. It was temporary relief only. She couldn't avoid them for ever.

Everyone had worn their ball attire to dinner and adjourned to the drawing room for dancing. Immediately after the meal, local guests had begun to arrive and the women had been given darling little dance cards done up in pale-pink card stock and embossed in gold trim to dangle from their wrists. It didn't take long for Channing to materialise at her side and claim two dances.

'I should like to claim more than two,' he drawled pleasantly, picking up the pencil and signing the card with a bold C.D. in the third and last slots. 'He returned the card to her. 'However, I realise we can't have anyone from the party carrying tales to London.' She understood he was daring her to a public breaking of the rules.

Alina lowered her voice to a seductive pitch. 'Does that mean I'll be drinking Moët in my room alone?'

Channing flashed her a quick smile. 'Absolutely not. It's only necessary to be discreet if there's something to hide. One implies the other, you see.'

Alina dropped her eyes in a demure pose. 'I must thank you for the clarification, Mr Deveril.' There were others beginning to approach. Channing couldn't overstay his welcome.

He laughed and raised her hand to his lips in a showy gesture. 'You don't fool me for a moment. Until then.'

Until then. When was that? Until the third dance when he brought up Seymour? Until the last dance when he'd bring up Seymour? She'd fully expected he'd take the first chance to ask her what she and Seymour had been discussing so avidly before dinner. But he hadn't. He'd merely signed her dance card, flirted a bit and moved on to sign other dance cards. Which he was expected to do—it was his job as a party guest to see that all the ladies were accommodated with all the dancing they desired.

She ought to take his coming to her first as a private sign of his esteem, a sign that he'd built his evening around her dance schedule, but she couldn't. She knew too much. They were playing a game, although it was hard to tell which one. Had this been about Seymour or had it been about the other game? Why hadn't he asked about Seymour? Or maybe it was just about getting even because now all she wanted to do was run across the drawing room and shake him and shout, 'Why won't you ask me about Seymour!'

Alina tried to set such thoughts from her mind and enjoy the dancing. He would ask her when he asked her and there was nothing she could do about it.

The thought was there at the back of her mind the whole evening, creating a layer of tension.

The third dance, a waltz, came and she fully expected Channing to mention it. A waltz was the perfect time to ask since there were no partners to move between. But all he did was flirt with his eyes and make love to her with the fluid movements of his body. She doubted anyone danced the waltz as well as Channing Deveril.

It was empirically true. The unbidden memory surfaced as he swept her through the steps. It had been at the ill-fated Christmas party, their last engagement before the contract officially ended. There had been dancing and Channing had been a most sought-after partner. She'd watched him dance with all the young ladies, each of them feeling like a queen when he was with them, the way she felt when she was with him. They were all just another job to him, even her, no matter what she wanted to believe.

That was when Alina had known with abject clarity she could have all the sex she wanted with Channing Deveril, but she could never have him. Not only because she was a widow with a scandalous Continental past, but because his heart could not be engaged, at least not by her. This time, she hoped to manage better, however. This time, she knew the limits. She could have all the earth-shattering, mind-bending sex she wanted, but nothing more.

The dance ended and he returned her to the group of people she'd been talking with before the dance. Not a word had passed between them about Seymour and the rest of the night loomed long before her. *Nothing is free.* This was how he was going to make her pay for keeping her secret.

The intervening dances were distractions, merely ways to count down until Channing claimed her once more, putting her night of waiting to rest at last. Surely *now* he would say something?

The last dance was to be a waltz, too, and, for special effect, Lady Lionel had the room dimmed, leaving only a few select candles burning to give the room a decidedly romantic feel. The effect was quite divine, Alina thought, as Channing led her out on to the dance floor.

Channing moved her into position, his hand at her back, her hand at his shoulder. His voice was low in her ear and she could hear the smile in it and the undercurrent of desire. 'For a hostess with a mediocre reputation, Lady Lionel has outdone herself. First the egg hunt, now this.'

Her own response was a little less friendly in nature. She wasn't ready to capitulate to his warm charm just yet after what he'd put her through this evening. She opted to get the issue out in the open. 'Too bad you're going to ruin it.' It truly was because it was positively heavenly to be danced through the turn by Channing.

'Exactly how am I going to do that?' Channing executed a sharp swirl to avoid a collision in the dark. The motion brought her up against him, creating an intimate awareness of his body, of his thighs where they brushed her skirts.

'You're going to ask me about Seymour.'

'No, I'm not.'

'You are, too. You were staring daggers before dinner.' Perhaps she'd imagined too much. Perhaps he really didn't care about her business with Seymour beyond curiosity's sake. Why would he? He was here with her on a job, just as he had been at the Christmas party. That had been her mistake then, too, assuming that it was more than a job.

He laughed softly. 'I assure you, I am not going to ask.'

Now her curiosity was piqued. 'Why not?'

He bent his lips to the spot below her ear, his breath light against her skin. 'Because, Alina, I don't want to ruin it.' He swung her into another turn and brought her up close against him, his voice husky with the desire she'd heard earlier. 'I have every intention of being in your room within the hour.'

And because that sounded much more promising than any argument over her business with Roland Seymour, Alina said, 'I do, too.'

Chapter Eleven

It might have been her room, but the seduction was all his. He seduced her with chocolate and a second bottle of Moët. There was no better aphrodisiac in the world than champagne and chocolate, if you were Alina Marliss, unless it was the sight of Channing Deveril naked in the candlelight, pouring that champagne. But it would have been remiss of her to assume he would make the night a repeat of what had gone before. That was a mistake only an amateur would make and Channing was no amateur. They'd already eaten bon bons together in the summerhouse and drunk Moët in the nude, which was why doing it again was such a tantalising prelude to the unknown. Alina smiled to herself, a low, simmering heat unfurling in her belly. She understood; this was his pay back for not being told about Seymour.

She'd made him suffer a bit this evening with curiosity and now he was doing the same, just the same as he had on the dance floor, making her wonder what would come next. But this was not her husband's fear-based wonder, this was wonder driven by titillation and there was a vast difference.

When her glass of Moët was almost gone, he rose from their chairs by the fire and issued his first command. 'Take off your clothes.'

Ah, so it was to be that sort of game tonight, Alina thought as he moved to another part of the room, his back to her. He wasn't going to watch as she disrobed. Of course not. That might derail the game, derail his control as the game master. She could hear him assembling supplies as she stripped out of her robe and underthings.

'Shall I sit?' she asked, fully willing to play whatever game he had in mind. Channing returned with a tray full of items. He made a great show of studying her, naked in the firelight, and then studying the chair.

'Yes, I think so,' he mused aloud. 'The chair is perfect.'

'Perfect for what?' she enquired, taking her

seat. She was more than a little aroused already just being naked in front of him and knowing that he watched her.

He knelt before her, the table and tray within easy arm's reach. *'Pour le petit mort avec chocolat.'* He spread her thighs, running warm hands along their insides and drawing them wide to the legs of the chair. It was arousing to be so vulnerable, so open to him.

He reached for the tray and took off a roll of cloth. 'Silk,' he murmured huskily, unwinding a long strip. 'Don't worry, I won't bind it too tight, just tight enough.'

Tight enough to hold her, tight enough to keep her from coming to her own aid. Alina's throat went dry, the prospect incredibly titillating as he bound her legs to the chair, her hands to the arm rests. He pulled at the bonds in an experimental tug, giving her a wickedly satisfied look when they held.

Her eyes followed his hands back to the tray. He picked up a bowl and a paint brush. A paint brush? His eyes held hers. 'Now, I shall paint you. You shall be my study in chocolate.'

She could smell it now, the scent of melted

chocolate, a most erotic scent on its own, but even more so when mixed with the salty, musky scent of sex. It was the smell of her, she realised. And of him. The smell of consent and excitement; a very different smell from fear. She knew. In the dim light of the fire, she could see the liquid bead of his own arousal lingering on the head of his phallus. There would be pleasure waiting at the end of this and the journey was part of that pleasure.

Channing rose up between her legs so that the two of them were close, so very close when he dipped the brush and drew it down her torso in a long stroke, leaving a warm trail of chocolate in its wake. Lord, it felt delicious on her skin, quite literally a sweet caress.

He painted her chest with curving whorls about her nipples, her breasts, her belly and then the sweetness became something more as the brush moved between her thighs, painting them, painting her private furrow in strokes that made it weep. Her desire rose, hot and demanding. There was nothing she could do but endure it. She understood at last just how helpless she was to resist any of the pleasure. None the less, she arched and bucked, feeble as the efforts were, in an attempt to give herself release, to no avail. She tried to calm her fevered body with the reminder that he would eventually bring her release.

But Channing had no intentions of letting the game end there. He meant for her to know tonight was his. She'd been the master last night, but only because he'd allowed it. He dipped a finger into the bowl and licked it with a wicked stroke of his tongue.

'It's time,' he murmured mysteriously. 'Perhaps you'd like something to drink first.' He rose and stepped back, ensuring that he could see her. He took himself in his hand, drawing his hand slowly along his length, and Alina understood. *Drink to me only with thine eyes and I will pledge with mine...*

Alina groaned, an arousal upon her so intense she thought *le petit mort* was far too small a concept for what she felt and it was clear Channing wasn't done, not even close to it.

He returned to her, kneeling once more and lowering his mouth to the flat of her belly, then to the silvery hillock between her legs, his breath warm against her skin as he spoke hot, decadent words. 'Sweet heavens, your pelt turns me on, Alina.' They were worship words and she'd treasured the first time he'd said as much. He'd told her then it was the North Star, that he'd never seen hair like that down there. Pure platinum silk, he called it, combed to smoothness, edges trimmed into a triangle of perfection, one of the many reminders that she was a woman who knew how to take care of herself in all ways.

He trailed a finger inside her cleft. She was wet for him; he would see it. She watched the pupils of his eyes dilate to black at the evidence. *Ah, bien,* this game was just as scintillating for him as it was for her. 'Taste me, taste us,' he whispered, dragging his finger across the top of his cock and then through the chocolate left in the bowl. He brought his finger to her mouth and she licked, running her tongue down the length of it. Surely, he would bring her off *now*. The chocolate was beginning to cool on her skin.

'Do you like licking?' he asked, but it was a rhetorical question only. 'Then you will like what comes next.' He rose on his knees and took her nipple in his mouth, his intentions clear. Oh, yes, there was no mistaking this was both pleasure and payback. After having painted her with chocolate, he was now going to lick it off her body, inch by inch.

'You're killing me, Channing,' she managed to say as he flicked his tongue over the dip of her navel. Had she ever been so well ravaged? Ever rendered so out of control of her own body? Had she ever *liked* it so much?

'Just wait,' he whispered, lapping at the chocolate on her thigh. 'The best is yet to come.'

Let it come soon, Alina thought, *before I explode from wanting, death by paint brush.* Although part of her was in no hurry to have this naughty seduction come to a head, as it were.

She gripped the arm rests, thankful in the exquisite moment for the bonds that held her in place. Without them, she might have slipped to the floor, completely undone. In the next, she wished she had her hands, wished she could bury them in his hair, wished she had an anchor in this storm of desire sweeping her. She wished she had use of her legs, wished she could squeeze them together, wished *le petit mort* would take her.

She got her last wish. Channing gave a final pull, the suction of his mouth, the light rake of his teeth over her nub, pushing her forward towards oblivion until she was there at last and he let her go, let the consuming tremor take her, a cry ripping from her throat and she was consumed.

She didn't recall when he untied her bonds, only that once she recovered herself she discovered she was free.

'How do you feel?' Channing sat across from her, sipping Moët casually from his glass as if nothing extraordinary had transpired in the last hour.

'Fine.' She watched Channing as he poured her a glass. She *did* feel fine and drowsy now that the crisis had passed, leaving her with that boneless sense of repletion.

'Glad to hear it.' He smiled over the rim of his glass. 'I have a little something I need you to do for me.'

'What might that be?' Alina asked, but she had a fairly good idea. A man couldn't pleasure a woman like that and not want a little something for himself. And she'd be happy to regain a little control.

Channing grinned and played with the stem of

his glass. 'You know, Amery told me you were too much for him. I'm starting to see why.'

'I never slept with Amery,' she reminded him. She was doubly glad she hadn't. She and Channing had certainly had other lovers, but it was better to not know explicitly who they were, better that they didn't have faces. Their past was haunted enough as it was.

'I know. I can't imagine what you would have done to the poor boy if you had,' Channing teased, but she could see that it was a relief to him, too. Amery was his co-worker, his friend, and she suspected that whatever she was to him or had been, she belonged to a very private part of his life he didn't share with others.

'I'm glad you're man enough for the task.' She smiled coyly, setting aside her glass and rising, her nudity blatantly displayed. He devoured the sight of her with his eyes, rising, too, and she could feel her desire for him stirring afresh as if the release she'd experienced minutes ago had not happened at all.

'Come to bed, Alina, and I'll show you what I'm made of.' Channing didn't wait for an answer. Instead, he swept her up in his arms and headed straight for the bed. She'd meant to take charge of this encounter, but any thought she had of regaining control was illusion only. This would be hard and fast, something that would give them both relief.

Channing drew her down on top of him. She reached to turn the lamp down, but he grasped her wrist. 'Leave it on.' His voice was husky, the request firm. He would brook no argument on this. Channing grinned, 'I want to see you fall apart on top of me.'

She might be on top, but he was still definitely in charge. 'I want to see all of you.'

That's what she was afraid of. They'd been naked together before, but never where there was full light. There'd always been dimness, darkness, to obscure her hidden flaws. She would have to work hard to keep him distracted, to keep him from thinking too much. She raised her hips over his phallus and slid down on him, her hair falling over her shoulders, her breasts, as she took him. She moved on him once, twice, then bent to take his mouth, but Channing restrained her.

'If you lay on me, I can't see you. Sit up,' he commanded gently. 'That's better. I can touch you, cup you and you can sheathe me.' He reached for her then, his hands taking her breasts from underneath, his fingers circling her nipples. She thought she might be safe. But she knew the minute she wasn't, knew the minute the palm of his hand found the imperfection under her breast

A question flitted across his brow. 'What's this?' He rolled her beneath him in a fluid motion. She thought of making a final stretch for the lamp, but it was too late. To turn the lamp down now would be tantamount to admitting there was something to see.

'It's nothing,' she murmured, but Channing would see for himself. He lifted her breast and studied the mark, the line between his brows creasing.

At length his eyes met hers. 'How did this happen?'

Alina shrugged. It was powerful and alluring to have Channing above her, his body braced over her on his elbows, but this was business she didn't want him in at all, even more than she didn't want him in the business about Seymour. He knew nothing of her marriage.

Channing pressed forward in the wake of her

silence. 'I'll tell you what it looks like to me and then you can decide if you want to disabuse me of the notion.' His voice was harsh, angry even. 'This looks like a burn mark. There's an image here or the remnants of an image. It's faded over time, but the skin is still puckered and a shadow of the image remains. At the time, it must have hurt. I can only think of one way someone gets such a specific mark in such a concealed place.' He paused, his gaze penetrating. 'It's not a mark anyone would give themselves.'

His blue eyes were hard, full of unconcealed anger. 'If this was not your husband's doing, you should speak now. You'd do his memory a disservice if you allowed me to think ill of the dead.'

She met his eyes with a hard stare of her own. 'He didn't want me to forget that I belonged to him.'

'Then it's a good thing he's dead already or else I'd have to kill him.'

Alina did reach for the light then. Not so Channing couldn't see her, but so she couldn't see him. When he looked at her like that, it was easy to pretend things could be different between them, like they'd been at Fontainebleau when anything had been possible. 'I don't need a champion, Channing. Besides, it's in the past. You can't do anything about it.'

Channing gathered her against him, her buttocks to the curve of his groin, his voice in her ear as the darkness cocooned them. 'You're wrong, everyone needs a champion. Even you, Alina.'

She fell asleep that way, cushioned against him, warm and safe in the pretence that tonight she could let him be hers.

Alina woke early. Something was wrong. For starters, the sun was up and Channing was still in her bed, snoring lightly. That did bring a smile to her face. London's finest lover snored. Nothing horrendous, mind; however, it did put a different construction on all that perfection one associated with him. Perfection. Champions. That's what was wrong. She remembered now. *He was going to be her champion.* Alina groaned. It had been a lovely pretence she'd fallen asleep to.

The problem with pretence was that it wasn't real. Pretence didn't last. In the light of day, it faded from a potent fantasy concocted in the dark to uncomfortable wishes in the light. Hers was no different. Channing knew about the brand. It had stirred an emotional reaction in him. In turn, his response had triggered one in her as well. She'd felt safe, secure, treasured even. But it was all a pretence.

Channing was very good at pretence. It was his job, after all, it was what made him such a success. He created fantasies women wanted to believe in, fantasies that went beyond the sexual, but encompassed their emotional lives, too. She'd seen it for herself when she'd hired him and she'd seen him at a distance with other women, too. She wasn't the only one he created that other fantasy for, yet she'd nearly fallen for it again last night.

She had to remember being here with her was a job, too, for him. It was not unlike the Christmas she'd first hired him. The only difference was that he was here as Amery's substitute. She could indulge in what he offered, but she had to keep a firm grip on precisely what that offering was—a fantasy that would end, a fantasy that wasn't real in the first place. This was business first and last for Channing. She'd do best to model that for herself. She would start reasserting a certain distance between her and Channing this morning.

Her brain registered a faint rustling somewhere in the room. It wasn't only the sensation of waking next to Channing that had drawn her from sleep with a feeling of unease. Something else was wrong. She caught the rustle again. Someone was in the room.

'Celeste?' Alina called out. Ugh, her voice sounded awful, proof of a late night.

'Comtesse.' Celeste hurried towards the bed, giving Channing's sleeping form an approving smile before launching into her news. 'I thought you would want to know at once. Roland Seymour's carriage left here at dawn with trunks and all.'

That got her attention. Alina sat up, her mind whirling. The bastard wasn't supposed to leave until tomorrow like the rest of them. He'd be in London this afternoon before the offices closed. She didn't want him discovering anything until she was back in town and had access to her team of solicitors. Damn and double damn. There was only one thing to do. Alina threw back the covers and jumped out of bed. 'We must pack, Celeste.'

She was going to have to go after him, that despicable bounder.

'Right now?' Celeste queried, nodding towards Channing.

'Right now. We can't have him reaching town before us. Lay out my travelling dress.'

This was not the morning she was hoping for. The day had been set aside for 'recovering' by their hostess. Guests would sleep the morning away, spend the day overseeing packing and perhaps taking a few quiet last walks with friends they'd made. She'd been looking forward to such a day, a day to celebrate that her efforts in regards to this party had been successful. A day to rest, to think of nothing before she had to think of what lay ahead in London; a Season she was obligated to attend just to prove to everyone her reputation was passable, reeling in Seymour and his dishonest heists. All she had wanted was one day of peace. What she had got was…

'I think it's time you tell me what is going on.' His voice sounded like gravel.

Channing. Wonderful. He was awake.

Alina turned from her dressing table. Celeste

had come to the doorway of the dressing room. 'It might be best, *madame*. You could use an ally.'

Alina gave Celeste a hard stare. She did not appreciate the vote of confidence in Channing, but Celeste's point was well taken. If she didn't tell Channing, he might seek out the information on his own and that could prematurely tip her hand before she was ready. Perhaps this was a case of keeping one's enemies closer. Not that Channing was an enemy precisely, but interference was.

If this was to be all business, she had to begin as she meant to go on. 'If you promise to let me do this my way, I'll tell you. But I must have your word, Channing.'

'It seems I have no choice but to agree.' Channing propped himself up on the pillows, the sheet falling to his waist. Celeste's eyes popped at the sight of his bare chest. Alina wished he had the decency to cover himself. It was one thing for her to see him naked, but she found she didn't like the idea of others seeing him in the same state.

Alina took a deep breath. 'Roland Seymour is a swindler and bankrupter of the unsuspecting. He offers to help people in distress by becoming a partner on deeds to their properties in exchange for loaning them money during the interim. Eventually the deed reverts full owner-ship back to the original holder and it does, just as agreed upon, but in the meantime he takes out huge loans, using the land as collateral. When he defaults on his loans, the banks come looking to possess the land, which is now back in the un-suspecting victim's hands, and, since Seymour is only a co-signer on the deed, the owner is now responsible.' She tried to keep the telling unemo-tional, tried to keep it devoid of the sordid way such a practice had affected her family.

Channing pushed a hand through his already-tousled hair and groaned, a far different groan than the ones he'd given the night before. 'Ce-leste, I'm going to need coffee.' He looked around the room. 'And I'm going to need my clothes. My valet will know what to send over. I think better when I'm dressed.' He gave her a once over in her white dressing robe. 'How about you, *comtesse?* Clothes?'

Alina shook her head and scowled. 'This is what I feared would happen.'

Channing cocked his head. 'What? Getting dressed or do you prefer to do your thinking naked? I could be persuaded to try, I suppose, although I can't guarantee which head I'll think with.'

Alina's frustration rose. She was trying to keep their 'morning after' interaction all business, absent of any reference to uncomfortable disclosures from the night before. Channing wasn't helping. He was using an entirely different script, wanting to play and flirt and interfere. 'This is no laughing matter. I've signed over a deed to him in order to catch him in action.'

What he ought to say was, 'I can see you have important matters to deal with, if you'll excuse me, I'll take my leave.'

What he said instead was, 'I suggest you get dressed. We have a lot of thinking to do.' Channing's grin vanished. 'It won't just be a disaster, it will be dangerous. A man like Seymour won't take kindly to being thwarted and he'll be even less appreciative of being exposed. Have you thought of that?' He sounded angry. He also sounded as if he understood everything after her brief summary. She'd forgotten how quick his mind was when it came to grasping nuances.

'I'd hate to think that the world would prefer

to ignore a wrong simply out of fear to right it,' Alina answered firmly. But she knew herself to be a hypocrite in that regard. She doubted she'd be so motivated to stop Seymour if he hadn't personally struck at her family. When it had happened she'd been in France, unable to stop it until it was too late. But she'd spent the year and a half of her return gathering the information she'd need to bring Seymour down. If she was for ever to be branded with her former husband's title, she was going to put it to good use. The Comtesse de Charentes was no longer powerless.

'Good God, you're set on this.' Channing sighed. 'Celeste, make that a lot of coffee.'

He was staying. So much for ridding herself of Channing's presence. It wasn't precisely the outcome she'd sought. But there were other ways of establishing distance, it wasn't only a consideration of proximity. If there was one good thing to come out of the morning, it was that she'd succeeded in keeping this all business. As long as they were discussing Seymour, they weren't discussing her or any of the foolish things she'd given vent to in the night.

Chapter Twelve

What had Alina got herself into now? Channing pushed his hand through his hair yet again a half-hour later. He was dressed, but his hair was going to be a tousled mess at this rate while he listened, questions darting through his mind. 'If it's him why hasn't anyone caught him before?' Channing sipped at his coffee.

'It's not him directly,' Alina explained. 'He is behind several syndicates that operate under different names. But he's used other aliases before so it's very difficult to catch him. Then there's the embarrassment factor. To catch him means exposing oneself to public scrutiny. He picks victims very deliberately, people who would be reluctant to let others know their finances were in trouble or that they'd been taken advantage of in an awkward business situation.'

'You are potentially courting scandal if your involvement in this becomes known,' Channing pointed out. Surely Alina had thought of that. If others worried over public censure, it ought to be a sign that she should worry, too.

'Only if I fail,' Alina reasoned. 'If I succeed, it might help my rather precarious reputation if it came out I had struck a blow for social justice.' She shrugged, but Channing could see the determined set of her jaw. She didn't believe she would fail.

'All right then, tell me how you're going to catch the thief.' Channing chose his pronouns carefully. He really meant 'we' or even 'he' if it came to that. Alina was not going to put herself in danger and for all her impressive research in tracking the man down, he didn't think she had any idea of what the villain might be capable.

'I've co-signed him on a deed to a property here in England that supposedly reverted back to me as part of the settlement and in turn he's loaning me funds to make improvements on the property for three months. My solicitors are on watch for the very second Seymour attempts to use the deed as collateral.'

'It seems risky—what if your solicitors simply miss their moment?' If it was that easy to spot, Channing thought, the man would have been caught by now, syndicate or not. Certainly, anyone's solicitor would notice activity involving a deed.

'Other solicitors are not as diligent as mine.' She paused here, her eyes sparkling with excitement. 'Besides, he won't be able to draw against the deed because the property doesn't exist.'

Channing spit out his coffee and gave up all pretensions to bland neutrality. 'You've forged a deed?'

'It's not really a forgery, it's just made up.' Alina said. 'It's not as bad as you think. The land actually exists and it's mine, it's just deeded under a false name.'

Channing relaxed slightly. 'Not that it makes it any better. Seymour will be furious to have been caught and duped. He will come after you. Did Amery know any of this?'

Alina shook her head. 'Absolutely not. It had nothing to do with him.' Channing understood the message completely. This had nothing to do with him either except for the fact that she was involved.

'What Amery knew or didn't know is irrelevant at this point.' Alina turned the conversation away from any ethical considerations he might raise, of which Channing felt there were a few.

Channing raised an eyebrow to indicate he didn't quite agree with her assumption. 'Oh?' Amery had only sensed he was outgunned in the arrangement and his instincts had served him well.

'What is relevant is that Seymour has bolted. I want to be in London, I *need* to be in London when he acts.' She started pacing. Maybe coffee wasn't such a great idea after all. He didn't need Alina to be more energised than she already was. She *would* go haring off to London without a thought for the consequences.

'He can't possibly do any harm today,' Channing argued. 'It will take more than an afternoon to get any paperwork through the banks and it's likely, since he wasn't planning on acquiring this deal with you, that he'll need time to think through what he wants to do. You have a few days at least.' He could see Alina didn't like his reasoning at all. It was far too sound.

'Think about your position. We can't both leave

the house party a day early. It will look suspicious and, quite frankly, you are not going to London without me. Whether or not you like it, you need a protector.'

'I had Amery,' Alina protested.

'Not a protector like Amery. He was only good for making you unavailable to the unwanted advances of others. You need someone to be your partner if you mean to do this mad thing.'

'And you think that partner should be you.' Alina faced him, hands on hips, looking most displeased.

'Yes, I do think it should be me.' Channing drew a deep breath. 'Alina, why not me? You know you can trust me.'

That earned him a steely blue stare. 'Do I? Well, it seems I have no choice.' That was his cue to exit.

Could she trust him? Could she trust him not? Alina picked the petals off a summer rose as she strolled around Lady Lionel's garden. It was good to be alone. The afternoon was warm, the weather and the walk had helped calm her nerves. She'd been agitated after Channing had left. How dare he insinuate himself into her business and *then* have the audacity to suggest she could trust him after…?

After what? She had to tread carefully here. After she'd come to England and then proceeded to engage him in a business arrangement, hiring his services to reintegrate her into English society? And all the while *she'd* mentioned nothing about the desire to establish an intimate arrangement akin to what they'd dreamed of in Fontainebleau? She'd made no overture and neither had he. Therein lay the rub. Of course, she'd been waiting for him to establish *his* desire to continue as they had been. No overture had come. At the Christmas party, she'd discovered why.

There'd been nothing between them but business, but Alina had acted as if there was. The argument that had followed the party had not been well done of her. She'd thrown several accusations at him and a vase or two for good measure simply because she'd let herself be convinced she wasn't just another job to him.

'What the hell do you mean by leaving the ball?' Channing shut the door behind him with

a resounding slam. She was sure the rest of the house would have heard it, if the music hadn't been playing.

'What do you mean by barging into a lady's bedroom?' she fired back, yanking the pins from her hair and making it clear she would not return to the festivities.

'I mean to settle this once and for all.' Channing was in rare form. He advanced on her with firm strides. She backed up, her knees hitting the back of her dressing table. 'You asked me to introduce you to society and I have. I have smoothed your way with introductions and with shaping the story of your return to downplay any scandal attached to it. I have done my job and you dare to walk away from me in a crowded ballroom where everyone is bound to notice.'

'You've done your job, absolutely, for me, and for every other woman at the party. You've made a fool out of me and you're right. Everyone is bound to notice.' She threw his words back at him.

'What did you expect? I couldn't possibly dance every dance with you and make you socially acceptable. Exclusivity was never part of the deal.'

'No, it never was. That's what your precious League is about, isn't it? An excuse for promiscuity.' She all but spat the accusation.

His blue eyes had narrowed dangerously. He gripped her arm for a moment. 'You don't understand anything if that's what you think.' He stepped back. 'The League is to protect men from women like you.'

She felt as if she'd been struck. 'You bastard, how dare you! This whole time, you made me believe...' Her voice threatened to break. She would not give him the satisfaction of knowing how much these weeks, this introduction to pleasure, had mattered, how close she'd come to thinking the impossible was possible when it had only been revenge to him, revenge for an act he couldn't comprehend. She was glad now she hadn't told him the whole of it: her marriage, that day in the park. He didn't deserve to know. Her hand closed over the vase on her vanity, the object an anchor while her mind reeled.

'What did I make you believe?'

That was when she threw it. The vase smashed on the door frame, satisfyingly close to his shoul-

der, close enough to make him flinch. She would not tell him, not ever.

It was the right decision. They'd returned to town and parted ways. The contract was fulfilled. But town society was not so large in January that she could avoid him. She saw him occasionally at events, always with a beautiful woman, always smiling, always handsome, always at a distance. She never stayed long if he was present. By February she'd succeeded in avoiding him altogether—that, too, was for the best, until now.

'Have you decided yet?' Alina jumped a foot and stifled an undignified yelp at Channing's approach.

'I hate it when you sneak up on me.' Alina said crossly. It hardly ever happened. She was usually in tune to his whereabouts whenever he was near. 'Decided what?'

'Decided if you can trust me?' Channing fell into step beside her, modifying his long step to hers.

Alina tossed aside the ruined rose and picked another. 'That's a foregone conclusion at this point. I told you my plans. I told you what Seymour was. There's nothing more to trust you with. Perhaps the real question is whether or not *you* believe me—do *you* trust me?' Trust was an enormous issue between them. They'd hurt each other with that trust before.

'You trust me in bed,' Channing pressed. 'You trusted me last night.'

'That was only a game,' Alina answered quickly. Games were short term, games had ends to them, clear victors and rules. She understood games. What Channing was suggesting went beyond those boundaries. It would bind them together once more for a length of time to be solely determined by them. 'I can see this through without any help. Your contract is up in two days. I wouldn't have asked Amery for assistance. I did not hire him for it. It's not his expertise and I doubt it's yours.'

'I doubt it's yours either,' Channing argued. 'Do you go after men steeped in fraud often?'

She gave him a wry look. 'Don't be facetious. You know I do not. It's different. This is my family, it's not yours. I have to do this for them.' Catching Seymour would change everything.

They had only invested with him as a means of helping her.

'Now we're getting to the heart of things.' Channing gave her a gentle smile, his eyes warm. It was a look that invited confidences. 'You think to avenge your family? Seymour took advantage of them? I did wonder after I left you this morning what had prompted such an interest in bringing the fellow to justice. Perhaps you might be so good as to tell me the details?'

'According to the marriage contracts, the *comte* was to pay them a large sum of money spread out over the course of several years. The payments would come monthly and they'd last as long as the marriage,' Alina began to explain. The *comte* had explained it as a way of providing for her in the future if anything happened to him. Her family could put the money in trust for her, something akin to a jointure or widow's portion. But the family hadn't the luxury of saving. They'd needed the income for bills and daily living.

'It became another way in which the *comte* bound you to him,' Channing offered succinctly when she finished. She'd left that part out. 'Those payments were another way to keep you from leaving him.'

She had not wanted to interject that analysis. It brought up other more delicate subjects that veered into the personal. 'There was my sister to consider. She will be eighteen next year and my parents wanted to give her a London Season and find her a good match. They could not have afforded that without the *comte*'s money.'

Beside her, Channing bristled. 'Even so, your family should not have allowed you to suffer.'

She was quick to leap to their defence. 'They did not forsake me. They'd hoped this investment would create an income that would free them from financial dependency on the *comte*. But it didn't work out that way and I couldn't allow them to be ruined.'

'So you stayed and endured whatever it was that bastard doled out,' Channing said with quiet anger. He didn't even know the half of it.

'Yes, I stayed. What else could I do? It was my desperation that caused them to turn to Seymour's offer.' In hindsight, she wished she had not confided in them. If they hadn't known how desperate she was, they never would have risked it. 'It was my fault it happened at all and it was my fault for what happened next.'

Channing caught her eyes in a solemn gaze. 'What was that?'

'Seymour offered to marry Annarose in exchange for clearing the debt that the property now carried. All my father had to do was allow the marriage and turn the property fully over to Seymour. The debt would disappear. Annarose was only fifteen.'

The last implied myriad things: the complete corruption of Roland Seymour to prey on an innocent girl as a means of 'resolving' a family's crisis and the intensity of her own desire to bring him to justice.

Channing nodded slowly, the slow blaze growing in his eyes affirming he understood entirely. Families were important to him. She'd seen him with his own at Christmas. He had sisters and an older brother. 'Do they know what you're planning?'

Alina shook her head. Her family wasn't like his. They'd defend each other to the death. Her family hadn't the strength or the resources to do that. 'They don't know and they can't know. My mother has enough to worry about besides that. You won't tell them?'

She didn't truly believe he would or that he'd ever have the opportunity to. She couldn't imagine on what occasion Channing would ever meet them. Her father's health had failed after the disaster with Seymour. They wouldn't come to London. It would be her job to bring Annarose out next year. She yearned to find Annarose a good man. Surely there was one out there, one that would keep her safe.

Channing's gaze studied her for a moment and she felt far too vulnerable as if he saw every secret she'd ever kept. 'You feel guilty.'

'Yes, it nearly ruined them. It did ruin my father. I should have stopped it. I *would* have stopped it if I'd been here. I should not have started it at all.' She should have kept her desperation to herself. She'd smelled a rat when her father had first written to her about it. If she hadn't been so far away in France, if her odious husband had given her leave to come home when she'd asked, it might all have turned out differently. Annarose would not have been endangered. 'I tried, you know. The *comte* would not hear of it. He feared I would not return and he denied me the permission.'

Channing's gaze had not moved from her. 'How did he deny that permission?'

'You don't want to know.' She moved away from him, trying to put a literal distance between herself and the conversation, but he reached out and took her arm. She'd not meant to share even that much, but it had tumbled out.

Channing's grip was firm. He was not going to let her walk away from him. 'Was that why he branded you or was that because of me?'

He'd kept his voice low, but Alina found herself looking around anyway. They were alone and yet she wanted to scold him, to tell him to hush for voicing such words out loud. They were horrible words that should not be uttered. Anger radiated through his touch, tightening his grip on her arm. 'Tell me, was it because of me?'

She held his gaze, the hard stare meant to scold him for invading her privacy. 'It was neither.' She wanted him to leave it alone. It was none of his business and the current nature of their relationship did not entitle him to make it so, but Channing disagreed.

Channing had set his jaw in a firm line, his arms crossed as he blocked the path. 'Tell me, Alina. What did he do?'

What had he said last night? Everyone needs a champion? She'd never told anyone. Now the *comte* was dead and she was here. That part of her life was over. 'Knowing can change nothing, not for the better any way.'

'Try me, let me decide.' Channing stood firm.

He would be repulsed when he heard. Perhaps that was what she needed in order to drive a wedge between them, one last reminder of why it could only be business between them. Alina drew a deep breath and spat out short, declarative sentences devoid of emotion and detail. 'He locked me in my room. He took away my clothes. For two weeks, he sent trays twice a day with the sparsest of meals until I had to choose between my own stubbornness and my health. I would be of no use to anyone sick, so I relented and stayed in France.'

Alina braced herself. He would pity her now, the one thing she hated above all else. It was why she'd not told anyone of the many things that had occurred. She didn't want pity, didn't want people looking at her and seeing the poor, misused wife. But Channing's face was impassive, unreadable, except his eyes. They burned.

'After that, I knew if I wanted to be free of him, I'd have to have something to hold against him, something to bargain with. It wouldn't be enough simply to defy him.' And she'd begun to plot, alone or almost so. There'd been no one in the household she could trust except Celeste. 'It didn't take long to discover how deep and how dark *le comte*'s vices went and then one night those vices worked in my favour.'

Channing was silent, his gaze thunderous in the sunny afternoon. 'I wish you'd come to me from the start.' It was one of those carefully layered comments gentlemen of good breeding made when they did not want to speak directly. He did not mean just the start of the Seymour gambit.

'How could I?' Alina replied softly, knowing he heard the layers in her response as well—*how could I have left the legal and religious promises of my marriage vows, made myself an object of bigamy, shamed my family, caused them certain financial ruin?*

Channing sighed, his hand curling over hers, conveying warmth and strength. 'I can wish for it, all the same.'

Chapter Thirteen

Roland Seymour could not have wished for better luck. Expenses were high with the Season starting and the Comtesse de Charentes's deed would come in useful. He'd left for London immediately and, a day later, sat ensconced with his syndicate in their offices on Fleet Street. 'I want to send someone out to the property right away so we can determine what improvements need to be made. Then we can show the bank our list of intentions in order to get a lien approved.'

Seymour winked at the young man who served as the syndicate's assayer. 'Look hard, we want a nice long list, Charlie.'

Charlie grinned—he knew the game. 'Yes, sir. I'll set out this afternoon if you like.'

'You may set out now,' Roland offered expansively. There was a practicality to the request that suited him. Charlie might know the game, but only on the surface. The fewer people who knew about the darker side of his business, the better. There were things he and the syndicate needed to discuss in a more private setting.

With Charlie gone, Roland leaned forward and fixed Mr Eagleton with a strong stare. Eagleton specialised in knowing all sorts of unsavoury details about everyone, a collateral that was often more useful than money. 'Well?'

Eagleton was a skinny weasel of a man with a sallow complexion. He usually looked avaricious. Today he looked contemplative and that worried Seymour. In fact, the whole atmosphere in the room had bothered Seymour from the start. He'd expected today to carry a celebratory air to it—he'd brought them a French countess, after all. But the tenor of the meeting had been quite serious.

'She's rich enough, I'll give you that much, Seymour,' he admitted slowly. 'However, need I remind you that this is not usually how we go about it? Typically, we pick the "client", not the other way around.'

Seymour fought back a grin. Client was a polite way of saying 'mark', but mark was far too much of a backstreet, St Giles sort of word and the syndicate wanted to paint themselves with a finer brush. 'I did pick her,' he answered quickly, his agitation building. They were questioning him? He'd been the making of them and now they doubted his judgement?

Eagleton looked about at the group as if waiting to take a cue from them and shrugged. 'Perhaps. We've heard your account of the house party.' He paused here and looked about the group before continuing. 'We believe from your account it's not entirely clear who picked whom. She made the first approach, did she not? She flirted with you across the dinner table, she sat with you for cards and she encouraged the walk about the room.' Eagleton ran through the key events leading up to the introduction of her business.

'She's a widow and she might as well be French for all the time she's spent over there. She's bound to be more forward than other Englishwomen,' Seymour defended his choice.

Eagleton steepled his hands. 'We are worried you may have been manipulated, that's all. We think we should proceed with caution until we know more about her. Even if she's just another widow, you picked her quite hastily without a background check.'

Hugo Sefton, the group's legal mind, leaned forward and joined the conversation. 'I concur with Eagleton, Seymour. She's not our normal sort. She's richer than most and that means she runs with a higher set of people. She may have connections that would protect her or fight for her should she be wronged.' He gave a harsh laugh. 'In other words, she might not be helpless enough.' Then he sobered. 'It would be a mistake to assume she's just a French *comtesse*. She was English before she married, but who was she? Who does she know? We haven't been caught because we've been careful.'

Seymour thought of his concerns over Mr Deveril and the summerhouse. He was glad he'd withheld that piece of information from his recounting. The group, in their overly protective mood, would have feasted on that titbit. He was banking on the *comtesse*'s assurances that Deveril was a house-party fling and nothing more. If he turned out to be more significant, that might be a problem. Then again, the summerhouse might be a delicious piece of blackmail to use against her when the time came.

'Surely the *comtesse* is not dangerous to us,' Seymour scoffed at Sefton's notion of caution. He decided to go on the offensive. 'Frankly, I'm disappointed. I would have thought by now, Eagleton, you would have ferreted out any juicy gossip about her, something to serve as leverage.'

'It's only been a day, Seymour. Even I can't spin straw into gold in that length of time,' Eagleton answered, affronted. 'But I will—no one is free of scandal.'

'I certainly hope so, it's what you're paid to do,' Seymour replied. That was more like it. Eagleton was getting a big head on him.

No plan was free of strings, not even hers, but Alina didn't need to be reminded of that as she paced the inner courtyard at Lincoln's Inn, waiting for Channing. They'd been back in London for three days and he'd finally convinced her to take a meeting with a barrister friend of his. She'd agreed at last. In part because she wanted Channing to drop the matter, but also because she was worried. If Channing was being so persistent, it was either because he felt obliged to be overprotective after her disclosures in the garden or because there was something she'd overlooked in her planning.

Alina looked up at the brick-and-stone structure rising in front of her, centuries of British legal wisdom housed inside its walls. With any luck there was some wisdom there for her. She hoped she wasn't making a mistake by involving yet another person in her pursuit of Seymour. She'd wanted to keep this a private matter, like her marriage. She'd had little success of that where Channing was concerned. Still, if this friend of Channing's could convince Channing the plan was sound, that would be a victory of sorts. She knew that was not Channing's intention in calling the meeting. His purpose was just the opposite. He wanted someone else to tell her how foolhardy her plan was.

Channing strode through the arch and waved. 'You waited, thank you. I had traffic,' he apologised, although he was only a few minutes late. She'd arrived early, wanting to get a sense of the place before the meeting.

'I thought it would be better if we went in together.' She smiled, but it was a tight smile. She might have consented to come, but she wasn't happy about it. 'I still don't see why we have to involve anyone else.'

Channing favoured her with a smile, more convivial than her own. 'You can never have too many friends, isn't that what the French think? Let's go see what Grey has to say.'

David Grey's offices were located off the main quadrangle of the building and once inside, Channing made the introductions while she studied this friend of Channing's. He was a slender man in his late thirties with sharp, kind eyes and an intelligent face that probably invoked confidence from his clients.

David Grey seated them at a long table in his personal library. It was a room designed to impress, another manifestation of that confidence, lined as it was with books. He folded his hands on the table and began immediately, fixing her with all the attention of his sharp eyes. 'Mr Deveril has discussed your situation with me in brief and I believe I have a good understanding of it, but I'd like to hear from you, *comtesse*.'

It was precisely the right thing to say. He was a

smart man, she could see that right away, or perhaps Channing had prepped him on her prickly nature. She would have hated David Grey to presume he knew everything without speaking with her first, no matter what Channing had told him in preface. Alina spoke, Grey took notes. When she ended her account, Grey sat back in his chair, gathering his thoughts before he delivered his verdict. It was not a verdict she was prepared to hear.

'It seems to me that you have a problem, *comtesse.*'

Her hopes sank. Ideally, she'd wanted him to validate her plan. At the least, she'd wanted him to lay out a legal course of action to follow.

'What sort of problem is that?' Alina asked coolly, meeting Grey's gaze with a challenge. She didn't dare look at Channing.

'Seymour isn't doing anything wrong.'

'What do you mean, he's not doing anything illegal?' Never had she imagined she would hear those words. She'd imagined hearing 'it's too dangerous' or 'you should leave this to the authorities', but not this.

Grey was patient, his voice quiet. 'Answer me

this, *comtesse*. May a deed have a co-signer or co-owner?'

'Yes.'

'Are the co-signers entitled to equal rights and privileges where the deed is concerned?'

'Yes.' Alina's hands tightened where she'd folded them in her lap. She didn't like where this was going.

'As such, does each co-signer have the authority to secure a loan against the property?'

'Yes.'

Grey nodded. 'Then tell me, what has Seymour done wrong in the eyes of the law?'

'The deception is in the details.' Alina cried. 'It's in *how* it's done.'

Grey raised thinning eyebrows at the exclamation. 'Does he force the holder of the deed into letting him co-sign?'

'No, not that I'm aware,' she had to answer honestly. From what she knew, her father had not been compromised into allowing a co-owner. It had been a private, mutual agreement of collateral.

'Does Seymour not honour his contractual obligations? For instance, does he not relinquish the property when his ownership has expired?' Grey had risen and was pacing. She had no trouble envisioning him cross-examining a witness and reducing the poor soul to the sum of his mistakes.

'No, he honours them in abstention. The property merely reverts back to the original single owner when the deadline arrives.'

'Does he advance the funds he's promised for improvements?'

'Yes,' she admitted glumly. He was prompt, too. Her father had sent her a letter saying how pleased he was when the money had been transferred to his account within the day. But the money was a red herring only; a small sum when weighed against the enormous amounts he took out against the property.

'Again, I ask you, what illegal act has Seymour committed?'

'He leaves the property indebted, mortgaged to the hilt!' Alina exclaimed. 'When he knows full well it would be a financial trial for the owner to pay back the funds.'

Grey shook his head sadly. 'Bad business is not illegal, it's merely unfortunate. We can't put the Exchange on trial for losing our money, can we?' He gave a sad chuckle.

'This is unacceptable.' She shot a fiery look at Channing, her anger boiling. 'You set this up. You knew what he was going to say; perhaps you've even asked him to say it. You haven't liked my plan from the start,' she accused. This is what she got for letting her guard down in the slightest, for trusting him even infinitesimally.

'Alina, it's not like that,' Channing began to protest, but she was having none of it. She didn't want to hear any explanation he could offer.

'I cannot believe there is nothing we can do. He is robbing people, *stealing* from them. The last time I checked those were crimes.'

David Grey thought for a moment. 'If you could prove there was a trend, something that showed it was more than a coincidence of bad business, perhaps you could get him on intent to defraud.'

It was the best news to come out of the meeting and Alina clung to it even through tea. Channing had taken her to a nice, upscale tea room in a Mayfair hotel, likely as a consolation. 'You don't have to pity me,' Alina said crossly as the tea was served.

'I'm not. I was hungry.' Channing smiled over his tea cup. Several women were looking in their direction. It was no doubt exciting for the women; to have a man as handsome, well positioned and single as Channing Deveril was a treat nonpareil.

He nodded to the women who passed their table. The women beamed and Alina grimaced. 'Do they know what you do for a living?'

Channing shrugged and she felt a satisfying twinge of gratification to have him squirm a bit for a change. They didn't discuss the agency. It was off limits like her marriage, but since he'd breached that bastion, she felt she had rights to do the same. 'Maybe, maybe not. It's hard to know how "secret" the League is these days. Nicholas D'Arcy's contretemps brought more exposure than I would have wished.'

She gave a light laugh. 'I heard about that.' All of London had heard about it. 'D'Arcy was the stuff of legends.' She paused. 'As are you. Do you still enjoy the "work"?'

'The administrative side of the business is very satisfying.' Channing answered. 'You may read into that all you wish.'

An elegantly dressed woman approached the

table with a friend. 'Mr Deveril, I've missed you these last weeks.' She shot an assessing, narrow-eyed look at Alina. 'I must have you over to the house.'

'Lady Bixley, it's good to see you.' Channing rose and bowed over her hand. 'Send an invitation around and I'll see what I can do. Have you met the Comtesse de Charentes?'

Lady Bixley didn't stay long after that. Alina watched her go, knowing competition when she saw it. 'Is she part of the "administrative work"?' Alina enquired once Lady Bixley was out of earshot.

Channing grinned. 'You weren't jealous, were you?'

Alina blew into her tea and slanted him a coy look. 'Hardly.' *Well, maybe just a little.* She hadn't been prepared for that stab of green envy. In the country, she'd had him all to herself. He had been there solely for her. But here in town, there was no contract anchoring his attentions. There was nothing to bind him to her except his own good will; something she'd assured him she didn't need or want. They were once more nothing to each other, not even business partners at this point. Yet she'd told him more than she'd ever told another. Her carefully set rules hadn't protected her.

Channing only laughed at her response to Lady Bixley's pass by their table. Nothing got under his skin and today it was damned well irritating. 'Does everything just roll off of you?'

'No, not everything.' Channing turned serious, his voice dropping, his eyes forgetting to scan the room and riveting on her alone. 'For instance, I haven't forgotten that you didn't mention to David Grey you'd given a counterfeit deed to Seymour.'

'He didn't need to know,' Alina said staunchly.

'Maybe not, but has it registered yet that while Seymour isn't doing anything illegal, *you* are?' Channing's intensity was chilling. Seldom had she seen him this avid about anything.

'It's not counterfeit. The land exists, just not under that name.'

'It will look that way and it was done *intentionally*. You did not accidentally misname the property, it was done on purpose with an intent to deceive and to entrap. On the surface it will look as if you are deliberately taking money from him for a property you know doesn't exist. If that isn't what fraud is, I don't know what is.'

'It's not fraud, it's a lure,' Alina argued but hearing Channing explain it in those terms *did* make her nervous. 'Besides, if there's any intent to defraud, the onus is on him. All we have to do is prove there's a trend.' She voiced the hope that had struggled to survive since they'd left Lincoln's Inn.

'Is that all? It's no little thing, Alina,' Channing said in disbelief. 'How are we to do that, exactly? It's my guess he's well aware of the risk a trend poses to him and that's why the syndicate operates under different names. Before we could prove a trend, we'd have to establish that the syndicate is the single entity behind all these failed properties. We couldn't even get our hands on those records without knowing the names the syndicate operates under. Even if we did, we'd still need people to come forward and testify they'd been taken advantage of. You said yourself people's lack of desire to expose their failures was a reason he'd been so successful. Proving this would be monumental, even if we had a team of solicitors and investigators working on it.'

She cocked her head and studied him. 'You look like a nice, ordinary man, Channing Deveril, but in reality you're the agent of doom.'

'Nice? Ordinary?' Channing laughed, unbothered by her foul temper. 'Is that what you see when you look at me? Do you want to know what I see when I look at you?'

It was an overt attempt at flattery and distraction. He didn't want her thinking about Seymour and, damn it all, it was working. Who wanted to think about Roland Seymour when Channing Deveril sat across from them? She felt a smile creep across her face whether she willed it or not. 'Well? What *do* you see? You'd better tell me now that you've brought it up.'

'I see hair asking to be released, one pin at a time; I see lips waiting to be kissed.' His voice dropped even lower, growing husky. 'I see a gown begging to be stripped from your body.'

He was a consummate flirt. Even in the middle of a tea shop in the light of day, he could make her burn. 'Where exactly do you see all that happening?' she couldn't help but ask, knowing full well if he had an answer, she'd be committed.

Channing rose and left money on the table. He

held out his arm. 'Right this way, *madame*.' Oh, yes, when she looked into those blue eyes, she was definitely committed.

Chapter Fourteen

Alina looked around as they stepped out into the sunshine. 'In your carriage?' She gave him a dubious look as his equipage pulled up to the kerb.

'I was not inclined to wait.' Channing gave her a private smile. 'When I see something I want, I go after it.' He nipped at her neck, his voice at her ear. 'And I want you.'

'People are staring,' she quietly admonished. But in truth she didn't mind. Something very different was at work right now that transcended her concern over passers-by gawking at a gentleman nipping the neck of a lady in broad daylight. Channing Deveril wanted her without any contracts between them, without any extenuating agreements. She was tempted to ask why, but she didn't want to know for fear the reason would ruin the illusion.

The steps came down and he helped her in. He shut the door behind them, his eyes intent on her. She felt her body tremble from the force of that gaze. The coach pulled out into slow traffic, taking her into uncharted territory where a man wanted her without games.

Channing reached for her, taking her face in his hands, covering her mouth in a long kiss. His kisses might be what she loved best: the taste of him in her mouth, the tease of his tongue as it caressed her, the press of his lips. Perhaps she loved it because the *comte* had never kissed, had never used his mouth the way Channing did. This was her discovery alone. She gave a contented moan. She would have been willing to settle for an afternoon of this; kissing Channing in a carriage with the curtains closed, but Channing had other ideas, better ideas.

He raised her arms and closed her hands over the steadying leather grips that hung from the coach walls. He hadn't asked, hadn't told her what to do, he'd simply done it and in doing so, he'd effectively moved them past kissing.

'Hold on, don't let go,' he murmured, his hands working the fastenings of her jacket, pulling free the white linen of the blouse she wore beneath it, only to meet with a chemise. 'You wear too many damn clothes, Alina.' His voice was hoarse with frustration and need. There was the tearing of cloth and she was free, Channing's hands at her bare breasts.

'I love you like this, Alina, your breasts falling into my hands, your nipples hardening when I stroke them before I take them in my mouth one by one, each a sweet berry for my tongue.'

Alina moaned, her body arching into him. Channing's words were a seductive litany of promises. His love talk was erotic, building an anticipation that started low in her belly and curled up throughout her until her entire body was on fire. Then, and only then, did he deliver on those promises.

He knelt between her thighs, her breast was in his mouth, his tongue driving her insane, his hand had taken pity on her and slipped beneath her skirts, sliding into the damp, warm core of her, moving in rhythm with his mouth. She wanted desperately to bite down on something, wanted an anchor amid the pleasure, but all she had were the straps and she'd promised not to let go. She groaned, her hips pushing against his hand.

But Channing knew what she wanted, *needed*, before she could even ask. He had only to raise himself up slightly to position himself at her entrance. Within moments, he was sheathed in her, sunk to the hilt in her wetness, her legs wrapped about him, rocking them with the movement of the carriage while she clung to the straps for dear life. Alina was vaguely aware she was screaming; his name, her pleasure, her release, her fulfilment. Never had she crested so wildly, so quickly, with so little control over herself. Channing had done this to her. No, not to her, *for* her.

She hadn't the strength to hold the straps. She let them go, falling into Channing's arms in a boneless heap as they both slid to the coach floor. He was sweaty and exhausted as he held her. For a long while neither of them spoke. Perhaps, like her, he wanted to hang on to the sensation, too, and there seemed to be no rush. It was hard to imagine so much pleasure could be found inside a coach. 'I was misinformed,' Alina said at last. 'I was told carriages were rather difficult arrangements for this sort of thing, highly overrated as rendezvous points.'

Channing gave a tired chuckle. 'Whoever told you that must not have known how to use one.'

She felt his arm tighten about her, felt the warmth of his body seep into her, felt a warning rise in her mind against all this comfort. 'Why did you do it, Channing?'

'Do what?'

'This.'

He laughed into her hair. 'I couldn't have you thinking I was nice and ordinary, now could I? Anyone can take a woman to tea, but to make love in a carriage afterwards? Let me qualify that—to make *good* love in a carriage afterwards, that takes talent.' He rapped on the ceiling, giving the signal to stop. 'Do you know what else takes talent? Carrying it off in the park as if nothing had happened.'

It wasn't an answer. It was a diversionary tactic and Alina recognised it as such immediately. Still, she was glad to get out of the coach a short while later, looking respectably decent. Tidying herself and focusing on the walk prevented her from thinking too much. Inside that carriage, the world had shifted to something more dangerous. In truth, it was not fair to blame it on the carriage ride. The shift had been in gradual evidence since they'd returned to London. Channing's obligations had ceased and yet his concern persisted.

No one required him to set up the meeting with David Grey. No one required him to take her to tea or to continue any social association with her. Yet he had done all that and now he was walking with her in Hyde Park, at the crowded hour none the less, as if it were the most natural thing in the world. He tipped his hat to a group of ladies as they walked by.

Alina laughed when they were out of earshot. 'Channing Deveril, you *are* the most wicked man I know. If those ladies knew what you'd been up to…' If they knew he'd been driving into her a half-hour before with nothing close to gentlemanly reserve, that he'd made her scream and then he'd made her question everything…

'They'd be jealous.' Channing disarmed her with a smile that had her already thinking about the next time. Perhaps they could get back in the coach right now.

'A little arrogant, aren't we?' she teased. It was

easier to tease than to ask questions, to think about what the afternoon meant, what being with him meant. She'd known what it meant when there'd been a contract. Now, she was at a loss. Perhaps she should simply leave it at impossible and move on.

Channing whispered at her ear, 'It makes you wonder what everyone else has been up to when they get out of their carriages.'

Alina gave him a playful shove. '*You* are the reason it's not safe for a girl to ride in a closed carriage with a man.'

He grabbed her hand and trapped it against his chest. 'I'm the reason a lot of things aren't safe.' He danced her around the back of a wide oak that hid them from view, his eyes full of mischief. She could handle this. This was good, this laughing with him, the flirting, but it *was* an illusion. It had been like this the last time, too, and it had led to nothing, nothing that she'd hoped for anyway.

'What are you doing, Channing?' She gave a breathless laugh as he pressed her against the tree trunk.

'Stealing a kiss.' Channing bent to claim

one, but she turned her head, his effort landing her cheek.

'I meant, what are you doing with me?' She was serious now. She needed answers before her emotions could become more entangled, more uncertain of the response she needed from them.

'You've already asked that question once today.' Channing nuzzled her with his nose.'

'But you haven't answered it,' Alina pressed him. She pushed at him. Something in her tone must have warned him she meant business. Reluctantly, he stepped away. 'I understood our arrangement at Lady Lionel's. That was business and I dare say we each had our own games attached to that business. But this? There is no more business, no more obligation, Channing. All that happens now, or doesn't happen now, is entirely up to us. So, what's it to be?'

She hoped her bluntness would pin him down, force him to confess to whatever his agenda was. But Channing was too wily for that. 'Do you want me to leave it alone, Alina? Do you want me to leave *you* alone?'

'That is *not* fair.' How dare he make it her place

to announce her intentions, her feelings, when she'd been the one to ask him first.

His eyes were sombre, studying her with a gravity one seldom saw in the public persona of Channing Deveril. 'None of it's fair. It's easy to talk about Seymour, isn't it? He's an external problem we can choose to solve together or not. Here's what I think. You need my help with him. You are blind to the potential danger you might be in. Period. I have connections and solicitors that you do not. Additionally, I have protection to offer you that you do not have on your own should it come to that.'

He made it sound so logical, so practical to lean on him, just a little. Something primal leapt within her at the sight of Channing Deveril standing before her, booted legs shoulder-width apart, hands behind his back in a powerful stance, as masterful in this as he was in bed. In spite of her desire for independence, there was something thrilling, something confiding in having her burden shared. She wasn't turning it entirely over to him, she could never do that, it wasn't in her nature. But to share it with someone strong and capable was a relief all its own. 'You'd be willing to help me with Seymour?' Alina ventured to be sure she understood him correctly.

He gave her a smile that spoke of irony and her new-felt relief faded. 'That's the rub, isn't it, Alina? Why would I be willing to invest myself in such a project? Especially, as you point out, when I am not obligated to do so by the agency or by any other standing between us.'

He paused and gave her a piercing look that made her want to shrink into the tree. 'That's the harder question to answer, isn't it? What's between us? *Is* there more between us than this contretemps with Seymour and the coincidence of encountering one another?'

Channing moved towards her, crowding her with his height, his size, making her entirely aware of his maleness, of what he was offering her; his body, tentatively even his heart, if she would answer those questions. Those two questions stood between her and Channing Deveril. 'But we both know to answer *that* question, we have to talk of unpleasant things.'

She drew a deep breath and placed a hand on the lapel of his coat. 'Not here. This is not the place.' She was not going to have such a critical conversation in the middle of Hyde Park at the crowded hour.

'Where?' Channing breathed against her ear, making her tremble with wanting all over again. He might have been asking her for an assignation.

'The Evert ball—are you invited?' She arched her neck and let him kiss its length, the spreading spring greenery of the tree allowing them to steal the indiscretion.

'Yes.'

Channing released her then. 'Have my driver take you home.'

She raised an eyebrow. 'Aren't you coming?'

Channing gave her a wicked grin and gave her back her own favourite cryptic response. 'What do you think?'

She smiled and shook her head. 'What a wicked creature you are.'

Channing swept her a bow. 'I will consider the afternoon a success, milady. I have risen above your estimation of being nice and ordinary.'

Chapter Fifteen

Nice and ordinary would have made things easier, Channing thought later that afternoon. He sat on his side of the desk at Argosy House and Amery DeHart sat on his, but their roles were decidedly reversed for once. It was Amery who pushed a hand through his hair and said with an angst Channing recognised as a tone he himself had used not long ago with Nicholas and Jocelyn, 'What the hell have you got yourself into?'

Channing hardly knew. One day he'd simply been taking over a standard assignment for Amery. The next, he was faced with a ghost from his past, the very inspiration for the agency. Even then, he might have been all right. He had his boundaries entrenched, the lessons he'd learned firmly in place. She would *not* sneak past his defences again. Yet she had. 'She's in trouble,

Amery. There's a man who has stolen from her family.' Channing went on to explain the situation with Roland Seymour, how she'd wanted the introduction as a means of anonymously insinuating herself into Seymour's influence in order to trap him, how she'd used a false deed.

'Don't you dare scold me,' Channing concluded with a pre-emptory argument when Amery would have protested. 'She would have asked you to do the same had you been there. It was what she'd hired you for.'

Amery gave him a wry look. 'Was that *all* she wanted with you?' He played idly with the pen on the edge of Channing's desk. 'She and I did not have a carnal relationship, merely a social one. She liked how I looked on her arm, nothing more. I am imagining from your tone, Channing, that she liked how you looked on more than her arm. In her bed, perhaps?'

It was Channing's turn to look discomfited. Amery's arrow had hit the mark most accurately and it was unnerving. He was used to being the one who read people so flawlessly. 'Originally, I was glad you were back a little early,' Channing replied drily, but Amery wouldn't be put off the scent.

'I was worried about you.' Amery's gaze was even now, unafraid to meet his. It was a sign of how Amery had matured in the past year, a sign, too, of how their friendship had deepened with Jocelyn's absence. Once, it would have been Jocelyn Eisley, co-founder of the League, who would have sat in Amery's chair, probing relentlessly for information from his friend. But Jocelyn had married and his wife held his attentions now.

'There's nothing to worry about,' Channing denied. But it was a blatant lie. There was everything to worry about, everything to sort through and reassess—not all of it was about Seymour, but also about that cruel cur of a husband.

'I disagree,' Amery answered. He leaned forward, hands steepling on the desktop as he fixed Channing with concerned hazel eyes. 'Consider the facts.' Amery ticked them off on his long fingers. 'You are gone barely a week to a standard house party, to carry out a standard assignment, one that didn't even expect physical intimacy, and yet you come home ready to slay dragons for a woman you didn't even know or want to know.

As I recall, I had to beg you to take the appointment.' He paused, a certain gleam in his eye. 'I'd have reconsidered taking time off, if I'd had any idea she was such a marvellous—'

'Don't you ever talk about her that way.' Channing was halfway out of his seat before he realised Amery had deliberately provoked him. He sat down, feeling foolish, and worse, exposed. Amery would know something was up now.

Amery leaned back in his chair, wearing a satisfied but sad smile. 'So it's that way, is it? She got to you. She's very beautiful, is she not? But there's something hard and unyielding in her. She's broken in some way. It's what gives her that edge she carries.'

'She's not broken,' Channing argued quietly. Far from it. She was strong, like a finely forged Damascus blade. 'I think she was betrayed by a husband who had destroyed her trust in marriage and in men.' He'd had time to think in the interim since the house party of what her disclosures meant, how those events had shaped her. Sex was power to her, the one weapon she had to turn men into playthings so they could not hurt her any more. It explained her hesitation today when things had moved beyond the lightness of flirtation.

'I never dreamed Elizabeth Morgan would appeal so strongly to you,' Amery put in.

Channing studied his hands. It wouldn't be fair to keep the truth from Amery. 'That's not her name. She gave a false name in order to keep her identity a secret from Seymour. She's Alina Marliss, the Comtesse de Charentes.'

Amery's body stilled. 'I know who that is. But I had never met her.' The *comtesse* might run in high circles, but she was socially reserved. Channing nodded. Amery would not have met her. 'It was why she waited to come to the agency when I was gone.'

'You knew her.' Amery's mind was racing. 'Not just from London circles, but from before, didn't you? She's the one Jocelyn told me about.' It was like watching a candle light the darkness and Channing regretted ever complimenting Amery's quick mind or trusting in Jocelyn's sense of discretion.

'Not by name,' Amery rushed on, trying to minimise Jocelyn's culpability. 'He told me once you'd met someone in Paris, years ago, but nothing had come of it—

'Nothing is coming of it,' Channing interrupted. 'It was an old and ill-timed affair.' One that had taken six years to consummate.

Amery laughed. 'Except that now she's back and she's in trouble and you want to help her the way you've helped all of us, from the footman at the door to the boys in the kitchen.'

'Is it so wrong to want to assist those in need?' Channing fired back, feeling entirely too vulnerable. Argosy House and the agency had become so much more over the years than just a strike against broken hearts.

Amery leaned forward. 'Of course not. What can I do to help?'

'After our meeting today with David Grey, I think we might need reinforcements,' Channing said. Alina had left the meeting with Grey dead set on establishing that nearly impossible trend Grey had mentioned and he'd all but promised her under the oak tree to help. 'I've already notified the agency's team of solicitors to get on it right away. I want her protected against charges of forgery.' He paused. 'We'll need protection of another sort, too. I don't think Seymour is the kind who will leave this battle to the court-rooms. When he finds out what she's done and what she knows, he'll be furious and strike out of self-defence, if nothing else.'

Amery nodded and grinned. 'No worries, I've already sent letters to Nick and Jocelyn. They're in town for the Season.'

Channing raised his brows in a bit of surprise. 'I didn't know.'

Amery shook his head and rose to take his leave. 'That's just how far gone you are, my friend. You're in over your head and you don't even know it.'

Ridiculous. He was Channing Deveril, London's luckiest man. Was he in over his head? Was that even possible? Not just with sexual games that offered overwhelming pleasure, not just with Alina's bedazzling beauty, both of which would have been enough to overwhelm any other man. It was the revelations that had him spinning. The marriage had not just been one of discontentment as he'd originally believed, but one of humiliation and degradation. Danger was not new to Alina. She'd lived with it before. No wonder she felt immune to whatever threat Seymour might pose, no wonder she didn't take the man seriously.

It still turned Channing's stomach to think of the faded brand pressed so cruelly into her skin, to think of the humiliation of being chained to her bed without basic comforts until she capitulated. Those were the only episodes she'd mentioned and only because he'd discovered the one and pushed for the other. Left to her own, she would not have told him.

She doesn't trust you, came the answer. And why should she? He'd told her he'd wished she'd come to him from the first, but that was hindsight speaking. When she had come to him for help re-integrating into English society, he'd been all business. Perhaps she had been looking for something more? He'd not understood at the time that her request to hire an escort had been a plea to start over.

He'd done his job, even indulged in physical intimacy with her at last. But he'd made sure he'd remained emotionally aloof and that she knew it. She was just another appointment in a ledger full of them. He'd even gone so far as to flirt with another, Catherine Emerson, the neighbour's daughter who'd gone on to marry his brother.

He'd kept his 'interest' in Alina purely professional and she hated him for it. He'd played a game of revenge just as he'd perceived she'd played one with him those years ago in Paris. But what he knew now called all that into question. Had she scorned him that day in the park or had she protected him? Even in the early days of her marriage, had she already been in danger from the *comte*'s cruel gambits? These were the details, the difficulties he'd alluded to today in Hyde Park, the things that must be discussed.

Alina felt knowing the details of her past couldn't change anything, but Channing disagreed. It had the power to change *everything*, to call into question all he'd assumed to be true. He hadn't known about the darkness of that marriage—could he assume the *comte* didn't know about him? If he did know, had he made Alina pay?

Channing felt his gut clench again, as his mind replayed the pivotal scene in the park. Had he really seen a young devoted wife, clinging affectionately to her husband after a long absence?

Had her husband draped her in jewels benevolently, or had there been a more malicious intent behind them? More importantly, what did those answers mean to him? He could not turn back the clock for her or for him. Was he in over his head? He could handle Roland Seymour, but where Alina and his emotions were concerned, maybe Amery was right. It was good to know, come what may, that his friends stood at the ready. All he had to do was say the word.

There was one word for the Comtesse de Charentes and that word was *bitch*. Roland Seymour swore it liberally and loudly, his hand coming down hard on the table surface where a few members of the syndicate had gathered for this meeting. He was calling it impromptu; the others were calling it an emergency. The *comtesse* had attempted to deceive him and she'd made him look the fool in front of Sefton and Eagleton, who would not hesitate to let the rest of the syndicate know what had occurred.

'This is why we must be cautious. Our system works. We have to be the ones who go to the clients, not the other way around. If clients are not carefully vetted, this is what happens,' Sefton preached.

Seymour wanted to shove all his caution up the man's ass except that, in this case, Sefton was justified. Charlie the surveyor had returned home late last night with the news: there was no land. The deed was just paper, it represented nothing. Charlie had checked the local records, talked with local people. No one had ever heard of such a place.

'It's not the duping that bothers me. It's the motives behind it which are clearly deliberate,' Eagleton put in. 'Our *comtesse* knew what she was doing. This was absolutely premeditated.' He smirked. 'She led you about the nose quite exquisitely from the flirtation to the walk about the room, right up to imparting the deed, which she happened to have with her at a house party.' He snorted there. 'That should have been the biggest red flag of all.'

Seymour tried to ignore the comment and he should have known better. He'd been overconfident. It had always been so easy, up to this point, to swindle the women. They were more desperate than men, they just wanted someone to come in and take care of everything for them and the *comtesse* had played the role to the hilt. Men, however, needed to feel this was business, that they were partners in this new and exciting venture that would revolutionise their finances.

Eagleton pushed a file folder at him. 'This explains it pretty neatly. Have a look.'

Seymour opened the brief and read, listening begrudgingly to Eagleton's commentary. 'You may recall the family name from a few years ago.'

Marliss. Sir Dylan Marliss. Seymour did remember him, vaguely; a gentry farmer with a comfortable income, but a property that was vastly under-developed and he knew it. Marliss had known he could be doing better, but he hadn't the ability or the financial connections to make it happen. Marliss and his wife were polite, quiet people with a younger daughter, just the sort the syndicate liked to do business with. They would neither suspect trouble nor make trouble once they discovered the syndicate's duplicity.

Seymour shoved the dossier back across the table. The *comtesse* was none other than Alina Marliss, their older daughter of whom there'd been not a single mention. Had the syndicate known there was a French countess in the family, they would not have approached Marliss. The syndicate made it a practice not to do business with peers. Peers were too well connected, too protected and they usually had a network of friends in high places. The syndicate preferred country men like Marliss. The country was isolating. Nothing happened quickly and that suited the syndicate perfectly.

'In my defence, Alina Marliss was never mentioned once in any of our conversations.' Seymour was desperate to save his image. He was starting to look like a fool in front of these men.

'The reason might be this.' Eagleton pushed another file across the table. Good lord, how many files did Eagleton have? He talked while Seymour scanned. 'At the time we were doing business with Marliss, the *comtesse*'s husband had recently passed away under a cloud of suspicion. It stands to reason that the family was trying to distance itself from any ensuing scandal. There was already some tension between the Marlisses and their daughter, but I'll get to that in a moment.'

Seymour looked up from the documents. 'It says here the cause of death was likely poisoning.'

'A long and gradual poisoning,' Eagleton added. 'Which means one needs to have regular and consistent access to the intended victim.'

'Are you suggesting the *comtesse* was suspected of such an act?' Seymour's mind began to move from defence to offence.

'She was, as were several others. It seems the *comte* was a man who was either intensely liked or disliked by his peers.'

This is where it got tricky. 'Did anything come of the suspicions?' Seymour asked, sliding the papers back into the folder.

'Nothing but rumour. It was never determined who might have done the *comte* in. The list remains long and distinguished to this day. It could have been anyone from the *comtesse* to his valet and several other nobles in between.'

That was disappointing, Seymour thought. 'I've already heard the rumours and they're fairly vague.' At the house party, he'd heard only that her husband's death had been quite unlooked for and, as such, it had struck people as unnatural. But there'd been no mention of poison or of suspects, only that it was suspicious in nature. 'If there are multiple suspects, that only seems to weaken the power of that rumour to do the *comtesse* any damage.'

Eagleton's eyes began to gleam. 'There is a bit more to it. You do recall that there was some pre-existing tension between the *comtesse* and her English family. It seems she wanted a divorce and her family disapproved of her pursuing one.'

That got Seymour's attention. There was something about divorce in France he was trying to remember. 'Isn't divorce illegal over there?' He didn't know exactly, it seemed to change with the wind. Under Napoleon, divorce had been legalised, but under the restored monarchy, the king had retracted the right to divorce. Seymour wasn't sure if that was still the case or if there might be exceptions.

'Oh, it's still illegal, all right, if you're French,' Eagleton said, 'but she's English. She was hoping to trade on her English heritage and get the divorce passed through Parliament. She hoped her parents might support it and help see the deed done, but her parents were scandalised. They wanted nothing to do with it. It would have been a long shot even if the *comte* had been game for it. But he was French and he would have none of it.'

It was all coming together now. Seymour nodded his head. 'With no option for divorce, our *comtesse* is left with only one way out.'

'Thus the suspicions. She asked for a divorce just three months before he died. The rumours have never been clarified—we could stir the pot a bit, rekindle some interest, give the rumours some teeth, some details, doesn't matter if they're true.'

Seymour gave a malevolent grin. It would be the perfect pay back for trying to draw him out. 'It would certainly be leverage, something that could be held against her to stop her from exposing us.'

Eagleton nodded. 'The best part is, we don't even have to have any real proof, we simply have to have her believe the rumours won't be so harmless as they were the last time. If she had real fear that she could be brought up on charges for murder, she would think twice about pushing her suit with us.'

'She should be thinking twice already. Don't forget—' Sefton spoke up for the first time in a while. He'd been quietly listening and thinking '—there's still the current issue of fraud. She deliberately put forward a false deed in an attempt to take money from us. Think how that will look to a court of law. If we coupled that with the suspicions about her husband's death, her character would look black indeed.'

Seymour liked where this was going. There was a certain irony in a fraudulent agency being able to legitimately prosecute someone else for fraud. But Eagleton was quick to ruin his mental celebration.

'Before we get overly confident in our position, I think we have to ask ourselves why? Why would the *comtesse* take such a risk? Is she that impulsive, or is she that sure of herself? If the latter is true, who does she have backing her? Protecting her?' Eagleton fixed him with a searching stare. 'Who are her friends?'

'No one. I'm sure of it. Women are too intimidated by her and men, well, men just want to bed her.' Seymour sounded more confident than he was. He wasn't sure at all that it was true.

Images of the summerhouse came to mind, but he wouldn't tell the syndicate about Deveril yet, not when there was no clear need. In the meanwhile, it wouldn't hurt to keep a watch of his own. Maybe there was a way to neutralise Channing Deveril before he became too attached to the *comtesse* or too involved.

'How soon can we strike?' Seymour asked, hoping not to appear desperate, but really, the *comtesse* left unchecked promised to be problematic.

Eagleton fingered the file and thought for a moment. He looked across the table to Sefton. 'Almost immediately, if we like. We just have to feed these rumours to the right sources and then we'll let the London gossips do their work.'

Seymour grinned. The sooner they could expose the *comtesse* and flush out Deveril's true position, the better. He shifted in his seat. Soon she'd be imploring him to forgive her. She'd be sorry she'd ever forged that deed. He knew exactly how he'd make her beg: on her knees, straddling his cock the way she'd straddled Deveril's in the summerhouse.

Chapter Sixteen

One, two, three steps and three steps again was all that separated her from him. Channing quietly shut the door to Lord Evert's library behind him and stepped into the dimly lit room. Alina stood at the console, her back to him as she played with the decanters. Ah, her delicious *bare* back. Well, her *almost* bare back. A stab of desire hit him hard, making him want to forgo the conversation and go straight to assignation. She'd worn peach chiffon tonight, tailored to perfection over the curve of her delicate shoulders, the low vee of her bodice mirrored by the low vee exposing her back.

She knew how to dress to her advantage from the combs in her hair to the slippers on her feet. Not a single item was haphazardly selected. But it wasn't only the clothes and the accessories, it was everything else: the buffed nails, just in case one saw her without her gloves, the light scent of her *toilette,* the discreet use of cosmetics. And yet a man would never mistake her for an empty-headed fashion doll. She was very much alive; it was there in her eyes when she looked at him, in her smile, in the sound of her laugh, in the way she'd risen against him today in the carriage in her passion. It made him feel *alive* in return.

There was no woman in London who compared and he wasn't the only man in the ballroom who'd noticed. Lady Evert's ball was an absolute crush, one of the biggest early events of the Season. People were eager to see and be seen after the long winter and Easter break. Plenty of people had noticed Alina. The sight of other men watching her, dancing with her, their hands at her waist or on her arm, had stirred something primitive and possessive in Channing.

No matter that she could handle herself in such a setting, he wanted to be the one, the only one, ever, to be the recipient of that smile, of that laugh. To know at the end of the night, he'd be the one to slip those beautiful gowns from her shoulders. Channing felt his groin tighten in response. She was lost in thought and had not heard him yet. It would be simple enough to come up behind her, bend her over the console and take her most thoroughly. It was wicked and fast and it did little cosmetic damage to one's appearance. One could be put to rights almost instantly.

'Don't even think it.' Alina's sultry tones were quiet in the dark room.

Damn. She'd noticed him. 'Don't think what?' Channing couldn't help but ask. She was right, of course. To do it now would completely derail what he'd come here for.

'Using the console as a staging area for something other than pouring drinks.' But there was no scold in her voice. There was the clink of stoppers being removed, followed by the sound of liquor flowing into glasses. She turned towards him and offered him a drink. 'Are you sure we're safe here?'

'No one reads at a ball.' Channing laughed. 'The Everts don't read at all. I think we'd be safe in this room in the light of day. We could probably *live* here before the Everts noticed.

Alina settled herself on the little sofa, her skirts pooling about her. 'Have you thought of your answers?' She was playing it cool tonight, putting the onus of the conversation on his shoulders.

Channing took the chair near the sofa. The dim light and the brandy was helping. He took the plunge, revealing a piece of his soul, but protecting the rest. 'When I ask myself why I would help you with Seymour, it is because my feelings are engaged yet again where you are concerned. Should my attentions not be welcomed, I would prefer to walk away now. I would leave you the services of my solicitors, but any further contact between us should be discontinued.' It sound fairly stiff, fairly formal when he couched it in those terms, a lot less like the lines running through his mind at present: *I could fall in love with you again. Indeed, there's no could about it—I have. What I feel with you is nothing I've ever felt with anyone else and I have to know— will you hurt me again?*

He waited, watching her process the carefully chosen words and then pick a carefully worded response of her own. He noticed everything about her in those tedious moments: how the firelight played on the white-gold of her hair, how her fingers played with the pearls at her throat.

'You've not thought this through, Channing. You only think you're in love with me,' she stated softly. 'But when you look at the practicalities you'll know better.' She was talking about the scandal that would follow her always. He didn't care. He'd quelled those silly rumours once before, he would do it again if need be. 'You will tire of fighting for me eventually. Although I appreciate the sentiment.' She'd read his mind. 'I don't deserve such a knight, Channing. I'm really quite ruined goods. I'm not capable of returning such sentiments.' Then she was cruel. 'Are you sure? I will cost you the agency, your lifestyle. I will not marry another man who treats his vows lightly.'

Her set down had been prettily done up until then. But that last was a slap in the face on two levels. She'd compared him to the *comte* and she'd done so by referencing the Christmas fight, that the agency was an excuse for promiscuity. Channing straightened. He'd known this would come up. It was one of the unpleasant things they had to discuss. 'Those words were a mistake on my part, spoken in the heat of argument,' Channing replied.

Alina set down her glass. 'I would hate to become another mistake. It would not be only your emotions that were engaged should we pursue anything. I would not want to wake up one day and discover you'd been wrong about your feelings.'

'It was not my feelings that were mistaken,' Channing corrected. 'I was unaware at the time that you would be jealous of any advances I made elsewhere. If I had understood what you really wanted from me, I would have pursued a different course of action.' Lord, this was a stilted conversation, but they were both trying so hard to protect themselves. There was consolation in that. He was not the only vulnerable party here.

'You should have asked.' Alina took a healthy swallow of the brandy.

'I did ask,' Channing snapped. 'I asked you to come away with me.' He rose to his feet and began to pace. A storm was rising between them, electric and swift. Now was the time for discretion and care, but caution seemed to elude him.

He was not alone. Alina was on her feet, facing him with fiery eyes. '*You* asked me to choose between bigamy and adultery by coming with you. Both fine lifestyle choices, don't you think?'

He would not stand for that. She would not turn his heartfelt offer into something sordid. 'Don't preach principles at me when you chose to stay for money and wealth. Remember, I saw you draped in your jewels and silks and you looked right through me.' The old anger, the old hurt was breaking free inside.

'Bastard!' Alina hurled her glass against the fireplace. It smashed, the sound of the crystal shattering loud in the quiet of the library. Her face was a mask of fury. 'Is that what you thought? I stayed for money?' She was moving towards the console with the decanter, sweeping up anything in her path. She had a vase in one hand. 'Alina!' Channing raced towards her, slowed momentarily by the sofa, her words starting to translate into meaning, but he needed more.

She threw the vase. He ducked and it crashed against a table. Channing charged on. 'Alina, stop!' But she was in full rage. She reached for a tumbler and threw, then another. Channing grabbed up a delicate Louis XV chair to use as a shield and counted. There were only six glasses. She couldn't hold him off for ever.

The sixth shattered against his chair shield and he tossed the piece of furniture aside. He was five feet from her when she grabbed the decanter. 'I'll throw it, I swear I will!'

'I know you will.' Then she'd be out of missiles, but Channing didn't relish smelling like a drunk the rest of the night, nor did he relish the idea of the damage the leaded crystal decanter could do to him. It *would* hurt. Channing held his hands out to his sides in a gesture of openness. 'Alina, please, put the decanter down and talk to me.' He kept his tone even. Angry women were an occupational hazard in the League. He'd dealt with his fair share.

'You thought I chose him!' she railed. 'That makes you a bastard and a stupid one at that.'

Channing stepped closer. Alina did not hesitate. Only the weight of the half-filled decanter gave Channing any warning. He leapt for her then, pinning her to the console, his hand closing around hers on the neck of the decanter.

'No!' Alina cried, but she was no match for his strength.

He felt her grip go slack, felt the decanter come under his control even as he saw the tears start to form in her eyes. His voice was quiet when he spoke. 'Tell me about Paris, about the park that day.'

He stepped back from her, giving her space and trust, but his eyes watched her intently. She started with simple words and he drank them up, piecing the story together. 'The *comte* knew. He knew there was an Englishman who had been at Fontainebleau. Someone had remarked on it to him. He did not know it was you, but he guessed that my affections might be engaged to some degree and he feared, as he always did, that I would steal away if given the chance.'

To protect you. Channing guided her back to the sofa. The words made him sick. To think he'd thought she'd played him false all these years, to think the worst of her. 'And what else?' he prompted.

'He'd brought me gifts from Italy: silks, jewels. He made me wear them, to show everyone I was his.'

'But that was not all,' Channing urged. She was holding something back. The man who had locked his wife in her room, taken her clothes and branded her skin, would not stop with a show of fine clothes and jewels.

'That I was only his, that only he had the right.' Alina pressed her eyes shut. 'Please don't make me tell you more.'

Channing gripped her hand. Remorse, anger and a host of emotions that refused to separate themselves coursed through him. His voice was low and insistent. 'Did you suffer for me?' God, he hoped not. But he thought of the brand on her skin and doubted there was any hope in that regard.

'He'd found the letters, you see. The ones you'd given me from Voltaire,' Alina said. The story was horrifying. The *comte* had stormed into her room, demanded she stand before him naked, while the room was searched for any item the *comte* had not personally given to her. Clothes had been taken, books had been seized, Voltaire included, and burned on the floor of her room in front of her while she'd shivered and his henchmen had stared. Then the physician had come to assure the *comte* there had been no consequences of any potential infidelity. There would not have been. He'd been chivalrous in those days and followed the lessons of his father. But his father had not met the *comte*.

The following day the *comte* had put her on display in the park in her satins and jewels. 'I had nothing left, but what he saw fit to give me,' Alina murmured. 'He'd promised me he would not seek out the Englishman if I performed well, dutifully.'

Channing's anger brimmed. 'I made it more difficult for you by showing up.' He should have listened to Henri and stayed away. He shook his head. 'I should have stormed the castle for you. I should have taken you away from Paris.' Self-loathing swamped him.

'And been killed or worse?' Alina flicked a sharp blue glance in his direction. 'The *comte*'s cruelty and power knew no bounds. He would not have hesitated to have had you castrated if he had any suspicions. I could not have watched that.'

No, but she could allow herself to suffer for him, Channing thought cuttingly. 'Why did you never tell me? When you returned to England?' But the words died on his lips before he could finish the thought. He knew why. He hadn't exactly been a picture of welcoming hospitality. There'd been no opening, just games and bitterness between them.

Alina shook her head. 'It's all in the past. But I don't know if we can move beyond it.' Channing knew what she meant. The events had shaped them, how they viewed the world and the choices they'd made since then. 'I will never be an asset to you, Channing. Nice English sons of earls don't associate with scandalous French countesses.'

Or marry them, Channing mused privately. She was being very delicate with her words. He needed a little distance and time to sort through the revelations. He was thinking with his temper at the moment, something he cautioned the men of the League not to do. He needed cool objectivity. He and Alina had been at cross-purposes, but explaining that didn't make everything all right, nor did it pave the way to a happy ever after, if that was even what they wanted. He knew what he wanted, though. He wanted her, games and pasts aside, he wanted her with a single-minded fierceness. How did he convince her she could want him, too?

Channing pulled her close. 'Oh, my dear, brave girl. I wish I could make it right.' Amery was right. He wasn't just in over his head, he was in head over heels and every other body part.

A sound at the door broke his thoughts. Alina looked up, alarmed. He shook his head. 'It's all right. It's Amery. The League has a special knock.'

A moment later, Amery stepped inside, his mouth a grim line of determination. He wasted no time. 'Channing, we have a problem. There are rumours. You need to come back to the ballroom.' He paused and looked at Alina. 'I don't think you should. It won't be pleasant and I fear we need to be careful about associations at the moment until we understand what we're up against.' Channing decoded the message swiftly. Amery must be concerned indeed if he was worried about them being seen with Alina.

'What are they saying?' Alina spoke up, her face pale in the candlelight.

Amery glanced at him. Channing nodded. 'Tell her.' He would spare Alina, but she'd hear the rumours, whatever they were, soon enough.

'They're saying the *comtesse* killed her husband.'

One look at Alina's stricken face and Channing's first inclination was to burst into the ballroom and call out the first man who dared to utter such a claim. But that would not solve the problem. It would, in fact, be the very worst thing he could do. It would call attention to the depth of his feelings for Alina. By doing so it would make her even more vulnerable to slander because now she'd think she had to protect him, *again*. No, the best thing to do would be to calmly walk into the ballroom and carry on as if nothing was wrong that affected him directly, gather information and plan accordingly, but damn it all if such a decision was easy.

Channing tugged at his waistcoat, gathering a semblance of control about him. 'Can you see Alina to Argosy House? I will go out and see what can be done—'

'I want to go out as well,' Alina interrupted. 'I want to face them.' Her chin was up, her eyes firing with anger.

Channing placed a soothing hand on her arm. 'I know exactly how you feel. But facing them while the rumour is as hot as your temper is not ideal.' He felt like a hypocrite. His temper was no less hot than hers and he had the satisfaction of going into that ballroom even if he couldn't fight anyone. He leaned close to her ear, breathing in the scent of her. The primal sensation of wanting to possess her, protect her, was filling him. *She was his.* 'You will be vindicated, my love, you may rest easy on that account. I give you my word.' She had been harmed enough, suffered enough on her own. But those days were gone. She had him now whether she wanted him or not.

Channing stepped away from her, the suddenness, the newness of the realisation swamping him along with the intensity of what it meant, but mean it he did. Alina was his.

The ballroom was seething with a frenetic energy when he entered. Channing bowed and nodded to acquaintances with ease, making his way towards his partner for the seventh dance, his hostess, Lady Evert. If anyone knew the gist of the gossip it would be her and she was the sort who would be in an immediate panic.

His instincts were spot on. They'd barely taken

the first turn of their waltz when Lady Evert broached the subject. 'It's about her. The *comtesse*.' Her tone was terse in its condemnation. Channing knew what was running through her mind; as hostess, this could ruin her ball—she had invited the woman, after all—or it could make her event an early highlight of the Season, the place where a delicious scandal had started. But she'd have to play it right.

She gave him a simpering look. 'I don't suppose you could be talked into rescuing her? Perhaps take her away after this dance. Out of sight, out of mind, I always say.' She shot a nervous look at the doorway, fearful that the *comtesse* would suddenly reappear from wherever she'd disappeared to. There was desperation in Lady Evert's command as she weighed her choices. That suited Channing.

'Perhaps I won't rescue her at all. She might have already sensed a change in the wind and left,' Channing suggested with a neutrality he didn't feel. He couldn't risk exposing his hand. But it was deuced difficult. Alina was in trouble again and this time he could protect her. People would think twice about crossing Mr Channing

Deveril. Such a move, however, would not be discreet. It would be a flagrant announcement of their association.

'I would consider it a personal favour if you did.' Lady Evert gave him a knowing look. In other words, if Channing could quietly manoeuvre the troublesome *comtesse* from the venue, she would be grateful. It would be excuse enough to exit the party. He could leave and Lady Evert would think it had been on her account.

'Then I suppose I could oblige.' Channing gave her a charming smile. He'd already obliged, in fact. By now, Amery should have quietly left with Alina for Argosy House.

When the dance was over, he wove through the ballroom, carefully making his way to the library to assure himself Amery had done exactly as instructed. He did not want to make his exit obvious. He had years of experience with this— stop and chat, nod to an acquaintance as if he had all the time in the world. He reminded himself this was not the first time Alina had faced society's scrutiny. There'd been questions when she'd returned two years ago. But he'd been beside her then, as her hired escort, able to diffuse rumours with his own stories. And she was no wilting wallflower, she'd meet society's censure with a show of strength. Still, the evening had been an emotionally draining one for her and it was bound to be more so before it was over.

Channing gathered his thoughts and plans as he'd made his way through the crowd, letting objectivity flow through him, calming his overheated emotions. Planning helped create perspective. He would drop a few casual responses to the rumour at his clubs over the next couple of days. If he could get Amery, Jocelyn and Nick to do the same, the rumour would defuse. He knew precisely how to handle this sort of thing. The agency was always quelling such cruel scandals. He was good at it.

He hoped it would be enough. There should be a statute of limitations on such things. Alina had worked hard to make herself socially acceptable, only to have to constantly brace herself against having that acceptability taken away at a moment's notice. Channing stayed an agonising hour longer to gather information, to hear how the rumour was playing out, what people's reactions were. But his thoughts were with Alina and his newfound knowledge.

By the time he called for his carriage and headed to Argosy House, one thought loomed larger than most. Quelling rumours was one thing, quelling doubt was another. Knowing what he knew, he began to wonder: had she done it? It was yet another telling factor as to how far he'd fallen where Alina was concerned.

Her culpability had not been his first thought when Amery had told him of the accusation. Neither had it been his second or third. Those thoughts had been about protecting Alina. It was only now with the crisis firmly in hand that the thought of potential, real guilt crossed his mind. Interestingly enough, what bothered him most about the rumour was not that she stood accused of murder. Her husband had been a mentally un-balanced brute of a man after all. What bothered him most was that he hadn't known. It was one more thing she'd omitted telling him, one more way in which she sought to distance herself from him. Just when he thought he knew her, he didn't.

Chapter Seventeen

Seymour knew. It could be the only explanation for the rumours. Who else would benefit from having such things surface now? But what did he know and how much?

Alina paced Channing's office at Argosy House while she waited for Channing to arrive. Amery was off getting tea. The place was quiet, all of the men out on nightly assignments. She ran through reasonably safe assumptions in her mind. Obviously, Seymour had discovered the deed was false. What did he know of *her*, though? Had he connected her to the Marliss family and now sensed she wanted revenge? Was that what was behind the rumours being spread tonight? Or had he simply dug up the old scandal as insurance against her and nothing more? If she knew the answers to those questions, she would have a better idea of what he meant to do with this information.

Amery returned, bearing a tray, his cravat hanging undone, his jacket off. 'I find tea helps in situations like this.' He gave a boyish grin that admitted he'd fought the kitchen for this assemblage of food and the kitchen had nearly won.

Channing took longer to arrive than she'd anticipated. She'd drank all of Amery's tea out of restlessness. Two hours had lapsed since she'd left the Evert ball. She'd had plenty of time to assimilate what had happened in the library, what she'd revealed. Had Channing had time to assess it? Had he had time to be repulsed by what the *comte* had done to her? Or was he still in the throes of his chivalry? Her heart ached. He'd believed the worst of her and still rallied to her cause even before tonight. What would it be like to have such a man as her own? He was offering it, of course, a man like Channing would. But she could not take it. She was so very dirty, sullied from her husband's vices, and now Channing knew the worst: she had murder on her hands. With that kind of scandal, she didn't dare to dream about a man like Channing Deveril.

At last, she heard his footsteps on the front steps, swift and urgent at the start, but slowing as he entered the hall to a regular pace. The alteration made her smile. Of course, Channing would never outwardly give the appearance of hurrying anywhere, it would be a sign that things were out of his control. For all his airs to the contrary, Channing Deveril was a man who liked to be in control. His manner in the bedroom affirmed it.

Alina could appreciate that. She liked to be in control, too, or at least to give the illusion of it. She heard him murmur something low and inaudible to Amery in the hall as she hastily took a seat in the chair, thumbing through a magazine as if she hadn't a care in the world. She looked up when he entered, giving the impression she was surprised to see him, that she hadn't heard a whisper of his presence on the stairs or that she'd even been listening for one.

Lord, he was devastating. She'd seen him just hours ago in full evening dress and thought it wasn't possible for him to look any more handsome. But here he was, wrecking that hypothesis in messy dishabille. His cravat was undone, its unravelled length hanging against the dark-grey silk of his waistcoat. He carried his jacket over one arm and a blond swathe of hair fell over one eye, having escaped the efforts of his valet to keep it in place.

Her second reaction was less positive: the news must be worse than she thought if Channing had gone to this effort to appear casual, to give the appearance nothing was wrong. He would try to spare her the brunt of it. She could not allow that. She couldn't help herself, or protect Channing if it came to that, if she didn't know all she was up against. She rose and straightened her shoulders. 'Was it foul?' It was best to begin with a show of strength. This was *her* problem, not his. Her life had been one mess after another. Not his.

Channing laid his coat over the back of his chair behind the desk, giving himself something to do while he gathered his thoughts, Alina guessed. 'I think we can safely assume Seymour has discovered the deed is a fake and that he has determined your connection to the Marlisses.'

Alina took the news calmly with a nod of her head. Such an outcome was not unlikely. Originally, she'd hoped Seymour would have put those pieces together later in the game *after* he'd tried to draw against the property. But that was no longer the issue. 'Why do you feel that conclusion is valid?'

Channing sat down in the chair and met her gaze with a seriousness she'd seen that afternoon behind the tree. 'The rumours are despicable, Alina. I won't lie to you. They cast you in the worst possible light.'

Alina played with her pearls. 'What are they saying tonight? That my husband's death is questionable? That he was poisoned? People said those things eighteen months ago. These are not new.'

Channing's tone was sharp. 'They are saying that and more. Seymour has put it about that you murdered your husband.' Accusation flashed in his eyes, not over any belief he had that she'd actually done such a thing, but accusation over her omission. Of course. He felt betrayed she hadn't told him when she'd first returned and hired him to ease her way. She'd been a bit vague about it back then. She wouldn't have chosen for him to find out this way. In fact, she wouldn't have chosen for him to find out at all.

'Seymour can't possibly have any proof of that,' Alina scoffed as if she found the premise ridiculous. But it did worry her that he'd unearthed so much so quickly. Her husband's death had occurred in another country and nearly three years ago. Even at the time of his death, the investigation had been done with a lukewarm intensity. Too many people had been too interested in protecting themselves. Her husband had not been well liked and the cousin who had unexpectedly inherited was all too keen to wrap any questions up in a neat package and move on with his new life as the Comte de Charentes to let any probing drag on.

Channing stretched and crossed his legs at the ankles. 'He doesn't have to. You know how rumours work. All it takes is repeating them enough and the damage is done. This could ruin you socially, Alina.'

She swallowed. 'It's not me I'm worried about. I'll live. I'll go to the country and re-invent myself.' She'd done it before. She'd re-invented herself inside her marriage as a *femme fatale* and after her marriage, even now, she had re-invented herself as an Englishwoman of independent means. One more incarnation would hardly matter. 'It's my family I'm concerned about.'

Seymour could hardly say or do anything to her that would be worse than what the *comte* had heaped on her. Her skin was thick. But her family was vulnerable. 'I am thinking of what a scandal would do to Annarose. She's to come out next year. I had hoped to have her come to London and make her début here where she could meet more eligible men.' Her sister wouldn't meet anyone if these rumours caught fire.

Channing nodded, his blue eyes thoughtful. He had sisters; he was close to his family. He would understand how important it was to her to be able to provide this opportunity for Annarose. 'We can attempt to scotch the rumours. I can put out counterclaims at the clubs. We can tell society what a horrible marriage it was.'

She shook her head. 'No details, I couldn't bear it.' It was bad enough to be privately humiliated. To have others know would be devastating.

'Of course, no details.'

But Alina heard something more in his tone. 'You don't think such a strategy will work this time.'

'No, I don't. There's more.'

'More than being accused of murdering one's

own husband? I can't imagine what "more" there could be,' Alina said with a lightness she didn't feel.

'There are other rumours that suggest you had motive for doing so, that you asked your husband for a divorce not long before his death.' Channing paused, his handsome face a study in consternation and anger. 'Why didn't you tell me? Why didn't you tell me any of it?' By 'any of it', he meant what she'd revealed tonight, this last part of being a suspect, albeit one of many of a very long list, and the request for a divorce.

'At the time, I didn't think it mattered.' Her eyes flashed with indignation. 'I don't care to have my decisions questioned. The fewer people who knew, the better. I wanted to leave my past in Paris and start a new life here. I hired the League to help me do that. I told you what you needed to know. I did not mislead you, I did not misrepresent myself.'

Channing shook his head, a shadow of sadness crossing his eyes. 'I don't mean then, I mean now, tonight, when there was no business between us.'

'It didn't seem like the right time. I didn't want it to seem as if I were making unrealistic expectations of you. Everything between us was new and heady and passionate, not the best circumstances in which to make decisions. I thought it was best to keep it to myself.' There was so much bad news when it came to her life, it was hard to know when to trot it out for consideration and up until today and the carriage, there'd been no reason to tell a man who would be moving on.

To his credit, Channing did not give in to a rant. It would have been so easy to shout cruel things, to throw the folly of that decision back in her face. She knew plenty of men who would feel justified in doing so. But Channing was not of the usual. He was silent for a long while, perhaps weighing his choice of response.

When he spoke, his voice was quiet. 'What do you think of that decision now?' His strategy was entirely disarming. She'd been prepared to fight, to defend her decision. But he would not be provoked. It was probably for the best—the tea set Amery had used was too pretty to throw.

Alina sat back down in her chair, her own fight going out of her. It was hard to stay defensive when there was no enemy. 'The divorce was my last stand, my last attempt to be free. The things

I've already shared with you were not isolated incidents. I would remind myself of all that I had: the house in Fontainebleau, the luxurious home in Paris, the fine clothes, the freedom to do as I pleased when he wasn't in town, which was often. I told myself I was lucky. I wasn't a rich girl with a lot to bring to a marriage and yet I'd managed to get this one. As long as I was with the *comte* I would want for nothing. My family would want for nothing.

'Was it too much to ask if he requested I sit at the table of his all-male dinners? Was it too much to ask if I wore the gowns he provided for those occasions, even if they were extremely provocative and not to my taste? Was it too much if he made certain demands in the bedroom? He was my husband after all. After a while, as you know, the demands became more prurient, more public. He had a particular fantasy in which I wore nothing but a diamond-studded dog collar and a matching leash. He would have me sit at his feet all evening and feed me from his hand. He was fond of reminding me that both the government and the church had given him dominion over me. I had no grounds upon which to refuse.

'That doesn't mean I didn't try. But it had ill effects. He curtailed my social freedom. No longer could I hold my salons, or be seen in the company of other men. He spent more time in Paris. Our drawing rooms were full of his orgies, the household staff was full of his spies, I couldn't go out without a full report being given to him of my activities. Anything would set him off and I'd be locked in my room for endless amounts of time, enduring a variety of deprivations.'

A fleeting thought crossed his blue eyes. 'You must have hated the prize at the egg hunt.' He'd put the pieces of that puzzle together. She could see Channing's fists clench, his jaw tighten.

'I don't tell you this to rouse your anger against a dead man. I tell you so you understand what I was up against, so you don't think the other incidents were random acts of rage. When I asked him for the divorce, he laughed and said, "On what grounds? Do I beat you? No. Have I ever laid a violent hand on you? No. Even if divorce were legal in France, you'd have no grounds and an annulment after so many years is laughable. I'd never attest to it. Do you have beautiful clothes? Are you married to a wealthy *comte?*

Do you have every luxury a woman could want? Do you have a husband who is attentive? Yes to all of that. If you say I keep you a prisoner here, I will say I don't let you go out for fear of your safety. Who is going to complain about that?"

'But there were other incentives to stay quiet beyond the hopelessness of his reasoning. He threatened my family. The *comte* had English friends. He told me he'd tell them to spread rumours of my infidelity, my inability to give him a child, of my debaucheries so that my family would not be able to hold their heads up in public. That was how he first cut me off from them. I could not write to them in case I'd be compelled to plead my case. You know already he denied me permission to go to them.'

Her hands had become white in her lap where they gripped one another. 'Channing—' her voice was a quiet whisper '—I didn't kill him, but it's only because someone else did. When he refused the divorce, I was desperate enough to do it. I just needed an opportunity, but someone else had an opportunity first. These are horrible things and horrible thoughts. Do you see now why I didn't tell you? A wife wanting to kill her husband? I didn't want another soul to know. I just wanted it all to go away, all the horror to be buried with him so I could start again. I didn't want the future tainted by him, it was the only thing I had that was truly mine.'

'We'll get Seymour and put a stop to this,' Channing said fiercely.

'This time, maybe. What happens next time? Channing, I'm ruined. I think the sooner you face that, the sooner we can be smart about the realities of a relationship. It just isn't going to happen between us.'

'I refuse to believe that,' Channing answered. His eyes held hers for a long moment. He was thinking again. 'I think it could happen if you would let it. Stop pushing me away. Stop using Seymour as an excuse, stop using the *comte* as an excuse, the quarrel at Christmas, all of it as reasons we can't be together.' He gave a warm laugh. 'You see Seymour as a barrier to our being together but I see it as a reason to be together. I can protect you. If you need to use excuses, use that one. I want you and I'm not above begging, Alina.'

She stood up wearily. She hadn't anything left

to fight him with. A truce would be victory at this point. If she let him keep arguing, he'd have them wed by morning and she'd be thinking it was a fine idea— another pretence that would fade in the dawn. 'It's been a long night, I'm going home to bed. Let's see what the morning brings.'

Channing rose and came around the desk, his hands settling at her shoulders, warm and firm. 'It's not a night for being alone.' He kissed her then, behind her ear along the sensitive line that ran to her belly. He might be done persuading with words, but he was a warrior at heart and he would not stop until he'd won. 'Stay and we'll see what the morning brings together.'

He led her through the dark halls to the room he kept for occasional stays at Argosy House, his hand warm over hers.

'Do you think this is a good idea?' Alina murmured her protest between kisses. Her body was sure Channing's hands were exactly the right remedy. Only her mind was uncertain—the one part of her that knew what sex really was and what it was best used for: power. It was a weapon she'd learned to wield over the years to her benefit. Sex was supposed to be a tool, a game. She understood that. By the very nature of his business, Channing knew that. It was the common ground they had between them, the one thing they understood about each other. He was probably using it right now to make her reconsider. But he only thought he wanted her.

Channing laughed against her throat, his hands at her hips drawing her against the cradle of his thighs where his phallus strained against his trousers, hard and insistent. 'I think it's the best idea ever.'

He turned her away from him, his hands working the fastenings of her gown, his mouth at her neck, at her ear. The gown loosened and he pushed it off her shoulders. His hands hooked beneath the straps of her chemise, working it over her head. He knelt at her feet to roll down her stockings. She'd spread her legs for him, thinking that he would take her with his mouth while he was down there, but Channing had confused her and gently closed her legs with a shake of his head. 'Not tonight,' he said softly.

There was something tender about his ministrations tonight as he undressed her. Channing had always been a considerate lover, but tonight was different. Tonight was not on pace to be a seduction. There would be no drinking Moët naked in the firelight, no silken ropes, no teasing temptations because Channing did not intend for tonight to be a game. It scared her even while it made her tremble. This would be like the carriage, like the declarations he'd made in Evert's library.

Channing stepped away from her. She could hear the sound of his clothes as they came off. She understood now why he was reluctant to light a lamp. A lamp would mean seeing one another and their responses, a lamp would bring back the element of gamesmanship. In the dark they could only feel, could only touch. The darkness would keep them honest.

Channing stepped towards her, naked and hot. She could feel the welcome heat of him as he danced her backwards to the bed. She went down on the mattress and he followed her, coming over her, covering her with his length, his heat, his body creating a sensual cocoon around her. There was a moment of rustling while Channing fitted a sheath over himself. Then she felt the slide of his skin on hers, felt the little adjustments of their bodies as they shifted to accommodate each other.

The darkness was not without its own eroticism, the tender slowness of Channing's efforts not without their own intense pleasures. He touched her with his hands, with his mouth, with his tongue, until the very languor of the foreplay was enough to drive her mad. When he finally moved to enter her, she was more than ready, her body clamouring for him, for the straightforwardness of this new lovemaking.

She moved beneath him, raising her hips in encouragement as he thrust deep. Her legs were about his hips, drawing him in tight as if she could hold him there for ever. She rocked with him, her muscles clenching about him, meeting each slick slide and return. This was an exciting, unexplored level of intimacy. 'Channing, take off your sheath. I want to feel you, every last part of you, naked against me.' She arched against him, her voice a mere rasp at his ear. She felt him comply, then felt him slide home, again and again until she could do no more but hold on.

She could feel the climax approaching, his body full of clues. It was there in the corded tension of his muscles where his arms braced over her, in the pulsing strength of his entry, the quickness of his breath, the pounding of his heart. She cried out his name, swept away at last while he spilled deep inside her.

The enormity of what they'd done came to her slowly in the post-climactic haze which followed. The 'best idea ever' was to make *love* in the dark, not sex. It was perhaps the most intimate, most true act she'd ever done with another person. This had not been a game, had not been abetted with external stimuli and that made it the most dangerous thing she had yet to do in bed. This could change everything if she wasn't careful, if everything hadn't already changed. What would happen if she dared to believe such a change was possible? If she dared one more time to believe in Channing Deveril?

Chapter Eighteen

Channing shifted in bed, careful not to wake Alina. If he had his way, he'd lie here all morning, basking in the sun that came through the window, wallowing in the contentment of lying abed with Alina. Channing couldn't help but laugh out loud at the image it created. Too bad not all problems could be solved as easily. There were plenty of them waiting outside of bed, one more reason he didn't regret getting *into* bed in the first place. There was a soft moan beside him.

'Ugh, you're awake already and thinking.'

'I always wake up thinking.' Channing drew her closer, liking how she fit perfectly in the notch of his shoulder, her body warm and lush against him. He sighed. This was all he really needed, Alina in his arms and a room to live in. The thought should have sent him bolting out of bed, but it didn't. It was merely a logical extension of thoughts he'd had last night. Last night hadn't been about sex. It hadn't been about two people competing for power and pleasure. It had been what he imagined a wedding night would be, something honest and strong and without artifice.

He moved over her, wanting that magic to happen again, for her. He wanted her to see, to *know*, sex could be more. He wanted it for himself, too, if he was truthful. Sex and pleasure, *physical* pleasure was his business. But with Alina, he'd discovered a pleasure that went beyond that, something which he couldn't package and sell. If he lost her, he would lose it as well.

Channing slid into her, revelling in her slickness. She gasped at the contact, her hands reaching over her head to grip the iron spindles of the bed frame. 'All right?' he asked, withdrawing slightly.

'Don't go!' she cried. 'It just felt so *delicious,* it's the only way to describe it. There's one little spot…' Channing smiled down at her. It *had* felt delicious, there'd been a delightful sensation as he'd entered her and slid towards her core. He did it again, relishing her cries of delight. His desire to bring her this new pleasure heightened his own. This morning interlude wouldn't last long, but it would prove to them both that they were just as good at this new, 'ordinary' sex together as they were at the other. This was physical genius indeed.

But the world was patiently waiting for them when it was over. Newspapers and scandal sheets were laid out with the food because they had to know. How badly had the rumours of last night hit? Clothes had materialised for them, thanks to Amery's forethought the night before. They dressed and faced the day.

It was early by Argosy House standards when they came down for breakfast. With a mutual look of consent, they filled their plates and each took a paper and turned to the society column. For a moment Channing was hopeful. The first two rumours weren't about her. But the third one was and his heart sank. 'You'd better read it out loud,' Alina said staunchly, catching his eye.

'New rumours percolated about the mysterious Comtesse de C. once more at Lady E.'s ball. Not only did the *comtesse*'s husband die suddenly, but she was considered suspect in the act. How is it that we did not know this sooner? What other lies has she foisted on us in a bid for acceptance?'

Channing threw the paper down in disgust. 'There's no proof, no truth to any of it.'

Alina was more sanguine. 'I think we must be careful not to go on the defensive just yet. Perhaps this is a sign of something else. Seymour has come out strong. He thinks to protect himself by discrediting me with rumours. He wants to use those rumours to force me to retreat in order to save my family from scandal. The issue is, *why* does he want me to retreat? I think he's scared; scared we know too much, scared we will not hesitate to come after him and expose him. He's overreached himself this time and he knows it.'

Channing peeled an orange and broke off a section, thinking out loud. 'He needs the rumours because he's afraid to come forward about the deed. If he complains about the false deed, there may be questions about his own dealings and that's too risky for him.'

Alina nodded, her words coming swiftly as her thoughts formed. 'If I were him, I'd use the rumours to pressure me in to withdrawing. The deed looks much more damaging if my character is under fire.'

'A sort of blackmail, if you will,' Channing added, thinking it over. 'Blackmail could be managed if one has the proper network. But we have to catch him at his trade, otherwise stopping the rumours won't yield us much.' He paused. 'We could stop him with a simple solution.'

She looked up, hopeful. 'What would that be?'

'You could marry me. No one would challenge Mrs Deveril.'

'No, Channing,' she said softly. He wasn't joking. He would really do it. She had to prevent that from happening. Easy solutions often had difficult repercussions.

Channing sighed. 'Since you won't marry me, we're going to need a team of brilliant solicitors and a set of society ladies who carry some sway among the *ton*.' Those were resources he had, but Alina wouldn't like it. He decided to break it to her gently.

Channing leaned forward and popped a bit of orange in Alina's mouth, dabbling at the dripping juice with a napkin while she chewed. 'Since your mouth is full, this might be a good time to tell you, Nick and Jocelyn will be over shortly and they're bringing their wives.'

'It's all over the scandal sheets this morning.' Seymour tossed down a pile of papers on the table. He faced the syndicate with a victor's confidence. 'The rumours are successfully planted. By tomorrow, London's rich will think a murderess walks among them. The *comtesse* will have no choice but to retreat the field. If she does, the rumours will slowly fade and she can work her way back into society's good graces. If not, she'll be finished. Even if she does come forward with any claims against us, no one will believe her.' He paused for effect. 'She's already in retreat from what I hear. She left the Evert ball almost immediately after the rumours began.'

Eagleton, the old killjoy, spoke up. 'The question is, where did she go? Do you know? I do.' He gazed around at the group. 'She went to Argosy House, a property owned by Channing Deveril, who showed up two hours later and the two did not emerge until morning.'

Seymour schooled his features into bland neutrality and waited. Was Eagleton going to reveal the last piece he had so judiciously withheld from the group?

'Mr Channing Deveril's brother,' Eagleton said, 'is Viscount Swale, his father is an earl. Their family is one of England's oldest and, when they choose, most influential.' The man sounded like a walking, talking version of *Debrett's Peerage*.

'That's no good,' Hugo Sefton bemoaned at the far end of the table, eliciting other nods of agreement. 'We don't deal with peers.'

'We don't know how involved he is. Perhaps he's just a lover. A woman of her background is likely to keep one or two on a string,' Seymour argued, trying desperately to keep his last *faux pas* from coming to light. He should not have believed the *comtesse* when she'd said Mr Deveril was of no account, not when proof to the contrary had been laid before his very eyes, quite literally, too.

'You've become quite the liar, Seymour,' Eagleton went on. 'What he has failed to mention to all of you is that Mr Deveril was at the Lionel house party. Mr Deveril is *not* someone she has taken up with since her return to town. While it is true that I do not yet know the depths of their association, having only had a few hours' knowledge of it—' this last was said in obvious contempt for Seymour and his extended knowledge of the association '—I suspect we will find there is more here than meets the eye.'

Seymour stifled a sigh of relief. 'Until then, there is nothing to do but wait and watch.'

Eagleton rounded on him. 'Wrong. There is plenty to do. She knows about us and if we are exposed it means prison or transport for every one of us. We cannot afford to sit back and wait. We have drawn her out and she will fire back. That is certain. The *comtesse* cannot afford to do otherwise. We cannot merely wait for that to happen and then carelessly lob our next volley. We must gather information, we must get to know all there is to know about Mr Deveril.'

Seymour scoffed. 'You make it sound like we're at war.'

Eagleton pointed a long bony finger at him. 'We are, my boy, and if you haven't figured it out yet, the casualties are you or her.'

This was war and Alina was waging it on two fronts. On one front there was Seymour and his horrid rumours, threatening to bring her down. The other was right here in the drawing room of Argosy House. She had to conquer Channing's friends. They were here to help him, even if that meant protecting him from her whether he wanted it or not. Alina was well aware she needed to pass muster before they gave their approval.

Alina preferred the battle with Seymour. He was an enemy she could see. She could think his thoughts, she knew how he operated. Channing's friends were a different type of enemy. They were polite enough to keep their thoughts veiled, making it difficult to anticipate what might come next.

They were all gathered at Channing's request. Across from her on the sofa sat Jocelyn Eisley and his bride, Cassandra. Nick D'Arcy's wife, Annorah, poured tea from a heavy silver service set while Nick beamed at her from his chair. Ah, Alina thought. So that's what love looked like. The group was impressive, all assembled, drinking their tea and chatting easily with one another.

It all served to remind her just how much of an outsider she was. She had to earn their respect, had to prove she was worthy of their dear friend's attention. She would try to make herself agreeable for Channing's sake, and for her own. She needed them if she was to fight Seymour. Her hand tightened on her tea cup as Channing moved the conversation towards the business they'd been assembled to discuss.

'I am glad we could all meet today,' Channing began. 'The Season gets busy and we each get involved in our own schedules. There's something I want to discuss with you before that happens. You all know the Comtesse de Charentes, Alina Marliss. She has told me of a terrible situation that I would like to see addressed before it goes any further.' He went on to explain Roland Seymour's land-and-loan syndicate, how her family had been one of Seymour's targets, how she was attempting to expose Seymour and how Seymour had struck back with vicious attacks to her character. 'Which I am sure you saw in the papers this morning,' Channing concluded with a wry smile.

It had been difficult for her to sit quietly by and let Channing do all the talking, but these were his friends. What they'd do for him would be more than what they'd do for her on her own. On her own, she would never have got in the front door.

'The rumours are absolutely vile,' Cassandra offered sympathetically when Channing finished.

'There have been rumours before,' Alina reminded the group. 'The difference is that those rumours were spawned from curiosity over a newcomer. These are spawned from strictly malicious intent and designed specifically to make me an outcast.'

'Rumours can be quelled,' Annorah said, offering a gentle smile. It wasn't exactly a promise that she would fight to quell them. That would come later, Alina suspected, once the lovely, blonde woman worked out why she should spend some of her social currency on this dubious acquaintance.

'We have to do more than stop rumours,' Jocelyn pointed out. 'Seymour must be stopped. Protecting the *comtesse* isn't enough. We might save her, but what of the others he's already taken advantage of and the ones to come? If we don't expose him, he will simply move on to others.'

Channing nodded. 'I already have our solicitors looking into the syndicate to see what they can discover. Although, in the end, we'll have to look beyond the syndicate. We have to find victims and proof that there is an intent to defraud. I've already talked to David Grey.'

That news surprised Nick. He gave Channing a sharp, approving look. 'You've been busy already.' But Alina thought she read another message in Nick's eyes about what might have prompted such haste. 'Perhaps this would be an opportune time for the three of us to talk in more detail,' Nick suggested with a quick look at Annorah.

Annorah took the cue and rose, signalling this was to be a male-only talk. She smiled at Alina. 'Let me show you the gardens. I've brought up new roses from Hartshaven this year and I think they've taken well to the city dirt. I planted some here for Channing, too.'

Alina understood. This was a chance to divide and conquer. The Eisleys and D'Arcys would not think of committing to this effort without understanding it in full or of letting Channing move forward without understanding the relationship between her and Channing.

The day was sunny. The unseasonably warm

spring had brought early blooms and bright colour to the small, private garden behind the town house. The group of women chatted casually, comfortably. Annorah talked about cross-breeding her roses, how she'd grown them in the hothouse at Hartshaven in Sussex and then transported them here. No one listening to them would guess so much was at stake or that they were all waiting for the other proverbial shoe to fall. Slowly, the conversation moved from flowers to men, to husbands and eventually to Channing.

'Channing must care for you a great deal,' Annorah said, her voice quiet, tinged even with a hint of admiration. It wasn't what Alina had expected. She'd anticipated the words, but not the tone. Those same words could have easily been edged with disbelief and disapproval.

'I'm sure you think we're being nosy, but Channing is dear to us,' Annorah said simply. 'If it weren't for him, I might not have gone after Nick.' She gave a becoming blush.

'He's responsible for helping Jocelyn and me out of a tight spot as well. If not for him, we might have decided we couldn't be together and given up. I was the niece of one of the League's most ardent enemies.' Cassandra laughed and looped an arm through Alina's, her eyes dancing. 'Don't think poorly of us, it stands to reason we would want to know everything about someone he's involved with. We want him to be happy just as we are.'

Alina couldn't help but smile at the other woman's warm intentions. She was not used to such openness. She was used to interrogation and deceit. She'd had few female friends in her life. Her marriage had not left room for friendships and she had not formed any friendships beyond acquaintances since her return to England. Still, it was a bit too soon to assume these fine women would be her friends. They might assist her for Channing's sake, but that was all she should hope for. When the investigation was over and it became clear there was no future between her and Channing, these women might change their minds.

Alina thought of Channing's offer that morning. If she were to marry Channing, his friends and family would work hard to make her socially acceptable. They wouldn't tolerate him being ostracised over his choice of wife. She opted for honesty. 'I did not ask Channing for all of you to come here today. This was his idea. In fact, his interference has been entirely his idea from the start. I had planned to manage Seymour on my own.'

She gave a wave of her hand. 'But you know what Channing's like when he sees someone in need.' Maybe these women knew about the boys at Argosy House whom Channing had saved from the streets, about the young gentlemen he'd helped, like Annorah's Nick, to pull their families out of genteel poverty with the agency.

Annorah smiled. 'I know Channing has a soft heart.'

'I wouldn't hurt Channing for the world,' Alina answered the unspoken challenge. 'What should occur to you is that I don't want him to risk anything more.'

'Don't worry,' Cassandra said evenly, placing a hand on her arm. 'Channing can take care of himself. He and Jocelyn once saved the League by pretending the League shipped Bibles to Africa.'

Cassandra regaled them with the story, since it had happened after Nick had left the League.

The group finished their walk in laughter and re-joined the men inside. Everyone mingled in the hall briefly but it was clear the visit was over. His friends would meet now and decide what was to be done. Jocelyn and Nick shook Channing's hand. 'We'll be at White's tomorrow around three. Why don't you stop in and have a drink?'

'I would be delighted. It's been a while since we've had a drink together.' Channing laughed. 'You've become old married men.'

Jocelyn glanced at his wife, his eyes filling with that indefinable something that made Alina's heart ache. 'It's not the worst thing to be,' he said. 'Until tomorrow, Channing.'

Alina watched them go with trepidation. It would be a long twenty-four hours while she waited for the League to pass their verdict. It wasn't only about helping her. She'd wade through the Seymour situation on her own if need be. This was a verdict about her, about whether or not she was worthy of Channing. She cast a quick glance at Channing and was suddenly overcome with the realisation of all he was willing to do for her.

'Shall we drive through the park?' Channing

suggested. It was an effort to distract her and perhaps a declaration of his own that he would stand by her regardless of his friends' decision.

'Are you sure? We'll be seen together.' She didn't want him to sacrifice himself needlessly.

He turned his head and smiled. 'Maybe it's time that happens. I meant what I said this morning.' He nudged her with his elbow, his eyes lighting up with mischief. 'Besides, it's not the first time Channing Deveril has been seen driving a beautiful woman.'

Chapter Nineteen

White's was a calculated move on Jocelyn's part, an all-male club and a long-standing bastion of titled men for one hundred and fifty years. It also ensured Channing would come alone.

Jocelyn and Nick were waiting for him when he arrived, already settled at a quiet table in a far corner where they wouldn't be disturbed. They rose and embraced him. There was no question of their loyalty to one another. Channing wondered how those values would play out now in the wake of Alina's scandal. Would they opt to advise him to distance himself from her or would his friends take her into the fold?

Jocelyn poured each of them a glass from the bottle on the table. 'A whole bottle?' Channing teased. 'We'll be here all afternoon.' He wasn't sure what kind of sign that was. None of them was a heavy drinker and a bottle seemed quite ambitious.

'We don't have to drink it all.' Jocelyn set the bottle down. 'I didn't want to be interrupted by a waiter. I thought a bottle would ensure our privacy.' He smiled, but his eyes were serious. 'It seems we have a lot to talk about.'

'I explained everything yesterday, Seymour has made a habit of taking loans out against properties that aren't his—'

'No,' Jocelyn interrupted. 'That's not what I was talking about. I was thinking of you and Alina. I want to know what your intentions are. Is this agency business or is it something else?' Jocelyn fixed him with a serious, dark-eyed stare. 'If it is agency business, I don't think the ladies can help, if you understand? But of course, you can count on Nick and I.'

Channing took a sip of the brandy—he did understand. 'It's not about the agency,' Channing assured him. 'I won't lie to you. It started as agency business. She hired Amery DeHart and he's been squiring her around town since February. Amery was called out of town so I stepped in for him, not knowing she was his client.'

'But it's not that way now?' Nick asked again. 'What changed?'

How did he explain it? There were so many pieces to his association with Alina. It suddenly seemed extraordinarily complicated. He wasn't sure where to start. 'I don't know that it's ever been agency business with her.'

Jocelyn gave him a quizzing look as if he didn't quite believe it. 'I seem to recall she was *your* client at the Christmas party a while ago.'

'She was, but I didn't see her again until this business with Amery came up.'

Jocelyn turned his glass by the stem in thoughtful contemplation. 'It seemed to me that she was rather angry over what transpired at the party for someone who had merely a working agreement with you to relaunch her back into society.' Jocelyn looked up at the last. 'Would you care to explain that? I have my guesses, but at this juncture, I don't think guesses are enough.'

Channing gave a dry chuckle. 'And all this time, I thought you only wrote bad poetry.' Nick laughed with him.

Jocelyn smiled. 'I do a lot more than that. When she showed up that Christmas I began to remember other things: how several years ago you went to Paris for your father and extended your stay; how you went back later that summer. When you came home you founded the agency. Something had changed in you.' Jocelyn shrugged. 'But there was nothing else for six long years. Then at last Alina Marliss arrived at the house party and I began to understand how all the little pieces fit.'

'You don't need me to tell you anything. You've got it all worked out.' Perhaps he could avoid telling Nick and Jocelyn anything deeper, anything more complicated.

'I disagree, there's plenty more to tell.' Nick urged quietly. 'She's beautiful, she's sensual, she's the kind of woman every man in a room dreams about, but that won't sustain a man like you for seven years, most of those years *in absentia.*'

'Wait—a man like me? What is that precisely?' Channing felt his hackles rise.

Nick leaned forward. 'You are surrounded by beautiful women all the time. You don't need to go to Paris if that's all it was.'

Channing studied his drink. Friends were damnable creatures. Sometimes they understood you better than you understood yourself. 'If you know it, what do you want me to say?'

'She's the one, isn't she? If we are to back you, and by extension her, with our reputations, I need you to say it. A woman accused unofficially of murder is no small thing to tackle.' Jocelyn's words came fast and urgent. Channing sensed a mounting frustration in Jocelyn's tone. His friend was tired of him dancing around the issue. Well, he was tired of it, too. But to stop dancing would require certain painful admissions he didn't want to make. Channing's answer came out sharper than intended.

'It hardly matters if she is, she won't have me if that's what you're asking. I asked her yesterday over breakfast.' His anger, perhaps years of it, was breaking loose. 'I can save her from this latest scandal, I can help her expose Seymour, but in the end she won't have me. If you're asking if I plan to marry her, the answer is no, she won't allow it.'

Channing pushed both hands through his hair, his head resting in his hands. He'd never spoken those thoughts out loud to anyone. The future seemed that much more bleak with the words uttered, the futile reality that much more tangible now that he named it. The man who could have anyone couldn't have *her* and there was nothing he could do, there'd never been anything he could do when it came to her.

He looked at Jocelyn and Nick, helplessness threatening to swamp him, and the years fell away. They were not grown men, two of them with wives, the other with a successful business and a notorious reputation in the bedroom. They were just close friends, simple boys again. Channing would have given anything in that moment to be a young buck again and drinking in London with Jocelyn and later Nick beside him. His throat was tight and it was hard to get words out. 'Have you ever felt like no matter what you did, you were going to lose something and you couldn't do a thing about it?'

There was silence before Nick spoke. 'Yes,' Nick said quietly. 'I thought I was going to lose Annorah. After all, why would she want me? I had nothing to offer that a decent man should have, no money, no estate.' Nick paused. 'I thought nothing would matter again if I lost her.'

Channing reached across the table and gripped his friend's hand. 'But you didn't lose her.' There was more he'd liked to have said, but emotions were too close to the surface. He'd never guessed. Nick had always seemed in control of everything, able to organise and command any situation, even surrounded by angry husbands.

'Are you sure there's no hope?' Jocelyn asked.

Channing shook his head. 'There's never been any hope for us. It's never been the right time. When I met her, she was married. Now, she's wedded to her freedom. She's fought so hard for it she's reluctant to give it up, reluctant to attach anyone else to her scandals.'

'Reluctant to attach *you* to her scandals.' Nick cocked his head. 'That sounds fairly hopeful to me. Have you thought about why she doesn't want to risk dragging you down? She cares for you, Channing. You can't give up yet.' Nick winked. 'Not now when our ladies are involved.'

It seemed the fates were determined to make him cry in White's that day. Emotion swamped Channing a second time. His friends had not deserted him and it was a novel recognition. He had spent so much time looking out for others, it was somewhat odd to have others look out for him. He took a moment to compose himself. 'What do we plan to do?'

Jocelyn sat back in his chair. 'For starters, the ladies will make the rounds. They'll put in a judicious word here and there to quell the rumours.'

'Good.' Channing nodded. 'That will buy us time to co-ordinate with Alina's solicitors and start the hunt for records of the syndicate's business dealings or any aliases Seymour used. We should see results within the week.'

Jocelyn gave him a thoughtful look. 'A word of caution though, I can't guarantee we'll find what we're looking for. If not, things may get rough. If I were you, I'd think hard about what my next steps need to be.' As heir to an earldom, Jocelyn was more cognizant of social standing than Nicholas. He was a lord. He had to think before he acted. A title offered social standing, but it also limited freedom in ways others might not comprehend. Channing nodded, appreciative of the perspective. His own family name was old and prestigious. He'd not bring scandal to it. He was also overcome. It was somewhat overwhelming to be on the other end of assistance. 'Thank you.' Was all he could manage.

'This is *not* what we hoped for.' Hugo Sefton's eyes blazed as he spoke to the group assembled about the meeting table. This was going to go badly, if Sefton's anger was any gauge. Roland Seymour shifted in his seat. Who would have thought so much trouble would have come from the *comtesse?*

'It's been a week and the rumours have all but died,' Sefton raged. 'They were supposed to be fanned to a fevered pitch by now. Since when has the *ton* been uninterested in claims of spousal murder?'

'Since Deveril's friends decided to get involved. They are not without influence.' Eagleton shot a disgruntled glare Seymour's direction. 'You neglected to tell us the truth about Deveril's involvement and now we have a whole handful of peers rallying to the *comtesse*'s side. The rumours were supposed to alienate her from any assistance, but they've done just the opposite—'

'That's only the beginning,' Sefton interrupted. 'I received a letter today from a firm of solicitors, Birnbaum and Banks, requesting a meeting to discuss some of our financial dealings with the *comtesse*. They're not the *comtesse*'s solicitors. They're Deveril's and they're not going to limit the discussion to her deed.'

'Which was a false statement of property,' Seymour put in. 'Everyone keeps forgetting she's the one with the lies here.'

Sefton, the group's accountant, grimaced. 'Don't be naïve. They will bring up the Marlisses' contract, too. The false deed is just the bait to make the meeting seem harmless. They know something. If they've established a trail, they could press charges regarding our intent to defraud.'

'*She* could press charges,' Eagleton corrected.

Sefton shook his head. 'I'm in no mood to have you mincing pronouns with me. All right, *she* can press charges. If there's a trail nothing will stop her.'

Eagleton fixed the room with a cold stare. 'Nothing but a moving vehicle in the middle of a very busy street.'

'What are you suggesting?' Seymour sat forward in his chair, somewhat surprised to find an ally in Eagleton. He'd half expected the syndicate to 'let' him take the fall for this disaster. It would be easy enough to distance themselves from him. He'd spent most of the meeting trying to figure out how to blackmail the members into having to support him.

'I'm suggesting that the best way to deal with Alina Marliss at this point is to silence her,' Eagleton said plainly. 'She has not taken our hints. The rumours were merely a warning of what could happen if she continued to pursue this course of action. She's had a week,' Eagleton reasoned with the group. 'Her answer to us has not been to retreat, but to amass an army against us.'

He stopped here and glared at Seymour. 'I'm not suggesting this for your benefit alone. It's what we all need if we're to come through this. Not one of us has any desire for prison or transportation. Are we in agreement?' He waited for the group to give their consensus. When he had it, he continued. 'Anderson, do you still have your contacts on the docks? Farley, do you still have your hired men in St Giles? Excellent. Here's what we are going to do. We must plan carefully, we'll only get one shot. If we miss, Deveril will be suspicious. Listen carefully, timing will be everything.'

Seymour was glad to listen. Within a few days, his problems were about to be solved. The next time the *comtesse* went shopping would be the last time.

Chapter Twenty

It hit Alina all at once: She was starting to feel safe. Cassandra Eisley looped an arm through hers and pulled her into a shop with an exclamation of, 'Oh look, what an adorable hat!' The middle of a shopping trip was the oddest of places for such a realisation, but there it was none the less.

It had been a week since Channing's friends had taken up her cause. Change had come within days. The scandal sheets stopped speculating about her character and she'd been to every social event of merit. The last had been at the insistence of Annorah and Cassandra, who had argued she needed to make her presence known. Nothing would be accomplished if people thought she'd crept off to lick her wounds. She'd been surrounded by Channing's minions at each occasion. Society would see that she had their backing.

Alina smiled, watching Cassandra try on the hat, turning her head this way and that in the mirror. 'Do you think Jocelyn will like it?' she asked as if there was any question.

'I think Jocelyn would like you no matter what you wore,' Alina answered honestly. One could not be in the same room as Jocelyn and Cassandra without seeing the great affection they had for each other.

Cassandra gave a cheeky smile. 'That's probably true.' She reached for another hat. 'What about this one? You should try it, it's just your colour.'

Alina tried the hat to please her. Feeling safe wasn't only about the rumours having died down or knowing that the men were busy delving into Seymour's affairs. It was also about the way she'd been welcomed into the fold. The wives of Channing's friends had taken her in wholeheartedly, attending events with her, taking her on calls with them and inviting her on personal errands like this shopping trip. When it had come to making their position clear, no one could say the attention had been pro forma. To anyone looking in from the outside the attention would appear to be quite genuine.

Maybe it was. That was one of the more dangerous thoughts she'd had this week. Maybe the ladies really did like her. Maybe she really could belong with a group like this. It wasn't as if she was low-born or had no breeding at all. Why shouldn't such friendships be within her grasp?

Just when she'd let herself believe such a thing was possible all the impossible reasons surfaced. The rumours would always be there, would always follow her. There was always the chance even worse would leak out. Heaven help the ladies if they knew what her marriage had been like, of the lurid things she'd been forced to do, or the things she'd done in the name of freedom. They would not want such a soiled creature in their association, not when it came to being a wife. She'd be tolerable as a mistress, someone they didn't have to see. Quite perfect even—a worldly, widowed woman. But that would put an end to all this. No one went on shopping trips with their husbands' friend's mistress.

Besides, Channing hadn't spoken of marriage

again. It was a ridiculous leap of logic. They were together until this episode with Seymour was finished. Familiar association with these fine ladies would end then, too. Alina took off the hat and set it aside, sadness unexpectedly swamping her. In August she would be alone again.

'Don't you like it?' Cassandra asked. 'I'm going to get this one.' She paused. 'Oh, my dear, what's wrong? Has something upset you?'

When had she become so transparent? Alina smiled in an attempt to recover. 'I'm fine, just a little peckish. Perhaps we might get something to eat?'

The excuse was enough to allay Cassandra and Annorah's worries and they set off for a place a few blocks down the street, Cassandra swinging her hatbox in her hand. It was a busy time of day, the pavements crowded with shoppers. There were people they knew along the way and they stopped a few times to exchange conversation with acquaintances.

As they neared the tea shop, a commotion broke out ahead of them. A man darted through the crowd, a package in his hand, followed by a shopkeeper brandishing a broom and yelling,

'Stop him! Thief!' The man was too fast, the shopkeeper too portly. The man barrelled towards them, head down, giving the appearance of a charging bull. Cassandra gave a little scream and pushed Annorah towards the wall of a shop out of the way, but the man collided directly with Alina. The force of the collision sent her reeling into the street, gasping and off balance.

Alina staggered. Oh lord, she couldn't breathe! In her panic, she tripped on the hem of her dress and fell. She managed to get to her hands and knees, her world spinning as she tried to focus, tried to breathe. She was going to die, right here in the street, suffocated by her own inability to draw a single breath. What was wrong with her? She wanted to cry, but that required air. She managed a short gasp and then another, each short breath reminding her of the air she lacked. The world continued to spin, black spots forming before her eyes. She was aware of a rumble in the distance like thunder, and the rise of screaming voices, but they were of no help to her.

Annorah's voice cut across the others. 'Alina! Get up!' She wanted to, she really did. She just couldn't. The rumbling was growing louder. She managed a glance down the street with her spotty vision and froze. A wagon was racing towards her, pulled by an enormous draughthorse. *Crawl!* her brain commanded. *Worry about breathing later, crawl now. Crawl back to Cassandra and Annorah.* Somehow she dragged herself a few feet, maybe it was only a few inches, the effort taking all her will. In the periphery of her vision she caught the blur of a flying object whiz past. She heard the cry of a startled horse. The horse shied, veering towards the left-hand side of the street.

It was Cassandra who ran forward, hauling her to her feet and shouting orders. She got an arm about her. Breathing was a little easier. 'You're all right, I've got you. Annorah's sent for Channing. He'll be here soon,' she murmured. 'You've had the wind knocked out of you, but it will be better soon.'

It was better; she was panting now instead of gasping. Alina tried to slow her breathing. Her gaze strayed to the street where a bright-pink striped box lay crushed, its ribbon ripped and smudged with dirt, its contents trampled. 'Your hat!' Alina cried.

Cassandra hugged her. 'Silly girl, better my hat than you. Channing would have had my hide if anything happened to you.' She gave a tremulous laugh. Her nerves were getting the best of her now that the crisis had passed. 'I didn't know what else to do. I only knew I had to stop that wagon.' Cassandra burst into tears.

The enormity of the near-accident swamped Alina then. She'd almost been the crushed hat box. If it hadn't been for Cassandra's quick thinking, it *would* have been her.

She was shaking by the time Channing arrived. He shouldered his way through the crowd that had formed around them, looking like a thunderous blond Apollo in his concern with Nick and Jocelyn behind him.

Channing took charge immediately, clearing the pavement of onlookers and wrapping her in his coat. 'Can you walk? The carriage isn't far.' His arm was tight about her.

'I'm fine, really. I'm just a bit mussed.' She tried for a laugh, but it came out reedy and shrill.

'You're shaking,' Channing scolded.

'Where are the others?' Alina tried to look around.

'Don't worry about them. They're coming. Jocelyn wants to ask questions.'

'Cassandra threw her hat box at the horse. Her new hat is ruined.' She was babbling when they reached the carriage.

'Shh. Never mind about that, Jocelyn will buy her a new one.' Channing bundled her into the carriage and gave the driver directions before climbing in beside her. He pulled her close and dropped a kiss on top of her head. 'You're safe now.'

'Hmm,' she said, feeling a little lightheaded from shock and adrenaline. 'I was thinking the same thing.' This is what she got for believing she was safe. If a random wagon in a street could end a life so precipitously, was anyone really safe?

Channing insisted on going to Argosy House and calling the family physician in spite of her protests to the contrary. She was fine, nothing a good bath and clean clothes couldn't fix.

'Cassandra and Annorah will want to see you and assure themselves you are all right,' Channing had answered her protests with a smile. Secretly, she thought he wanted to assure himself. He had even carried her upstairs to a spare room before turning her over to the doctor, another gesture that was entirely unnecessary.

'Let him fuss,' Annorah said later when they came to call. 'No doubt Channing feels guilty he wasn't there to protect you.'

'There was no way he could have known. It was an accident. He can't be with me always,' Alina argued, letting Annorah pick up a brush and comb out her hair.

'Well, there's no reasoning with a man in love.' Annorah smiled at her in the mirror.

Alina smiled back, not wanting to argue. She couldn't very well tell Annorah that she was wrong. Channing Deveril wasn't in love with her—even if he was, she couldn't allow it.

'We have to allow for the fact that Cassandra is right.' Jocelyn paced the office downstairs at Argosy House with an agitated stride. Channing pushed a hand through his hair, thinking through all his friends had reported.

Jocelyn and Nick had stayed behind and questioned people at the crash site. The information they'd brought back was disturbing, but not necessarily reliable. 'Cassandra might be overwrought. It wouldn't be unusual for her to have imagined what she saw,' Channing argued.

Jocelyn shot him a censorious look. 'If Cassandra says she saw the man deliberately push Alina, then she did.' Jocelyn was stubbornly block-headed when it came to his wife.

Channing studied his friend. Jocelyn was a good critical thinker. 'You believe Seymour was behind this,' Channing surmised. It was a conclusion he was unwilling to draw simply for its implications— mainly that the game had escalated.

'I do,' Jocelyn said seriously. 'Nick thinks so, too. Seymour is scared. He knows his rumours have been rendered insignificant. He knows the *comtesse*'s popularity is growing thanks to her association with our women. He can no longer fight her alone. Alone, she wasn't much of a threat. There was no one she could rally except for a paid team of solicitors. But now—' Jocelyn waved a hand to indicate an invisible army of people who could rise to Alina's cause '—Seymour knows all the *comtesse* has to do is whisper her concern and he will be exposed. It is only her discretion that has kept her from publicising the situation thus far and Seymour knows it.'

Jocelyn stopped here and gave a smug smile. 'He also suspects we are doing more damage to him behind the scenes. Any day we're going to find proof about who he really is and what he really does. He's in a race against time and he's decided the best way to win that race is to eliminate Alina.'

Channing's anger started to boil. 'When will we have enough go after Seymour? Surely the solicitors have uncovered enough by now? Perhaps we can even bluff him into confession if we can serve up a tasty enough deal.'

'Soon,' Jocelyn affirmed. 'Don't rush this. We'll only get one chance. We have to make it stick. A man like him has got out of jams before. He'll know all the loopholes. This has to be airtight.'

Channing slammed a fist down on the arm of his chair. 'I can't sit here doing nothing. I don't want Seymour to think for a moment that I will tolerate such a blatant attempt to harm someone under my protection.'

Jocelyn stopped and fingered a paperweight. 'Under your protection? Those are strong words, Channing. What are you prepared to do in order to provide that protection?

Channing met Jocelyn's gaze slowly. 'Anything, everything. With my body if need be, with my name. If I'd been there today—'

'With your name,' Jocelyn interrupted. 'I don't mean in the way we're doing now with the girls playing their part. I mean more permanently. You have to talk her into it. She doesn't have a choice now.'

To make her Mrs Alina Deveril, wife of Mr Channing Deveril. It was a dream he'd never allowed himself to contemplate for too long. It wasn't distasteful, it was just improbable. 'Marriage would be complicated.'

Nick gave a wry smile. 'All marriages are complicated in their own way. If love was easy, everyone would do it.'

'Aside from whether or not Alina would have me, it would mean giving up the agency,' Channing said slowly. It was one thing to know that in theory, to actually do it would be hard, but he would for Alina. To truly be Mr Deveril, he would need a different presence in society. The agency could go on, but he would have to remove himself from any attachment. 'I've been thinking of retiring.' But he was also thinking perhaps the reason he hadn't asked Alina before was fear of rejection. He didn't know if she'd say yes.

'I'd put the question to her in terms she can understand, like her safety.' Jocelyn pinned him with a hard stare. 'While you're thinking, think about this. The afternoon's effort wasn't a warning. It was an attempt on her life and it was botched.

'Now, ask yourself what are you prepared to do? Convince her to do the same.'

Anything, everything. The words like a litany through his brain. 'I'll put the question to her to-night.' It would take all of his considerable skills at persuasion, but he was prepared to give up everything for Alina Marliss, even the agency. He understood Jocelyn's comment fully. Alina was alive either because someone had made a mistake or because Cassandra had an incredibly good aim.

* * *

Who would have thought Cassandra Eisley had such a good aim? Seymour was seething with anger when the news came. Eagleton was with him, his mouth set in a grim line. The attempt to trample the *comtesse* had failed, the only casualty being a hat box.

'Send a letter,' Eagleton said in quiet tones. 'We must act now while she's frightened, before she can think clearly.'

Seymour gave Eagleton a puzzled look. 'A letter? Why?'

'We can't make another attempt on her life. It would look too suspicious. They'll be alert to it if they even remotely think the accident today was foul play. We can't threaten her, but we can threaten someone she cares about.'

'Her sister? Her family?' Seymour went to the desk and drew paper and ink, thinking he was starting to understand Eagleton's train of thought.

'No, you idiot. Think for a moment. Do we want her to have allies? No. Does she have allies? Yes. Those damn rakes out of Argosy House have chosen to champion her. We want her alone, the way she was before. Alone, she has no protection. We have to separate her from her allies. Now, tell me, who do we eliminate?'

'Channing Deveril,' Seymour answered smugly then the reality hit him. 'We're going to kill a peer's son?' That seemed very unlike the syndicate. At heart, they were cowards, preying on those who couldn't defend themselves.

'Hopefully, we won't have to. We just have to convince the *comtesse* any association with her puts him at risk.' Eagleton gestured to the blank paper. 'Now, write. Take this down just as I say it.'

Chapter Twenty-One

The worse things are, the better one has to dance. Alina had learned that adage years ago in France. No matter what the *comte* did to her, come evening, it was time to put on a pretty dress and jewels and dance as if nothing was wrong; the more wrong it was, the prettier the dress, the bigger the jewels. No one must see beyond the perfect façade.

There was no *comte* here, but the lesson applied. She'd rather be at Argosy with Channing, tucked away in the little room, instead of Lady Houghton's ball. Cassandra and Annorah had argued otherwise; it would be difficult to convince everyone the accident on Bond Street was nothing if Alina were to absent herself from their scheduled events.

In the end, she put on a pale-blue gown she'd

yet to wear, had Celeste pile up her hair and off she went, ready to pretend.

Attending the Houghton ball was a special kind of torture. News of her narrow escape had circulated and everyone was eager to have her relive the details. Didn't people think about how horrifying it was for the victim to keep retelling the experience? It was made even more terrifying by the knowledge that it wasn't an accident at all. Channing had told her of Jocelyn's suspicions and Cassandra's belief she had been pushed.

Seymour wanted her dead. He must be very frightened indeed to resort to those lengths. Well, she was frightened, too. When she'd begun this game she'd not anticipated it going to this level. Now she feared for herself, she feared for Channing, she feared for all the people involved. She knew from experience, one did not operate well from a position of fear. This had to end quickly.

The League had done its part tonight. She'd danced with Amery, with Jocelyn and Nick. She'd danced with Channing, too. Between the four, they had kept her dance card empty of partners who would importune her with curious questions about the afternoon.

They'd also kept her safe. These men had appointed themselves as her guard, not that anyone was going to threaten her at a ball. She did feel those chances were slim, but apparently Channing did not agree. He was drawn tight tonight, his trademark ease and good humour forced, if anyone took time to notice.

'I'm going to go to the retiring room for a moment,' Alina whispered to Channing after the last group of visitors moved on.

'Take Cassandra with you, or Annorah,' Channing urged.

Alina shook her head. 'I'll be fine. I need a few minutes to myself.' It was true. All the socialising, all the pretending that everything was fine, had worn her out. She wanted to regroup.

The retiring room was thankfully empty. It was close to the supper waltz and everyone was on the floor dancing. She could have some privacy. Not that Channing's protection was unwanted. She just wasn't prepared to have so many people care about her. It took some getting used to.

Alina sat down in front of a vanity and went through the motions of checking her hair. It didn't really need checking. Celeste's pins always held. She took a deep breath, closed her eyes and let her posture sag.

'Comtesse de Charentes?' A timid voice broke her peace.

Alina straightened and opened her eyes. Of course, the one time she wasn't perfectly poised, someone would see. Channing had probably sent a maid up to check on her.

The maid was young, maybe not even a regular employee of Lady Houghton's, but hired for the evening. She held out an envelope and bobbed a curtsy. 'This arrived for you. I was to give it to you immediately.'

Alina took the envelope warily. This was out of the ordinary and, given the course of the day's events, there could only be one reason for it. She forced her brain to function. 'Thank you, did the messenger wait for a reply?'

'No, milady.'

Of course not. If the messenger waited, he'd have to contend with Channing and the other members of the League. There would be questions, assuming she told them about the note at all. Alina gave the maid permission to retire and slid the note out of the envelope.

It was short and direct, its intent clear. She crumpled it in her hand. She was *not* telling Channing about this. He would never tolerate the choice that had to be made. She'd been right about the need for this to be resolved before it escalated.

Alina fingered the crumpled paper. Seymour was attempting to blackmail her into dropping everything in return for leaving Channing unharmed. Well, she would see this not as blackmail, but as an opportunity to confront him and finish him. Alina folded the paper into small quarters and put it in her reticule. She was tired of those she loved being used against her. Her family had suffered for her; her sister had suffered for her; Channing would not die for her. She wasn't worth it. She drew a deep breath. Whatever her feelings were for Channing, they were over now. This had to end and she would end it. She would give herself one last night and then she would say goodbye.

She danced with Channing when she returned to the ballroom. It was the supper waltz and everyone would be going in to eat afterwards.

'Do we have to?' she asked Channing. 'Surely it would be acceptable if we left. We've done our duty.'

Channing smiled. 'Your town house, one hour. There's something I want to discuss with you.' Alina thought of the note in her reticule. She had twenty-four hours in which to confront Seymour before his threat became real. Whatever he wanted to discuss or do, this would be goodbye. She would make it count for the rest of her life, however long that was.

'Alone at last.' Channing took the champagne she offered. He kissed her on the cheek. 'You were marvellous tonight. I know it can't have been easy.' He'd already got rid of his coat and cravat. His shirt was open at the neck and the sleeves were rolled up. She had a sudden image of what it would be like to go home with him after every ball. It would be like this: champagne and dishabille.

At the sofa, he set down his champagne and reached for her foot, pulling off her slipper. He ran his hand down her foot, kneading the ball of her heel. 'How does that feel?'

'Divine.' Alina sighed. Far too divine. He was making it hard to leave him and yet what choice did she have? To choose otherwise meant Channing was a dead man. She couldn't protect him from a bullet. Even if the League managed to bring down Seymour, there was no guarantee of safety for Channing. In fact, it would be worse. Seymour had made that clear. He *wasn't* the gunman. The gunman was a random fellow, hired to shoot if a signal didn't come from Seymour within the allotted time. Any time after that was fair game. It wouldn't even have to be immediate. But Alina had one chance to stop it all.

'I think this has to stop,' Channing began in low tones.

'Of course it does. It has become too dangerous,' Alina answered slowly, unsure of where Channing was going with it. She'd let her thoughts wander for the briefest of moments and she'd missed some key piece of information.

'I don't mean Seymour.' Channing glanced at her, his hand halting in its massage. 'I mean us, slinking around to libraries, Argosy House, your house, oak trees in parks, carriages.

'I like the excitement,' Alina answered warily. He had her thoroughly off balance now.

'I like it, too, because we're together.' Channing went on, resuming his massage. 'I've been thinking about being together a lot and I've decided I want to be with you always, not slinking off to places, not playing games of discretion so no one finds out and makes a scandal out of it. I want to legitimately be with you. I want to dance with you more than twice, I want to arrive at functions with you, leave functions with you and not need a reason to.'

'What are you saying?' Alina's mind raced. She was pretty sure she knew, but she wanted him to say the words in the hope that she was wrong. She didn't want this, not now when she should be leaving him. She thought this had been settled.

'I'm saying that I would like to marry you. Would you do me the honour?' Channing's eyes held hers, intense and penetrating as if they could wring the right answer from her. They almost could. But they were destined to disagree on what the right answer would be.

She tried to pull her foot away, but he held it tight. 'Don't back away, Alina.' His voice was hoarse, a sign of the emotion behind his proposal. 'This isn't about Seymour and scandals.'

Alina swallowed. She didn't want to hurt him. Would he understand that? Maybe later. She doubted he'd understand it now when he believed he had his heart on the line, but she had to try. 'You don't want to marry me, Channing. You want to save me.' She gave a small smile and shook her head. 'I appreciate it, but I don't need saving. I can save myself.' *I can save you, too, if you'll let me.*

'This isn't about saving,' Channing interrupted.

'Yes, it is,' Alina fired back. 'It's what you do. Just look at the agency. You save young boys from the street and teach them job skills, you give them a respectable future. You save young gentlemen on the brink of a poverty they won't be able to cope with and help them create fortunes. You give women a few hours of pleasure against the loneliness of their lives. You are doing this because you want to protect me. When the threat passes, you will be stuck with me and you'll wonder why. You are reacting out of fear because of what happened today.'

'You are not about saving, Alina. You are about

loving,' Channing said softly. She did yank her foot away at that and tucked her feet up underneath her skirts. If he touched her again, she'd be lost. She'd expected him to shout, to argue the claims she'd made. She'd wanted to make him angry, wanted to fight, maybe even throw a few things. There was a pretty little vase on the table. It was easier to walk away when she was angry. But he hadn't played fair. He'd said the word 'love'. It was the first time either of them had used it out loud with each other.

'You shouldn't love me, Channing. I'm not worth it.'

'Give me one reason why,' Channing persisted. She saw now that he'd anticipated her far better than she'd anticipated him. He'd known she would resist. He'd even guessed the grounds on which she would resist.

'I can probably do better than that, but to start, there's the agency. You'd have to give it up. A married man can't be part of the League of Discreet Gentlemen.'

'I will retire,' Channing answered easily, without a moment's hesitation. 'I'd been thinking of it for some time now, anyway. Next?'

She had not expected such abject capitulation. 'Society will talk. They will say you married poorly. There will be scandal.'

'How could they say that of you? You're a French *comtesse* and I'm a second son. The match is equal enough.'

Alina stood up and began to pace. 'You're being obtuse, Channing. You know what I mean.'

Channing arched his eyebrows in superiority. 'A few minutes ago you knew I was proposing marriage and you made me say it anyway. Now it's your turn. If you're going to refuse me, you'll have to come right out with it.'

'It's not my title that's not good enough. It's me. I'm not good enough. I'm nothing but a high-class whore, Channing. I've done things no decent lady would consider doing, I've used sex for manipulation.' Her voice started to break.

Channing exploded to his feet. 'Stop it, Alina. That is the *comte* talking, that's what he wanted you to believe. You did those things to survive. It's not part of who we are, it's not part of what we do. It's never been a part of that.'

'We've played games,' Alina cautioned. 'You can't say that.'

'Because we like to, it's our nature. But it's also in my nature to recognise when the game ends and it becomes something more.' Channing gripped her shoulders. 'I played games because it was the only way I could have you, the only way you were available to me. I want *you*.'

There was only one way to win this argument and that was to shut him up. Alina reached up and kissed him hard on the mouth, her arms about his neck as she pulled him down to her. 'Show me, Channing Deveril.'

He didn't need to be asked twice, although she'd been prepared to ask as many times as it took. A 'love them and leave them' strategy didn't work so well without the first part. Channing's mouth ravaged hers in hard kisses, his hands ripping at the fabric of her gown in their haste. Her own hands were in a tearing frenzy, working the buttons of his waistcoat, dragging out the tails of his shirt.

She understood the need for haste. The events of the day, the emotions of the evening, had them exposed and vulnerable. Their bodies were hungry for any antidote to the unresolved issues that lay between them,even if the antidote was only temporary. She was hungry, too, for this last souvenir of one good man. She did not doubt Channing's words. He wanted her, he might truly love her. But she would be his undoing even if he couldn't see it. She had to be strong enough for both of them.

Her hands went to the waistband of his trousers, freeing his phallus. There was no question of readiness. He was long and hot in her hand. Channing had her skirts up, her bodice down, his mouth over one breast. Her own arousal was already intense. He bit at her nipple, his tongue following the tiny, shiver-inducing nip. Alina moaned.

'Wrap your legs around me,' Channing instructed. He lifted her then, bearing her backwards to the wall, the bed too far to contemplate in their current state. This joining would be fast, powerful, consuming. There was no time for details, just raw, unleashed passion. Up against the wall.

Alina felt the brick surface at her back, hard and unyielding, not unlike Channing himself. He kissed her roughly, his cock making a swift penetration that left her gasping. More, she needed more. She wanted the ramming force of him deep in her, wanted the power of him to drive out every other consideration until all she could do was scream his name.

Chapter Twenty-Two

The bed was empty. Channing awoke to the morning with a groan, his body late to acknowledge what his brain had already registered in its subconscious. Perhaps it was the emptiness itself that had awakened him. He rolled over and tested the pillow, the sheets for signs of her heat. They were cold.

Channing sat up and looked around the room. Alina was not an early riser and last night should have given her every reason to sleep late. After the rather frantic but explosive coupling against the wall, they'd adjourned to the bedroom for another bout of lovemaking, this time at a more sedate and lingering pace. It had left them both exhausted, he'd thought. Apparently she was a bit less exhausted than he was. 'Alina?' he called out, taking the lazy man's approach to searching the house. Why get up when he could just shout? He fell back on the pillows, still tired. He'd like to curl back up with her and sleep for another few hours, then talk about marriage when he had her at her most compliant.

'Alina?' he called again when there was no response. This was truly worrying. Channing threw off the sheets and padded through the bedroom naked. Out in the other room there was no sign of her. Where else could she be? Downstairs? He grabbed a sheet and descended. He tried the front sitting room. His eyes lit on the chair where a spare shawl had been draped the night before. The chair was empty. His stomach knotted.

Channing bent in half, hands on knees as the reality swept him. Alina was gone! Not just gone as in having stepped out to get breakfast. She was gone; disappeared. Alina had left *him* while he slept in her bed, in her house. Surely she had to come back? The proposal, his confession of love, had it been too much? Was she truly not interested? Had she left because he hadn't taken no for an answer or was there another reason?

Back in the bedroom he felt the sheets. How

long ago? The sheets again. They were cool, so damnably cool. It could have been an hour ago, or more. Thoughts raced through Channing's head as he pulled on clothes. Where would she have gone? Why hadn't she wakened her maid? It would take time to check out the possibilities. He could not think straight, concern and puzzlement warring for his attentions. He called for Celeste.

An hour later, Channing was out of luck. He'd been reduced to shamelessly interrogating the poor maid. The only luck he had was that Alina had awakened Celeste. But there was little she would tell him. Celeste repeated everything for the fifth time. 'Now she is gone. She packed a small valise with papers and left.'

'Where?' Channing pushed a hand through his hair. They'd already been over this. He knew what Celeste would say before she said it.

'I don't know. She wouldn't tell me.' That fact was clearly as distressing to her as it was to him.

'It's ten o'clock in the morning. Where would she go at eleven?' How did one behave mysteriously in the bright light of day? How did one simply vanish? 'Did she plan to come back?'

Channing tried another tack. Perhaps he'd focused too much on where she went. It might be better to focus on the aftermath, what happened after she completed her errand.

'She didn't say, milord. She didn't pack anything for a journey, though.' Celeste answered. 'All of her things are still here.'

Cold fear tightened its grip on his stomach. Was that because she would be back or because she knew she wasn't coming back? *And things like gowns and hairbrushes weren't needed.* He didn't dare voice the thought out loud. Celeste was on the brink of tears as it was. What kind of woman got out of her lover's bed and walked straight to her doom?

A woman like Alina de Charentes. A woman who was fiercely independent, who wouldn't let anyone else fight her battles, who would not tolerate anyone suffering for her. Channing knew in a flash of insight where she'd gone. 'Oh God, she's gone to confront Seymour.' What was she thinking? Seymour had proven himself to be dangerous. Seymour had ordered an 'accident' yesterday. Did she think the broad light of day would protect her? It hadn't protected her yesterday.

Channing pulled out a calling card from the case in his coat pocket. He scribbled on the back. 'If there's any news, or if she comes back, send word.' He dressed swiftly. He had to go somewhere to think and to plan. Outside, he hailed a cab and gave the address for Argosy House.

He wanted to go after her, but he had no idea where she might intend to confront Seymour. Was there an arranged meeting? Before he could go charging after Alina, he needed his team of researchers. They would have an address he could at least try.

Channing leaned back against the squabs of the cab. The slowness of his progress was driving him mad. Alina was in danger and he was stuck in London traffic on his way to an intermediary stop. That settled it. He was six streets from Argosy House. He could cover that distance faster on foot. Channing jumped out of the cab and tossed the driver a coin. Then he began to run, never mind the stares of people who found the sight odd, never mind that his boots weren't made for running but riding or that he was going to have blisters. It felt good to run, good to be doing something.

Amery was waiting for him when he bounded up the steps to Argosy House. 'She's gone, Alina's gone,' Channing panted in the hall. His well-trained staff were trying hard to ignore the sight of him, sweaty and dishevelled, hands on knees as he fought for breath. They were not used to seeing him with even a hair out of place no matter what the crisis.

Amery had a hand on his shoulder, guiding him into the front parlour. He barked an order for tea and sandwiches and shut the parlour door firmly behind him.

'I've been expecting you.' Amery reached into his coat and pulled out a letter. 'This was delivered early this morning.' There was a scold embedded there. *I couldn't find you.*

'I think she's gone to confront Seymour. Her maid said she took papers from her town house,' Channing said, his thoughts starting to settle with his breathing. He unfolded the paper and read. The letter was short. It had been written in haste this morning, he guessed. She'd not had time to invest in a lengthy missive without risking he'd catch up.

He handed the letter to Amery. 'She's gone to confront Seymour to protect me.' Channing's head sank into his hands. Was this why she'd fought so hard against his proposal last night? Why there'd been an extraordinary edge to their lovemaking? She'd known she was leaving him. 'All the while I was thinking last night would be a new beginning for us, and she knew it was the end.'

Channing groaned. 'Last night, she knew. She'd already decided.' When had Seymour got to her? She'd been with him all night except for when she'd gone to the retiring room. Had someone slipped her a note then? They must have, not that such details mattered at this point. All that mattered was that she'd gone out to face Seymour alone to protect him.

'Why would she believe such a thing? Why would she do such a thing?'

'Because she loves you.' Amery went to open the door and let the tea tray in. 'Quite a lot, too, if she went to all this trouble to slow you down.'

Channing raised his head. 'What?'

'Why didn't she just leave this note at what is it, the Piccadilly house? Is that why I couldn't find you this morning? It would have saved a lot of time if she'd left it propped up on a table.

Damn her. She'd led him on a deliberate goose chase, knowing full well the places he'd look for her, the place he'd go if he didn't find her.

Amery passed him a plate of sandwiches. 'Eat something. It will help. I'll pour a little something stronger in the tea to make it worthwhile. Nick and Jocelyn will be here soon. I sent a boy to get them.' He paused. 'It might be best to say this out loud before they get here. You do understand Seymour will not hesitate to kill her? He's already tried to do it once. To him, it's the most expedient answer to a messy problem.'

Channing nodded. 'It might be best to say *this* out loud. She will not die for me.'

'Understood,' Amery replied. 'Did the maid say what she took with her?'

'Papers.' He wished the maid had said Alina had taken a weapon.

'Papers aren't much good at stopping bullets.' Amery was grim.

'She must have thought they were her best

chance,' Channing argued, not wanting to agree with Amery's rather dire comment. But then it hit him. Hope flickered for the first time since waking up. 'She took papers because she had a plan. She thinks she has something she can use to stop Seymour.' He only hoped it would also be something that would keep her alive until they could find her.

Alina had a plan. She was going to bluff Seymour into compliance. Actually, it wasn't entirely a bluff, she was just going to exaggerate the truth a little. She ran through it one more time as the hired cab slowly wound its way through the London streets, imagining how the scene would play out. It was always good to visualise. Was there an argument she'd forgotten? An angle she hadn't anticipated?

So far so good. She'd made a clean getaway, although it hadn't been easy to leave Channing. She'd laid a time-consuming trail for him in case he followed her. She had to eat up the clock. The meeting with Seymour wasn't until one. She had to outwit Channing long enough to make the meeting and then she'd have to outwit Seymour. What happened with Channing after that remained to be seen.

Channing would be furious. He would wake up and find her gone *after* he'd offered marriage. That was exactly why she had to do this. She had accused him of proposing because it was a potentially expedient solution, but she knew better and it frightened her. Channing loved her. He'd spoken the truth last night. Their relationship had stopped being a series of games for him. Now, he was prepared to give up everything that mattered to him *for her.*

She'd never been loved like that. *Channing* had never loved liked that. He was a man who would love like the wolves that prowled the French woods in winter: ferociously, loyally and he would love only once. Those wolves mated for life. They protected each other, they died for each other. The *comte* had shot one that had crept too close to the château looking for food at the end of a cold January. For the next month, when the moon rose, she'd heard the howling of a lone wolf on the edge of the forest, crying for its mate. The wolves had moved on in the spring, but she'd not forgotten the utter desolation in that howl. The cry had penetrated her heart. It was not merely the cry of being alone, of being one, but the cry of a soul ripped in half, the cry of a being who knew they would never be whole again.

She didn't want that desolation for Channing. It would be better to stop it before it went too far. She could save him from himself if she could face Seymour alone and distance herself from Channing. She would leave London and Channing would eventually find someone else, someone worthy of his all-consuming ability to love. He was meant to love, to be the leader of a pack. But not her, she was meant to be alone.

She couldn't hurt anyone then with her scandals and her sordid past. It didn't mean it was easy to be alone, only that it was best, even if her heart broke over the prospect. Channing had offered her the dream and it was a potent one, one she yearned to accept; a happy marriage, a marriage without fear, maybe even a family of her own in the future. *It's a dream only. You can't really have all that. What would children think of a mother accused of murder, who did the things you did? They will find out. Society will never let you forget what you were.* That was true, too.

She would ruin whatever she touched. She was like the wolf who was cast out of the pack because of its ability to taint the entire group. She'd saved the Deverils the trouble of doing it. She'd cast herself out before they were forced to do it.

The cab rocked to a halt. Alina drew a breath and reminded herself, so far so good. Channing hadn't caught up to her, or perhaps he hadn't followed her after all. Perhaps he was regretting his proposal already or perhaps his friends had helped him see reason; they'd tried. They'd done their part. If she wished to go on alone, they should let her. All she had to do now was walk into the building and confront Seymour with her bluff.

Alina stepped down from the cab and paid the driver. She looked up at the building, shielding her eyes from the bright glare of the day. Her nerves quickened. She wasn't naïve. She knew danger lay inside, although the prospect seemed surreal. It was daylight, the office building looked like every other brick building on Fleet Street, which was home to various businesses, newspapers and printers. She couldn't bring herself to believe that Seymour would attempt anything violent in such circumstances. Everything looked *normal*.

'*Comtesse.*' A man approached her on the pavement, dressed in a businessman's standard dark suit, but businessmen didn't travel with two burly henchmen. She noticed them right away, even though they stood at a distance. 'If you'll come with me?' He gestured in the direction of the alley to the left of the building.

They wouldn't be going inside after all. Alina wasn't sure if she should feel relief or panic. Finally there was the air of the sinister about this meeting or panic for exactly the same reason. There was no real choice. She had to go with them, the two guards would ensure it, as would she. This was what she'd come to do. She had to see it through.

The alley was narrow, the bright glare of the street didn't extend into this gloomy corridor. The man took her arm none too gently and guided her to a black door. She was tempted to jerk her arm free, but for a man who looked like a weasel, there was a wiry strength to him.

Seymour was inside. He was alone, but she felt vastly outnumbered by the two hulking men, and the weasel. With Seymour, it was four against one and who knew what weapons they carried. All she carried were papers to make her bluff believable. The door shut behind her with an ominous thud. She couldn't see the guards. They must be behind her, standing sentry at the entrance, a reminder that she was in this alone now. Let the games begin.

'Four to one, Roland?' Alina gave a coy smile. It would be best to pretend they were alone, build the illusion of intimacy and rapport. 'Is that really necessary to discuss business with an old friend?'

'You're not an old friend and you know very well what you've attempted to do,' the weasel answered.

Alina fixed him with a glare of contempt. 'Who is this impertinent fellow, Roland? Don't say he's a friend, you can do better.' She caught the gleam of satisfaction in Seymour's flat, dark eyes. That was useful. Seymour and the weasel might be in business together, but they were not friendly with one another.

'This is Leonard Eagleton, he manages certain aspects of my affairs.'

The dirty aspects, Alina thought. Seymour wasn't the sort to actually do his own dirty work.

'No names!' Eagleton hissed.

Seymour turned towards Eagleton with a cold laugh. 'It won't matter what or who she knows in a few minutes.'

The words chilled her. There was no mistaking their meaning. She wished the guards were in front of her. At least she would see it coming. It was extraordinarily unnerving to think she might simply be shot in the back at any moment. A man like Seymour, who stole from the unsuspecting, would not hesitate to order a shot from behind. He had no code of honour to satisfy. When the end came, would she have done enough to protect Channing from the threat in the letter? It wouldn't be worth it otherwise. Channing was all that mattered in these final minutes. Channing was all that had ever mattered. If he was safe, he'd protect her family, he'd protect Annarose. Were things always this clear at the end?

She could not appear daunted, or distracted. She must be brazen and bold. Dealing with Seymour was not unlike dealing with her husband. She'd learned early any show of fear was anathema. Alina sauntered forward towards the desk, rolling her hips slightly. 'I think there are things you should know first.' She drew her hand down the low, round neckline of her bodice, her hand slipping inside. She watched Seymour lick his lips, an entirely involuntary gesture on his part as she slowly withdrew a slip of paper. She unfolded it. 'Do you know what this is? It's a set of instructions to be carried out if I do not return home by three o'clock this afternoon. Instructions have been left to assume a failure to return is a sign of my demise and people should behave accordingly.'

'What, may we assume, constitutes "accordingly"?' Eagleton asked.

'What a fine question.' Alina gave him a smile for him alone, something for him to bask in while she played with Seymour. 'I have left three sets of instructions in three different locations that certain documents be released to *The Times* immediately. These documents contain names of your former clients and the amounts of money you obtained against their properties. These documents will also be released if Channing Deveril *ever* comes to harm. Furthermore, should either of the two events I've described come to pass, a warrant for your arrest is waiting to be carried out, not just for swindling and intent to defraud, but for murder.'

Alina gave a cold smile, her hand fingering the low-hanging pendant at her neck, drawing Seymour's eyes to her cleavage. Her voice was husky when she spoke. 'You kill me, but I'll kill you next. When I say, I'll see you in hell, Mr Seymour, I literally mean it.'

She watched Seymour's eyes slide sideways towards Eagleton. He was nervous. Her threat had got to him. 'Perhaps we can negotiate—'

'Negotiate, my foot,' Eagleton interrupted roughly. 'She's bluffing. She doesn't know half of what she's claiming.'

Alina sat her hip on the corner of the desk and turned her charms full force on Seymour. Now was the time to divide and conquer. She ran a finger down the line of Seymour's jaw, her eyes holding his, her voice low, private, as if Eagleton wasn't in the room. 'You disappoint me, Roland. Is this how you run your business, by letting others run it for you? You led me to believe you made all the decisions,' she purred.

'Perhaps we can create a mutually beneficial agreement,' Seymour sputtered, arousal evident in his eyes. The allure of danger and sex combined to make a potent aphrodisiac and he was desperate to salvage his pride, to prove he was in charge. 'You agree not to release any of your information and we'll drop the threat against Deveril.'

'I'll need to have that in writing.' Alina rose from the desk and stepped away. Her heart did a little leap of victory, but she couldn't celebrate too soon. She still had to get out of the room and she couldn't leave without securing the agreement.

'She's bluffing, I tell you! Seymour, don't be a nodcock. She's playing you,' Eagleton argued.

Alina gave Eagleton a cold smile, her hand resting lightly at her throat while she played with the chain of the pendant. 'Do you think you can afford to find out, Mr Eagleton?'

Eagleton eyed her with a beady stare. She'd overplayed her hand. Eagleton was not as easily distracted as Seymour, or as easily cowed by the suggestion of ruin. 'The real question is, can you?' Something silver flashed in the weasel's hand. 'Let me assure you, my gun is not a bluff.'

In a fluid motion that gave no warning, Eagleton aimed the pistol and fired. Seymour slumped forward on his desk, shot through the head. Eagleton put the gun on his desk. 'Now, you were saying?'

Alina fought back the bile rising in her throat, her mind trying to grasp the horror of the cold-blooded act she'd just witnessed. Seymour hadn't been warned, but she had. She was going to die just like that, her life snuffed out in a fraction of a second as if she'd never existed, unless she came up with something extraordinary in the next few moments. She gathered all of her courage and leaned forward, letting the bodice of her gown gape a bit. 'I was saying, Mr Eagleton, that you and I are going to need a new arrangement.' She trailed a hand lightly down her throat to the exposed neckline of her gown. 'Something just between us. We can strip away any tendency towards pretext.'

He gave her an oily smile, lust rising in his eyes. 'I find the prospect of doing business with you a very seductive one, *comtesse*.'

Alina stepped back from the desk. She pushed the sleeve of her gown down one shoulder and then the other. There were still the guards to contend with, but she'd worry about that later. Once she had the gun, they'd change their minds. For now, let them watch. She could do this. She was the Comtesse de Charentes. She'd done worse and she wanted to live so very much.

Chapter Twenty-Three

Channing heard the gun fire, but only barely. If he hadn't been expecting trouble he wouldn't have been on the lookout for it. No one else was. Fleet Street was crowded with clerks and businessmen bustling about their day. Carriages and wagons jammed the street. Noise was everywhere: the yells of men, the rumble of drays, the neighs of horses. A gunshot would easily be missed.

He waved for Nick and Jocelyn to join him, his heart pounding. Was he too late? They'd gone into the office building only to find nothing. The address the solicitors had acquired for the syndicate's 'office' was nothing more than a room with a table and chairs in it. They might meet occasionally, but they did not do business there. Channing had suspected something of that nature. It would have been too easy. But they'd been obliged to check it out, just in case, and it had cost them time. Too much time, by the sounds of the gunfire. 'It came from the alley.'

'At least now we know where she is,' Jocelyn offered as they jogged through the crowded pavement, weaving between people. It was some consolation. Channing had feared they wouldn't know where to look next. If the office was a front, Seymour could have taken her anywhere. Then the search would have taken on a needle-in-the-haystack mentality.

At the alley, Channing slowed. All of his instincts wanted to dart down the narrow strip between the buildings but his brain counselled caution. If Alina needed him, he would do her no good charging in like a bull. 'Wait,' he told the others. 'Let's do a little reconnaissance first. See if there's a door, see if there's anyone in the alley.'

They joined the crowd passing by and casually scanned the alley. There was a door, but no men. Channing was thankful there was just the one door. There could have been more and that would have taken time they might not have. His gut churned even now, thinking that Alina could be lying somewhere, hurt, unable to help herself.

Jocelyn put a restraining hand on his arm as they reached the door. 'Keep your wits about you. We don't know what or who or how many we might find behind that door.'

Channing nodded. 'The element of surprise will be our best weapon and we'll only get to use it once.' All three men drew their pistols. Their initial entrance would be a show of force. In the early moments of their arrival it would be crucial to survey the room, take stock of how many were present and who was in charge. If they were outnumbered, it would be crucial to focus their efforts on putting the leader at risk.

It was decided Nick and Channing would enter first, followed by Jocelyn, who would protect the door, keeping it clear for a smooth retreat. Nick and Channing exchanged a quick glance. 'You don't have to go,' Channing said at the last. He was thinking of Annorah and the baby. Perhaps he should not let Nick risk this.

'You can't wrap me in pink wool, Channing.' Nick grinned. 'But thanks for the thought anyway.'

Together, they burst through the door, using the

noise and the suddenness of their appearance to catch the room's occupants off guard. The force of the door ploughed down one of the guards, Channing's pistol, used as a club, took the other one. 'Alina!' Channing's eyes found her immediately, but the weaselly-looking man was closer, faster, and Alina had made a tactical error that put her within his reach. Instead of using their entrance to retreat, Alina had used the distraction as a chance to grab for the gun on the desk.

The man's reflexes had been excellent. He seized the gun and dragged Alina to him, a shield and leverage all in one. Three well-built, armed men to one skinny weasel suddenly meant nothing. It could have been fifty to one and still meant nothing as long as the weasel held Alina. 'Looking for something, Deveril?' The man laughed and jabbed the gun at Alina's temple.

That was when Channing noticed Seymour's form crumpled over the other desk. The weasel was certainly bloodthirsty. And full of lust, too. Now that the initial force of the attack was over, he took in the details: Alina's gown in disarray, her hair falling from its pins. Her eyes were twin blue flames, but her face was pale.

'The *comtesse* and I were just reaching an accord,' the weasel said. 'I think, my dear, we'll have to put that on hold.' He yanked hard on Alina's hair, pulling her head up, her gaze forced away from Channing's. Channing watched her exposed throat work as she swallowed her fright.

Channing went rigid with fury at the sight of the bastard's mouth at Alina's ear. He would shoot the man right there if it weren't for the risk to Alina. He had no compunction about doing it, but there was no shot to take. Channing searched his mind, his vast stores of knowledge about human nature. He was usually so good at reading people. He'd been reading them all his life, his business thrived on his ability to do so. Everyone wanted something. What did this man want?

His eyes fell on Seymour's corpse again. 'I can see you're a man of action,' Channing stated, an idea coming to him.

'I will shoot her, too.'

'I'm sure you would.' Channing kept his voice calm, his tone casual. 'But that would be shortsighted.' He began to pace the room.

'Shortsighted?' The weasel pivoted with him. It was what he hoped for. It would be awkward to pivot and hold Alina to him. If Alina saw an opening to escape, would she take it? If the movement exposed her captor, Channing would take the shot, or Nick would. Jocelyn had to keep his sights trained on the guards in case they recovered consciousness.

'We're not here for the *comtesse*. We're here for you. You can only shoot her once and then your shield is gone.' Channing frowned. 'I can see you thought to use her for leverage, but that only works if we came for her.'

'You're bluffing, just like her,' Weasel sneered. 'I didn't believe her and I don't believe you.' He tightened his hold on Alina and she fought back a gasp.

Channing shrugged and moved. 'She's working with us, certainly, but make no mistake, we were here for Seymour. You'll do just as well.' Channing would use the man as leverage against himself. Self-preservation had motivated the Weasel's shooting of Seymour. Anything he thought he could do to save his own hide he would do.

Channing reached the end of the room. He had to turn and Weasel would have to turn, too. It would be the one place in the room where he'd be vulnerable. There would be an angle, a moment, where Channing would have his chance. 'Alina, my dear, you know what to do,' he said, hoping to give her some kind of warning, oblique as it was. 'You know your part in this.' Let that give Weasel something else to worry about. Weasel was a coward at heart.

The turn came and Channing orchestrated it as carefully as a turn in the ballroom, partnering Weasel every step of the way. Weasel made the turn, his clumsy movement putting Alina off balance. She stumbled. She used her weight to drag herself down and away from Weasel while he groped for a chair to stay upright. His shoulder, the left half of his body was exposed for the slightest instant. Channing shot. There was no time to aim, only react. He just had to make contact. He didn't have to kill, only wound.

The idea must have occurred to the Weasel as well. He heard Jocelyn shout, saw a blur of movement out the corner of his eye, the report of his pistol seemed extremely loud and he was down, pain searing his shoulder. He dropped his pistol, his hand instinctively going to the source of the hurt. It came away coated in red. One thought occurred to him as his strength ebbed. He had to get to Alina, had to get her away before he couldn't any more. 'Alina.' His voice was a hoarse rasp. He tried to speak louder and couldn't.

Alina was beside him, Nick and Jocelyn on the other. 'Get him up, Alina, let's get out of here.' Nick was gruff. 'Help me out here, Channing, get your legs under you. We have to get you home.'

'Is it that bad?' he tried to joke, but his words slurred and the world spun into darkness.

Alina screamed his name. 'You will not die for me, Channing, do you hear me? You will not!'

No, he would live for her. Somehow. But not right now. Right now he had to rest. Alina was safe, Seymour was dead and he had to rest. He sagged against Nick's arms.

She was going to kill him for scaring her to death. The last three days had been the worst three days of her life. She still showed signs of it, Alina thought, checking her appearance in the mirror. She'd stayed by Channing unceasingly until he'd regained stable consciousness and there was no sign of fever. The doctors had been confident from the start that if he could avoid fever, the wound would heal well. It had looked worse than it was and Channing had been lucky. The bullet had gone straight through. Not that Alina would ever be convinced of that.

She smoothed the skirts of her apple-green afternoon gown. She was unexpectedly, but perhaps understandably, nervous. This would be the first time she'd seen Channing with both of them fully recovered. He'd been given permission to sit upright in a chair for a few hours and she'd slept last night for the first time since the confrontation. The danger posed by Seymour was past, but much else remained unsettled between them. She walked the short distance between their rooms and knocked on the door before pushing it open.

Channing was ready for her and the sight of him brought a smile to her lips. Not even a shoulder wound could dim his golden good looks. His hair was brushed and he was dressed in shirt and waistcoat. A jacket was difficult to manage, but he was otherwise his usual, immaculate self.

She went to him. She knelt in front of him and took his hand, wanting to touch him, wanting to assure herself he was real. 'You are a sight to behold, Channing Deveril.' She smiled, overwhelmed by the waves of relief sweeping her. She'd not thought to be so moved by the sight of him healthy and safe, her beautiful, golden English lion. Then, horror of horrors, she began to cry for the second time.

'Why the tears? It's all over, Alina. Eagleton told Finn and the solicitors everything they needed to know. The syndicate is destroyed.' Channing's good hand played with her hair.

'All I wanted was for you to be safe. They were going to kill you.' Alina's tears wouldn't stop.

'You should have told me about the note,' Channing scolded softly. 'You were very brave, but very foolish, too.'

'I couldn't risk you. I could never risk you. I have to know you are out there in the world somewhere, all golden and goodness.' She kissed his hand. 'I'd never met anyone like you. That first day in Paris, I felt like you knew me, that when you looked at me you saw all of me and all of me was enough.' Her eyes dropped. 'But I knew, too, that I couldn't have you. It would have to be enough just to know you were out there.'

'It doesn't have to be that way. I believe there's a proposal on the table.'

Alina looked up. 'Are you sure? There's no need. The crisis is passed, the sacrifice is not necessary any more.' She'd understood Channing had been willing to cover her in his name, not that she would have allowed it.

Channing held her gaze. 'There's no need, only want. You may find it hard to believe, but I do not consider marriage to you a sacrifice. The only sacrifice is having had to wait this long to do it.'

Alina smiled. 'I don't know, Channing Deveril, marriage to me will be very demanding. The sex might kill you.' Saying yes would be the bravest thing she had yet to do. It took strength to reach for one's dream even if that dream sat just inches from her.

Channing laughed. 'I certainly hope it does. Does that mean yes?'

'What do you think?' She slanted him a coy look and reached for him. She had his trousers open with a flick of her hand.

Channing let out a satisfied moan. 'I think taking a bullet for you was worth it.'

Epilogue

London's finest rake had married splendidly. It was the best kind of wedding: big, spectacular, complete with a handsome groom, a beautiful bride and enough gossip to make it interesting. Among the guests were the bride's parents. Her father gave her away, her mother cried and her sister stood up with her in a pretty dress of primrose. But London had turned out to see the other two sets of guests: Nick D'Arcy and his wife, Annorah, and Jocelyn Eisley and Cassandra. Even with such notoriety in attendance, it had regretfully not been enough to deflect any attention away from the main focus.

Alina assured Channing he'd better get used to it. A beautiful woman and a handsome man were always interesting. Alina had garnered all the attention. She'd worn her signature colour, the bright blue that brought out her eyes, and people were already speculating about the enchanting blue-eyed children that would come of that union sooner or later. One of those children would come into that world rather promptly, Channing thought, if Alina was correct. It was a bit early to tell, but Channing hoped she was right.

They would spend their honeymoon at the Deveril hunting box in Scotland, enjoying the autumn colours of the Highlands in peace and quiet. But there was a stop they needed to make before they could leave London behind.

Channing's travelling coach pulled up outside Argosy House. He helped Alina out. 'What are we doing here?' she asked.

Channing merely grinned and opened the door. 'You'll see.' Inside, a great round of applause went up. Everyone was assembled in the hall from the footmen to the escorts, Nick and Jocelyn at the head of each column. He was moved, he really was. 'Is this your idea of a quiet drink?' Channing joked, taking a glass of the champagne that was circulating on trays. Nick and Jocelyn had asked them to stop by, but Channing had not expected this. It was the perfect way to go out.

Channing drew Alina to him and raised his glass. 'A toast, everyone, to new beginnings. I am the luckiest of men today to marry the woman I love. I will leave the agency a happy man. But there is still a job that needs doing and the League must go on. I leave that task to the most capable Amery DeHart. Cheers.'

Glasses clinked, men clapped Amery on the back in congratulations and good-humoured teasing. Over their heads, Channing's eyes met Nick's and Jocelyn's in mutual accord and in farewell. Their journeys were complete and they were satisfied men. He bent to Alina's ear. 'Let's go. The future awaits and I can hardly wait to get there.' They slipped out to the carriage, a clean getaway just the way the League preferred.

Except for one pair of eyes. Nothing escaped Amery DeHart's attention. He watched the carriage roll down the street. He might have imagined the carriage rocking slightly, but he didn't imagine the laughter floating back to him. That was real enough. He raised his glass in a silent salute to his friend and his mentor. In the falling dusk of evening, Amery DeHart drank to his vow. As long as women were in need of pleasure, there would be a League of Discreet Gentlemen.

* * * * *